Dear Reader,

As a high-school English teacher, I once chaperoned high-school dances to make a little extra cash. One of the experiences I will never forget is the time I chaperoned Prom.

Held at the city's courthouse, a beautiful old building full of stone columns and smooth marble, the dance was the most anticipated event of the school year for many. It was a glittering, promise-filled night – parents waiting outside to take pictures during the promenade, girls floating across the floor in elegant dresses, boys in tuxedos, everything a bit more beautiful and exciting than usual. You could almost hear them thinking, *What happens next?*

Later, when I had the idea for *Matched*, this scene came back to me. All the lovely girls, all the handsome boys, everyone poised on the edge of the steps waiting for their names to be called, right on the brink of their adult lives. In *Matched,* Cassia also attends a similar event – her Match Banquet – but the stakes are even higher. In her world, the Society chooses who she marries, where she lives, and when she dies. And it all begins at the Banquet.

I hope you will join Cassia on her journey as she discovers *what happens next.*

Best wishes,

Ally Condie

ALLY CONDIE

is a former high school English teacher
who lives with her husband and three sons
outside of Salt Lake City, Utah.
Visit her online at www.allycondie.com

ALLY CONDIE

MATCHED

PENGUIN BOOKS

PENGUIN BOOKS

Published by the Penguin Group

Penguin Books Ltd, 80 Strand, London WC2R ORL, England

Penguin Group (USA) Inc., 375 Hudson Street, New York, New York 10014, USA

Penguin Group (Canada), 90 Eglinton Avenue East, Suite 700, Toronto, Ontario, Canada M4P 2Y3
(a division of Pearson Penguin Canada Inc.)

Penguin Ireland, 25 St Stephen's Green, Dublin 2, Ireland (a division of Penguin Books Ltd)

Penguin Group (Australia), 707 Collins Street, Melbourne, Victoria 3008, Australia
(a division of Pearson Australia Group Pty Ltd)

Penguin Books India Pvt Ltd, 11 Community Centre, Panchsheel Park, New Delhi – 110 017, India

Penguin Group (NZ), 67 Apollo Drive, Rosedale, Auckland 0632, New Zealand
(a division of Pearson New Zealand Ltd)

Penguin Books (South Africa) (Pty) Ltd, Block D, Rosebank Office Park, 181 Jan Smuts Avenue,
Parktown North, Gauteng 2193, South Africa

Penguin Books Ltd, Registered Offices: 80 Strand, London WC2R ORL, England

penguin.com

First published in the USA by Dutton Books, a member of Penguin Group (USA) Inc., 2010
First published by Penguin Books Ltd, 2010
Published in this edition 2011

017

Text copyright © Allyson Braithwaite Condie, 2010
'Poem in October', by Dylan Thomas, from *The Poems of Dylan Thomas*, copyright © 1945
by The Trustees for the Copyrights of Dylan Thomas, first published in *Poetry*.
Reprinted by permission of New Directions Publishing Corp.
'Do Not Go Gentle into That Good Night' by Dylan Thomas, from *The Poems of Dylan Thomas*,
copyright © 1952 by Dylan Thomas. Reprinted by permission of New Directions Publishing Corp.

Set in Minister-Light
Printed in Great Britain by Clays Ltd, St Ives plc

British Library Cataloguing in Publication Data
A CIP catalogue record for this book is available from the British Library

ISBN: 978-0-141-33478-3

www.greenpenguin.co.uk

Penguin Books is committed to a sustainable
future for our business, our readers and our planet.
This book is made from Forest Stewardship
Council™ certified paper.

For Scott,
who always believes

ACKNOWLEDGMENTS

My deep gratitude and appreciation to:

Scott, my husband, who makes writing not only possible but probable;

My three boys, who make everything exciting—I love you, and you, and you;

My parents, Robert and Arlene Braithwaite; my brother, Nic; and my sisters, Elaine and Hope, who read every word, every time (and in Elaine's case, over and over again);

My reader friends and writer friends, who give essential feedback and encouragement;

Alec Shane, who went the extra mile even though he is a fourth-degree black belt, not a distance runner;

Jodi Reamer, who is brilliant and down-to-earth (and fun!), the advocate of every writer's dreams;

Julie Strauss-Gabel, a woman of unparalleled graciousness and genius, who makes every page better;

And the wonderful team at Penguin who all believed and who exercised their myriad talents on the behalf of this story, including, but not limited to, Theresa Evangelista, Lauri Hornik, Rosanne Lauer, Linda McCarthy, Shanta Newlin, Irene Vandervoort, Don Weisberg, and Lisa Yoskowitz.

MATCHED

CHAPTER 1

*Now that I've found the way to fly, which direction should I go
into the night? My wings aren't white or feathered; they're green,
made of green silk, which shudders in the wind and bends when
I move—first in a circle, then in a line, finally in a shape of my
own invention. The black behind me doesn't worry me; neither do
the stars ahead.*

I smile at myself, at the foolishness of my imagination.
People cannot fly, though before the Society, there were
myths about those who could. I saw a painting of them once.
White wings, blue sky, gold circles above their heads, eyes
turned up in surprise as though they couldn't believe what the
artist had painted them doing, couldn't believe that their feet
didn't touch the ground.

Those stories weren't true. I know that. But tonight, it's
easy to forget. The air train glides through the starry night
so smoothly and my heart pounds so quickly that it feels as
though I could soar into the sky at any moment.

"What are you smiling about?" Xander wonders as I
smooth the folds of my green silk dress down neat.

"Everything," I tell him, and it's true. I've waited so long
for this: for my Match Banquet. Where I'll see, for the first

time, the face of the boy who will be my Match. It will be the first time I hear his name.

I can't wait. As quickly as the air train moves, it still isn't fast enough. It hushes through the night, its sound a background for the low rain of our parents' voices, the lightning-quick beats of my heart.

Perhaps Xander can hear my heart pounding, too, because he asks, "Are you nervous?" In the seat next to him, Xander's older brother begins to tell my mother the story of his Match Banquet. It won't be long now until Xander and I have our own stories to tell.

"No," I say. But Xander's my best friend. He knows me too well.

"You lie," he teases. "You *are* nervous."

"Aren't you?"

"Not me. I'm ready." He says it without hesitation, and I believe him. Xander is the kind of person who is sure about what he wants.

"It doesn't matter if you're nervous, Cassia," he says, gentle now. "Almost ninety-three percent of those attending their Match Banquet exhibit some signs of nervousness."

"Did you memorize *all* of the official Matching material?"

"Almost," Xander says, grinning. He holds his hands out as if to say, *What did you expect?*

The gesture makes me laugh, and besides, I memorized

all of the material, too. It's easy to do when you read it so many times, when the decision is so important. "So you're in the minority," I say. "The seven percent who don't show any nerves at all."

"Of course," he agrees.

"How could you tell *I* was nervous?"

"Because you keep opening and closing *that*." Xander points to the golden object in my hands. "I didn't know you had an artifact." A few treasures from the past float around among us. Though citizens of the Society are allowed one artifact each, they are hard to come by. Unless you had ancestors who took care to pass things along through the years.

"I didn't, until a few hours ago," I tell him. "Grandfather gave it to me for my birthday. It belonged to his mother."

"What's it called?" Xander asks.

"A compact," I say. I like the name very much. Compact means small. I am small. I also like the way it sounds when you say it: *com-pact*. Saying the word makes a sound like the one the artifact itself makes when it snaps shut.

"What do the initials and numbers mean?"

"I'm not sure." I run my finger across the letters *ACM* and the numbers *1940* carved across the golden surface. "But look," I tell him, popping the compact open to show him the inside: a little mirror, made of real glass, and a small hollow where the original owner once stored powder for her face, according to Grandfather. Now, I use it to hold the three emergency tablets that everyone carries—one green, one blue, one red.

"That's convenient," Xander says. He stretches out his arms in front of him and I notice that he has an artifact, too—a pair of shiny platinum cuff links. "My father lent me these, but you can't put anything in them. They're completely useless."

"They look nice, though." My gaze travels up to Xander's face, to his bright blue eyes and blond hair above his dark suit and white shirt. He's always been handsome, even when we were little, but I've never seen him dressed up like this. Boys don't have as much leeway in choosing clothes as girls do. One suit looks much like another. Still, they get to select the color of their shirts and cravats, and the quality of the material is much finer than the material used for plainclothes. "*You* look nice." The girl who finds out that he's her Match will be thrilled.

"Nice?" Xander says, lifting his eyebrows. "That's all?"

"Xander," his mother says next to him, amusement mingled with reproach in her voice.

"*You* look beautiful," Xander tells me, and I flush a little even though I've known Xander all my life. I *feel* beautiful, in this dress: ice green, floating, full-skirted. The unaccustomed smoothness of silk against my skin makes me feel lithe and graceful.

Next to me, my mother and father each draw a breath as City Hall comes into view, lit up white and blue and sparkling with the special occasion lights that indicate a celebration is taking place. I can't see the marble stairs in front of the Hall yet, but I know that they will be polished and shining. All my life I have waited to walk up those clean marble steps and through the doors of the Hall, a building I have seen from a distance but never entered.

I want to open the compact and check in the mirror to make sure I look my best. But I don't want to seem vain, so I sneak a glance at my face in its surface instead.

The rounded lid of the compact distorts my features a little, but it's still me. My green eyes. My coppery-brown hair, which looks more golden in the compact than it does in real life. My straight small nose. My chin with a trace of a dimple like my grandfather's. All the outward characteristics that make me Cassia Maria Reyes, seventeen years old exactly.

I turn the compact over in my hands, looking at how perfectly the two sides fit together. My Match is already coming together just as neatly, beginning with the fact that I am here tonight. Since my birthday falls on the fifteenth, the day the Banquet is held each month, I'd always *hoped* that I might be Matched on my actual birthday—but I knew it might not happen. You can be called up for your Banquet anytime during the year after you turn seventeen. When the notification came across the port two weeks ago that I would, indeed, be Matched on the day of my birthday, I could almost hear the clean *snap* of the pieces fitting into place, exactly as I've dreamed for so long.

Because although I haven't even had to wait a full day for my Match, in some ways I have waited all my life.

"Cassia," my mother says, smiling at me. I blink and look up, startled. My parents stand up, ready to disembark. Xander stands, too, and straightens his sleeves. I hear him take a deep breath, and I smile to myself. Maybe he is a little nervous after all.

"Here we go," he says to me. His smile is so kind and good; I'm glad we were called up the same month. We've shared so much of childhood, it seems we should share the end of it, too.

I smile back at him and give him the best greeting we have in the Society. "I wish you optimal results," I tell Xander.

"You too, Cassia," he says.

As we step off the air train and walk toward City Hall, my parents each link an arm through mine. I am surrounded, as I always have been, by their love.

It is only the three of us tonight. My brother, Bram, can't come to the Match Banquet because he is under seventeen, too young to attend. The first one you attend is always your own. I, however, will be able to attend Bram's banquet because I am the older sibling. I smile to myself, wondering what Bram's Match will be like. In seven years I will find out.

But tonight is *my* night.

It is easy to identify those of us being Matched; not only are we younger than all of the others, but we also float along in beautiful dresses and tailored suits while our parents and older siblings walk around in plainclothes, a background against which we bloom. The City Officials smile proudly at us, and my heart swells as we enter the Rotunda.

In addition to Xander, who waves good-bye to me as he crosses the room to his seating area, I see another girl I know named Lea. She picked the bright red dress. It is a good choice for her, because she is beautiful enough that standing out works in her favor. She looks worried, however, and she keeps twisting her artifact, a jeweled red bracelet. I am a little surprised to see Lea there. I would have picked her for a Single.

"Look at this china," my father says as we find our place at the Banquet tables. "It reminds me of the Wedgwood pieces we found last year . . ."

My mother looks at me and rolls her eyes in amusement. Even at the Match Banquet, my father can't stop himself from noticing these things. My father spends months working in old neighborhoods that are being restored and turned into new Boroughs for public use. He sifts through the relics of a society that is not as far in the past as it seems. Right now, for example, he is working on a particularly interesting Restoration project: an old library. He sorts out the things the Society has marked as valuable from the things that are not.

But then I have to laugh because my mother can't help but comment on the flowers, since they fall in *her* area of expertise as an Arboretum worker. "Oh, Cassia! Look at the centerpieces. Lilies." She squeezes my hand.

"Please be seated," an Official tells us from the podium. "Dinner is about to be served."

It's almost comical how quickly we all take our seats. Because we might admire the china and the flowers, and we might be here for our Matches, but we also can't wait to taste the food.

"They say this dinner is always wasted on the Matchees," a jovial-looking man sitting across from us says, smiling around our table. "So excited they can't eat a bite." And it's true; one of the girls sitting farther down the table, wearing a pink dress, stares at her plate, touching nothing.

I don't seem to have this problem, however. Though I don't gorge myself, I can eat some of everything—the roasted vegetables, the savory meat, the crisp greens, and creamy cheese. The warm light bread. The meal seems like a dance, as though this is a ball as well as a banquet. The waiters slide the plates in front of us with graceful hands; the food, wearing herbs and garnishes, is as dressed up as we are. We lift the white napkins, the silver forks, the shining crystal goblets as if in time to music.

My father smiles happily as a server sets a piece of chocolate cake with fresh cream before him at the end of the meal. *"Wonderful,"* he whispers, so softly that only my mother and I can hear him.

My mother laughs a little at him, teasing him, and he reaches for her hand.

I understand his enthusiasm when I take a bite of the

cake, which is rich but not overwhelming, deep and dark and flavorful. It is the best thing I have eaten since the traditional dinner at Winter Holiday, months ago. I wish Bram could have some cake, and for a minute I think about saving some of mine for him. But there is no way to take it back to him. It wouldn't fit in my compact. It would be bad form to hide it away in my mother's purse even if she would agree, and she won't. My mother doesn't break the rules.

I can't save it for later. It is now, or never.

I have just popped the last bite in my mouth when the announcer says, "We are ready to announce the Matches."

I swallow in surprise, and for a second, I feel an unexpected surge of anger: I didn't get to savor my last bite of cake.

"Lea Abbey."

Lea twists her bracelet furiously as she stands, waiting to see the face flash on the screen. She is careful to hold her hands low, though, so that the boy seeing her in another City Hall somewhere will only see the beautiful blond girl and not her worried hands, twisting and turning that bracelet.

It is strange how we hold on to the pieces of the past while we wait for our futures.

There is a system, of course, to the Matching. In City Halls across the country, all filled with people, the Matches are announced in alphabetical order according to the girls' last names. I feel slightly sorry for the boys, who have no idea when their names will be called, when they must stand for girls in other City Halls to receive them as Matches. Since my last name is Reyes, I will be somewhere at the end of the middle. The beginning of the end.

The screen flashes with the face of a boy, blond and handsome. He smiles as he sees Lea's face on the screen where he is, and she smiles, too. "Joseph Peterson," the announcer says. "Lea Abbey, you have been matched with Joseph Peterson."

The hostess presiding over the Banquet brings Lea a small silver box; the same thing happens to Joseph Peterson on the screen. When Lea sits down, she looks at the silver box longingly, as though she wishes she could open it right away. I don't blame her. Inside the box is a microcard with background information about her Match. We all receive them. Later, the boxes will be used to hold the rings for the Marriage Contract.

The screen flashes back to the default picture: a boy and a girl, smiling at each other, with glimmering lights and a white-coated Official in the background. Although the Society times the Matching to be as efficient as possible, there are still moments when the screen goes back to this picture, which means that we all wait while something happens somewhere else. It's so complicated—the Matching—and I am again reminded of the intricate steps of the dances they used to do long ago. This dance, however, is one that the Society alone can choreograph now.

The picture shimmers away.

The announcer calls another name; another girl stands up.

Soon, more and more people at the Banquet have little silver boxes. Some people set them on the white tablecloths in front of them, but most hold the boxes carefully, unwilling to let their futures out of their hands so soon after receiving them.

I don't see any other girls wearing the green dress. I don't mind. I like the idea that, for one night, I don't look like everyone else.

I wait, holding my compact in one hand and my mother's hand in the other. Her palm feels sweaty. For the first time, I realize that she and my father are nervous, too.

"Cassia Maria Reyes."

It is my turn.

I stand up, letting go of my mother's hand, and turn toward the screen. I feel my heart pounding and I am tempted to twist my hands the way Lea did, but I hold perfectly still with my chin up and my eyes on the screen. I watch and wait, determined that the girl my Match will see on the screen in his City Hall somewhere out there in Society will be poised and calm and lovely, the very best image of Cassia Maria Reyes that I can present.

But nothing happens.

I stand and look at the screen, and, as the seconds go by, it is all I can do to stay still, all I can do to keep smiling.

Whispers start around me. Out of the corner of my eye, I see my mother move her hand as if to take mine again, but then she pulls it back.

A girl in a green dress stands waiting, her heart pounding. Me.

The screen is dark, and it stays dark.

That can only mean one thing.

CHAPTER 2

The whispers rise soft around me like birds beating their wings under the dome of City Hall. "Your Match is here this evening," the hostess says, smiling. The people around me smile as well, and their murmurs become louder. Our Society is so vast, our Cities so many, that the odds of your perfect Match being someone in your own City are minuscule. It's been many years since such a thing happened here.

These thoughts tumble in my mind, and I close my eyes briefly as I realize what this means, not in abstract, but for me, the girl in the green dress. *I might know my Match.* He might be someone who goes to the same Second School that I do, someone I see every day, someone—

"Xander Thomas Carrow."

At his table, Xander stands up. A sea of watching faces and white tablecloths, of glinting crystal glasses and shining silver boxes stretches between us.

I can't believe it.

This is a dream. People turn their eyes on me and on the handsome boy in the dark suit and blue cravat. It doesn't feel real until Xander smiles at me. I think, *I know that smile,* and suddenly I'm smiling, too, and the rush of applause and smell of the lilies fully convince me that this is actually happening. Dreams don't smell or sound as strong as this. I break protocol a bit to give Xander a tiny wave, and his smile widens.

The hostess says, "You may take your seats." She sounds glad that we are so happy; of course, we should be. We *are* each other's best Match, after all.

When she brings me the silver box, I hold it carefully. But I already know much of what is inside. Not only do Xander and I go to the same school, we also live on the same street; we've been best friends for as long as I can remember. I don't need the microcard to show me pictures of Xander as a child because I have plenty of them in my mind. I don't need to download a list of favorites to memorize because I already know them. Favorite color: green. Favorite leisure activity: swimming. Favorite recreation activity: games.

"Congratulations, Cassia," my father whispers to me, his expression relieved. My mother says nothing, but she beams with delight and embraces me tightly. Behind her, another girl stands up, watching the screen.

The man sitting next to my father whispers, "What a piece of luck for your family. You don't have to trust her future to someone you know nothing about."

I'm surprised by the unhappy edge to his tone; the way his comment seems to be right on the verge of insubordination. His daughter, the nervous one wearing the pink dress, hears it, too; she looks uncomfortable and shifts slightly in her seat.

I don't recognize her. She must go to one of the other Second Schools in our City.

I sneak another glance at Xander, but there are too many people in my way and I can't see him. Other girls take their turns standing up. The screen lights up for each of them. No one else has a dark screen. I am the only one.

Before we leave, the hostess of the Match Banquet asks Xander and me and our families to step aside and speak with her. "This is an unusual situation," she says, but she corrects herself immediately. "Not unusual. Excuse me. It is merely uncommon." She smiles at both of us. "Since you already know each other, things will proceed differently for you. You will know much of the initial information about each other." She gestures at our silver boxes. "There are a few new courtship guidelines included on your microcards, so you should familiarize yourselves with those when you have an opportunity."

"We'll read them tonight," Xander promises sincerely. I try to keep from rolling my eyes in amusement because he sounds exactly the way he does when a teacher gives him a learning assignment. He'll read the new guidelines and memorize them, as he read and memorized the official Matching material. And then I flush again, as a paragraph from that material flashes across my mind:

If you choose to be Matched, your Marriage Contract will take place when you are twenty-one. Studies have shown that the fertility of both men and women peaks at the age of twenty-four. The Matching System has been constructed to allow those who Match to have their children near this age—providing for the highest likelihood of healthy offspring.

Xander and I will share a Marriage Contract. *We will have children together.*

I don't have to spend the next few years learning everything about him because I already know him, almost as well as I know myself.

The tiny feeling of loss deep within my heart surprises me. My peers will spend the next few days swooning over pictures of their Matches, bragging about them during meal hour at school, waiting for more and more bits of information to be revealed. Anticipating their first meeting, their second meeting, and so on. That mystery does not exist for Xander and me. I won't wonder what he is like or daydream about our first meeting.

But then Xander looks at me and asks, "What are you thinking about?" and I answer, "That we are very lucky," and I mean it. There is still much to discover. Until now, I have only known Xander as a friend. Now he is my Match.

The hostess corrects me gently. "Not lucky, Cassia. There is no luck in the Society."

I nod. *Of course.* I should know better than to use such an archaic, inaccurate term. There's only probability now. How likely something is to occur, or how unlikely.

The hostess speaks again. "It has been a busy evening,

and it's getting late. You can read the courtship guidelines later, another day. There's plenty of time."

She's right. That's what the Society has given us: time. We live longer and better than any other citizens in the history of the world. And it's thanks in large part to the Matching System, which produces physically and emotionally healthy offspring.

And I'm a part of it all.

My parents and the Carrows can't stop exclaiming over how wonderful this all is, and as we walk down the steps of City Hall together, Xander leans over and says, "You'd think they'd arranged everything themselves."

"I can't believe it," I say, and I feel opulent and a little giddy. I can't believe that this is me, wearing a beautiful green dress, holding gold in one hand and silver in the other, walking next to my best friend. My Match.

"I can," Xander says, teasing me. "In fact, I knew all along. That's why *I* wasn't nervous."

I tease him back. "I knew, too. That's why I *was*."

We're laughing so much that when the air train pulls up neither of us notice for a moment, and then there *is* a brief moment of awkwardness as Xander holds out his hand to help me climb aboard. "Here," he says, his voice serious. For a moment, I don't know what to do. There is something new in touching each other now, and my hands are full.

Then Xander wraps his hand around mine, pulling me onto the train with him.

"Thank you," I say as the doors close behind us.

"Any time," he says. He does not let go of my hand; the little silver box I hold creates a barrier between us even as another one breaks. We have not held hands like this since we were children. In doing that tonight, we move across the invisible divide that separates friendship from something more. I feel a tingle along my arm; to be touched, by my Match, is a luxury that the other Matchees at Banquets tonight do not share.

The air train carries us away from the sparkling, icy white lights of City Hall toward the softer yellow porch lights and streetlights of the Boroughs. As the streets flash past on our way home to Mapletree Borough, I glance over at Xander. The gold of the lights outside is similar to the color of his hair, and his face is handsome and confident and good. And familiar, for the most part. If you've always known how to look at someone, it's strange when that directive changes. Xander has always been someone I could not have, and I have been the same for him.

Now everything is different.

My ten-year-old brother, Bram, waits for us on the front porch. When we tell him about the Banquet, he can't believe the news. "You're Matched with *Xander*? I already know the person you're going to marry? That's so strange."

"You're the one who's strange." I tease him, and he dodges me as I pretend to grab him. "Who knows. Maybe your Match lives right on this street, too. Maybe it's—"

Bram covers his ears. "Don't say it. Don't say it—"

"Serena," I say, and he turns away, pretending that he didn't hear me. Serena lives next door. She and Bram torment each other incessantly.

"Cassia," my mother says disapprovingly, glancing around to make sure that no one heard. We are not supposed to disparage other members of our street and our community. Mapletree Borough is known for being tight-knit and exemplary in this way. *No thanks to Bram*, I think to myself.

"I'm teasing, Mama." I know she can't stay mad at me. Not on the night of my Match Banquet, when she has been reminded of how quickly I am growing up.

"Come inside," my father says. "It's almost curfew. We can talk about everything tomorrow."

"Was there cake?" Bram asks as my father opens the door. They all look back at me, waiting.

I don't move. I don't want to go inside yet.

If I do, that means that this night is coming to an end, and I don't want that. I don't want to take off the dress and go back to my plainclothes; I don't want to return to the usual days, which are good, but nothing special like this. "I'll come in soon. Just a few minutes more."

"Don't be long," my father says gently. He doesn't want me to break curfew. It is the City's curfew, not his, and I understand.

"I won't," I promise.

I sit down on the steps of my house, careful, of course, of

my borrowed dress. I glance down at the folds of the beautiful material. It does not belong to me, but this evening does, this time that is dark and bright and full of both the unexpected and the familiar. I look out into the new spring night and turn my face to the stars.

I don't linger outside for long because tomorrow, Saturday, is a busy day. I'll need to report to my trial work position at the sorting center early in the morning. After that I'll have my Saturday night free-rec hours, one of the few times I get to spend with my friends outside of Second School.

And Xander will be there.

Back in my bedroom, I shake the tablets out of the little hollow in the base of the compact. Then I count—one, two, three; blue, green, red—as I slide the tablets back into their usual metal cylinder.

I know what the blue and green tablets do. I don't know anyone who knows for certain what the red tablet does. There have been rumors about it for years.

I climb into bed and push away thoughts of the red tablet. For the first time in my life, I'm allowed to dream of Xander.

CHAPTER 3

I've always wondered what my dreams look like on paper, in numbers. Someone out there knows, but it isn't me. I pull the sleep tags from my skin, taking care not to tug too hard on the one behind my ear. The skin is fragile there and it always hurts to peel the disk away, especially if a strand or two of hair gets caught under the adhesive on the tag. Glad that my turn is over, I put the equipment back in its box. It's Bram's turn to be tagged tonight.

I did not dream of Xander. I don't know why.

But I did sleep late, and I'm going to be late for work if I don't hurry. As I walk into the kitchen, carrying my dress from the night before, I see that my mother has already set out the breakfast food delivery. Oatmeal, gray-brown and expected. We eat for health and performance, not for taste. Holidays and celebrations are exceptions. Since our calories had been moderated all week long, last night at the Banquet we could eat everything in front of us without significant impact.

Bram grins mischievously at me, still wearing his sleep-clothes. "So," he says, shoving one last spoonful of oatmeal

into his mouth, "did you sleep late because you were dream-
ing about *Xander*?"

I don't want him to know how close he is to the truth;
that even though I didn't dream of Xander, I wanted to. "No,"
I say, "and shouldn't you be worrying about being on time for
school?" Bram's young enough that he still has school instead
of work on Saturdays, and if he doesn't get going, he'll be late.
Again. I hope he doesn't get cited.

"Bram," my mother says, "go get your plainclothes on,
please." She'll breathe a huge sigh of relief when he moves on
to Second School, where the start time is half an hour later.

As Bram slouches out of the room, my mother reaches
for my dress and holds it up. "You looked so beautiful last
night. I hate to take this back." We both look at the gown
for a moment. I admire the way the fabric catches the light
and plays it back, almost like the light and the cloth are both
living things.

We both sigh at exactly the same time and my mother
laughs. She gives me a kiss on the cheek. "They'll send you
a little piece of the fabric, remember?" she says, and I nod.
Each gown is designed with an interior panel that can be cut
into pieces, one for each girl who wears the dress. The scrap,
along with the silver box that held my microcard, will be the
mementos of my Matching.

But still. I will never see *this* dress, my green dress, again.

I knew the moment I saw it that it was the one I wanted.
When I made my selection, the woman at the clothing

distribution center smiled after she punched the number—seventy-three—into the computer. "That's the one you were most likely to pick," she said. "Your personal data indicated it, and so did general psychology. You've picked things outside of the majority in the past, and girls like their dresses to bring out their eyes."

I smiled and watched as she sent her assistant into the back to retrieve the dress. When I tried it on, I saw that she was right. The dress was meant for me. The hemline fell perfectly; the waist curved in exactly the right amount. I turned in front of the mirror, admiring myself.

The woman told me, "So far, you are the only girl wearing this dress at the Match Banquet this month. The most popular gown is one of the pink gowns, number twenty-two."

"Good," I told her. I don't mind standing out a *little*.

Bram reappears in the doorway, plainclothes wrinkled, hair askew. I can almost see the wheels turning in my mother's mind: Is it better to comb his hair and make him late, or send him as he is?

Bram makes the decision for her. "See you tonight," he says, sprinting out the door.

"He's not going to be fast enough." My mother looks out the window toward the air-train stop, where the tracks light up to indicate the approaching train.

"He might," I say, watching Bram as he breaks another rule, the one about running in public. I can almost hear his footsteps pounding on the sidewalk as he runs down the street, his head lowered, his school pack bumping against his skinny back.

Right when he gets to the stop, he slows down. He pats his hair into place and walks casually up the steps toward the train. Hopefully, no one else has seen him run. A moment later, the air train pulls away with Bram safely inside.

"That boy is going to be the end of me." My mother sighs. "I should have gotten him up earlier. We all overslept. It was a big night last night."

"It was," I agree.

"I have to catch the next City air train." My mother pulls her satchel over her shoulder. "What are you doing for your free-rec hours tonight?"

"I'm sure Xander and everyone will want to play games at the youth center," I say. "We've seen all the showings, and the music . . ." I shrug.

My mother laughs, completing my sentence. "Is for old people like me."

"And I'm using the last hour to visit Grandfather." The Officials don't often allow a deviation from the usual free-rec options; but on the eve of someone's Final Banquet, visiting is encouraged and permitted.

My mother's eyes soften. "He'll love that."

"Did Papa tell Grandfather about my Match?"

My mother smiles. "He planned to stop by on his way to work."

"Good," I say, because I want Grandfather to know as soon as possible. I know he has been thinking as much about me and my Banquet as I've been thinking about him and his.

After I hurry and eat my breakfast, I make my train with seconds to spare and sit back. I may not have dreamed about Xander while I slept, but I can daydream about him now. Looking out the window and thinking about how he looked last night in his suit, I watch the Boroughs slide by on my way into the City. The green has not yet given way to stone and concrete when I notice white flakes drifting through the sky.

Everyone else notices them, too.

"*Snow?* In *June?*" the woman next to me asks.

"It can't be," a man across the aisle mutters.

"But look at it," she says.

"It can't be," the man says again. People twist, turn to the windows, looking agitated. Can something wrong be true?

Sure enough, little white puffs drift past on their way to the ground. There is something strange about this snow, but I'm not exactly sure what. I find myself holding in a smile as I look at all the worried faces around me. Should I be worried, too? Perhaps. But it's so pretty, so unexpected, and, for the moment, so unexplainable.

The air train comes to a stop. The doors open and a few pieces drift inside. I catch one on my hand, but it does not melt. The mystery of it does, however, when I see the little brown seed at the center of the snow.

"It's a cottonwood seed," I tell everyone confidently. "It's not snow."

"Of course," the man says, sounding glad to have an explanation. Snow in June would be atypical. Cottonwood seeds are not.

"But why are there so many?" another woman asks, still worried.

In a moment, we have our answer. One of the new passengers sitting down brushes white from his hair and plainclothes. "We're tearing out the cottonwood grove along the river," he explains. "The Society wants to plant some better trees there."

Everyone else takes his word for it; they know nothing about trees. They mutter about being glad it isn't a sign of another Warming; thank goodness the Society has things under control as usual. But thanks to my mother, who can't help talking about her work as a caretaker at the Arboretum, I know that his explanation *does* make sense. You can't use cottonwood trees for fruit or fuel. And their seeds are a nuisance. They fly far, catch on anything, try to grow everywhere. Weed trees, my mother says. Still, she harbors a particular affinity for them because of the seeds, which are small and brown but cloaked in beauty, in these thin white tendrils of cotton. Little cloudy parachutes to slow their fall, to help them fly, to catch the wind and glide them somewhere they might grow.

I look at the seed resting in the palm of my hand. There is still mystery in it after all, in that little brown core. I'm not sure what to do with it, so I tuck it into my pocket next to my tablet container.

The almost-snow reminds me of a line from a poem we studied this year in Language and Literacy: "Stopping by Woods on a Snowy Evening." It is one of my favorites of all the Hundred Poems, the ones our Society chose to keep, back when they decided our culture was too cluttered. They created commissions to choose the hundred best of everything: Hundred Songs, Hundred Paintings, Hundred Stories, Hundred Poems. The rest were eliminated. Gone forever. *For the best*, the Society said, and everyone believed because it made sense. *How can we appreciate anything fully when overwhelmed with too much?*

My own great-grandmother was one of the cultural historians who helped select the Hundred Poems almost seventy years ago. Grandfather has told me the story a thousand times, how his mother had to help decide which poems to keep and which to lose forever. She used to sing him parts of the poems as lullabies. *She whispered, sang them,* he said, *and I tried to remember them after she had gone.*

After she had gone. Tomorrow, my grandfather will go, too.

As we leave the last of the cottonwood seeds behind, I think about that poem and how much I like it. I like the words *deep* and *sleep* and the way they rhyme and repeat; I think to myself that this poem would be a good lullaby if you listened to the rhythm instead of the words. Because if you listened to the words you wouldn't feel rested: *Miles to go before I sleep.*

"It's a numbers sort today," my supervisor, Norah, tells me.

I sigh a little but Norah doesn't respond. She scans my card and hands it back. She doesn't ask about the Match Banquet, even though she has to know from my information update that it happened last night. But that's nothing new. Norah barely interacts with me because I'm one of the best sorters. In fact, it's been almost three months since my last error, which was the last time the two of us had a real conversation.

"Wait," Norah says as I turn toward my station. "Your scancard indicates that it's almost time for your formal sorting test."

I nod. I've been thinking about this for months; not as much as I thought about my Match Banquet, but often. Even though some of these number sorts are boring, sorting itself can lead to much more interesting work positions. Perhaps I could be a Restoration supervisor, like my father. When he was my age, his work activity was information sorting, too. And so was Grandfather's, and of course there is my great-grandmother, the one who participated in one of the greatest sortings of all when she was on the Hundred Committee.

The people who oversee the Matching also get their start

in sorting, but I'm not interested in that. I like my stories and information one step removed; I don't want to be in charge of sorting real people.

"Make sure you're ready," Norah says, but both she and I know that I already am.

Yellow light slants through the windows near our stations in the sorting center. I cast a shadow across the other workers' stations as I pass by. No one looks up.

I slip into my tiny station, which is just wide enough for a table and a chair and a sorting screen. The thin gray walls rise up on either side of me and I can't see anyone else. We are like the microcards in the research library at Second School—each of us neatly tucked into a slot. The government has computers that can do sorts much faster than we can, of course, but we're still important. You never know when technology might fail.

That's what happened to the society before ours. Everyone had technology, too much of it, and the consequences were disastrous. Now, we have the basic technology we need—ports, readers, scribes—and our information intake is much more specific. Nutrition specialists don't need to know how to program air trains, for example, and programmers, in turn, don't need to know how to prepare food. Such specialization keeps people from becoming overwhelmed. We don't need to understand *everything*. And, as the Society reminds us, there's a differ-

ence between knowledge and technology. Knowledge doesn't
fail us.

I slide my scancard and the sort begins. Even though I
like word association or picture or sentence sorts the best,
I'm good at the number ones, too. The screen tells me what
patterns I'm supposed to find and the numbers begin to
scroll up on the screen, like little white soldiers on a black
field waiting for me to mow them down. I touch each one
and begin to sort them out, pulling them aside into different
boxes. The tapping of my fingers makes a low, soft sound,
almost as silent as snow falling.

And I create a storm. The numbers fly into their spots
like flakes driven by the wind.

Halfway through, the pattern we are looking for changes.
The system tracks how soon we notice the changes and how
quickly we adapt our sorts. You never know when a change
will happen. Two minutes later, the pattern changes again,
and once more I catch it on the very first line of numbers. I
don't know how, but I always anticipate the shift in pattern
before it happens.

When I sort, there is only time to think about what I see
in front of me. So there in my little gray space, I don't think
about Xander. I don't wish for the feel of the green dress
against my skin or the taste of chocolate cake on my tongue.
I don't think of my grandfather eating his last meal tomorrow
night at the Final Banquet. I don't think of snow in June or

other things that cannot be, yet somehow are. I don't picture the sun dazzling me or the moon cooling me or the maple tree in our yard turning gold, green, red. I will think of all of those things and more later. But not when I sort.

I sort and sort and sort until there is no data left for me. Everything is clear on my screen. I am the one who makes it go blank.

When I ride the air train back to Mapletree Borough, the cottonwood seeds are gone. I want to tell my mother about them, but when I get home she and my father and Bram have already left for their leisure hours. A message for me blinks on the port: *We're sorry to have missed you, Cassia,* it flashes. *Have a good night.*

A beep sounds in the kitchen; my meal has arrived. The foilware container slides through the food delivery slot. I pick it up quickly, in time to hear the sound of the nutrition vehicle trundling along its track behind the houses in the Borough.

My dinner steams as I open it up. We must have a new nutrition personnel director. Before, the food was always lukewarm when it arrived. Now it's piping hot. I eat in a hurry, burning my mouth a little, because I know what I want to do with this rare empty time in this almost-vacant house. I'm never really alone; the port hums in the background, keeping track, keeping watch. But that's all right. I need it for what

I'm going to do. I want to look at the microcard without my parents or Bram glancing over my shoulder. I want to read more about Xander before I see him tonight.

When I insert the microcard, the humming takes on a more purposeful sound. The portscreen brightens and my heart beats faster in anticipation, even though I know Xander so well. What has the Society decided I should know about him, the person I'll spend most of my life with?

Do I know everything about him as I think I do, or is there something I've missed?

"Cassia Reyes, the Society is pleased to present you with your Match."

I smile as Xander's face appears on the portscreen immediately following the recorded message. It's a good picture of him. As always, his smile looks bright and real, his blue eyes kind. I study his face closely, pretending that I've never seen this picture before; that I have only had a glimpse of him once, last night at the Banquet. I study the planes of his face, the look of his lips. He *is* handsome. I'd never dared think that he might be my Match, of course, but now that it's happened I am interested. Intrigued. A little scared about how this might change our friendship, but mostly just happy.

I reach up to touch the words *Courtship Guidelines* on the screen but before I do Xander's face darkens and then disappears. The portscreen beeps and the voice says again,

"Cassia Reyes, the Society is pleased to present you with your Match."

My heart stops, and I can't believe what I see. A face comes back into view on the port in front of me.

It is not Xander.

CHAPTER 4

W*hat?*" Completely startled, I touch the screen and the face dissolves under my fingertips, pixelating into specks that look like dust. Words appear, but before I can read them the screen goes completely blank. *Again.*

"What's going on?" I say out loud.

The portscreen stays blank. I feel blank, too. This is a thousand times worse than the empty screen last night. I knew what it meant then. I have no idea what it means now. I've never heard of *this* happening.

I don't understand. The Society doesn't make mistakes.

But what else could this be? No one has two Matches.

"Cassia?" Xander calls to me through the door.

"I'm coming," I call out, tearing the microcard from the port and shoving it into my pocket. I take one deep breath, and then I open the door.

"So, I learned from your microcard that you like cycling," Xander says formally as I close the door behind me, making me laugh a little in spite of what just happened. I hate cycling the most out of all the exercise options, and he knows it. We argue about it all the time; I think it's stupid to go riding on something that doesn't move, spinning your wheels endlessly. He points out that I like to run on the tracker, which is almost the same thing. "It's different," I tell him, but I can't explain why.

"Did you spend all day staring at my face on the portscreen?" he asks. He's still joking, but suddenly I can't catch my breath. He viewed *his* microcard, too. Was *my* face the one he saw? It feels so strange to be hiding something, especially from Xander.

"Of course not," I say, trying to tease back. "It's Saturday, remember? I had work to do."

"I did, too, but that didn't stop me. I read all your stats and reviewed all the courtship guidelines."

He unknowingly throws me a lifeline with those words. I am not drowning in worry anymore. I am neck deep and it still washes over me in cold waves, but now I can breathe. Xander still thinks we are Matched. Nothing strange happened to him when he viewed his microcard. That's something, at least.

"You read all the guidelines?"

"Of course. Didn't you?"

"Not yet." I feel stupid admitting this, but Xander laughs again.

"They're not very interesting," he says. "Except for one." He winks at me significantly.

"Oh?" I say, distracted. I see other youth our age mingling and gathering on our street, walking to the game center like us. They're waving, calling, wearing the same clothes we wear.

But there's a difference tonight. Some are watching. Some are watched: me, and Xander.

The others' eyes glance at us, hold, flicker away, look back.

I'm not used to it. Xander and I are normal, healthy citizens, part of this group. Not outsiders.

But I feel separated now, as though a clear thin wall rises up distinctly between myself and those staring at me. We can see each other, but we can't cross over.

"Are you all right?" Xander asks.

Too late, I realize that I should have responded to Xander's comment and asked him which guideline he found interesting. If I can't pull myself together soon, he'll know something's wrong. We know each other too well.

Xander reaches for my elbow as we turn the corner and leave Mapletree Borough. When we've walked a few steps more, he slides his hand down my arm and interlaces his fingers with mine. He leans closer to my ear. "One of the guidelines said that we are allowed to express physical affection. If we want."

And I *do* want. Even with all the stress I feel, the touch of his hand against mine with nothing to separate us is still welcome and new. I'm surprised that Xander is so natural at this. And as we walk, I recognize the emotion that I see on some of the faces of the girls staring at us. It's jealousy, pure and simple. I relax a little, because I can understand why. None of us ever thought we could have golden, charismatic, clever Xander. We always knew he would be Matched with another girl in another City, another Province.

But he's not. He's Matched with *me*.

I keep my fingers locked in his as we walk toward the game center. Maybe, if I don't let go, it will prove that we are meant to be Matched. That the other face on the screen means nothing; that it was simply a momentary malfunction of the microcard.

Except. The face I saw, the face that was not Xander: I knew him, too.

CHAPTER 5

T here's an opening over here," Xander says, stopping at a game table in the middle of the room. Apparently the other youth in our Borough feel the same way we do about this Saturday's recreation options, because the game center is crowded with people, including most of our friends. "Do you want to go in, Cassia?"

"No thanks," I say. "I'll watch this round."

"What about you?" he asks Em, my best girlfriend.

"You go ahead," she tells him, and then we both laugh as he grins and spins around to give his scancard to the Official monitoring the game. Xander's always been this way about the games—completely alive with energy and anticipation. I remember playing with him when we were little, how we both played hard and didn't let the other win.

I wonder when I stopped liking the games. It's hard to remember.

Now, Xander settles himself at the table, saying something that makes everyone else laugh. I smile to myself. It really is more fun to watch him than to play yourself. And this game, Check, is one of his favorites. It's a game of skill, the kind he likes best.

"So," Em says softly, the sounds of laughter and talking covering her words from everyone but me, "What is it like? *Knowing* your Match?"

I knew she would ask me this; I know it's what everyone would like to know. And I answer the only way I can. I tell her the truth. "It's Xander," I say. "It's wonderful."

Em nods in understanding. "All this time none of us thought we could ever end up with one another," she says. "And then it happens."

"I know," I say.

"And *Xander*," she says. "He's the best of us all." Someone calls her name and she drifts toward another table.

As I watch, Xander picks up the gray pieces and puts them out on the gray and black squares of the board. Most of the colors inside the game center are drab: gray walls, brown plainclothes for the students, dark blue plainclothes for those who have already received their permanent work positions. Any brightness in the room comes from us: from the shades of our hair, from our laughter. When Xander sets down his last piece, he looks across the board at me and says, right in front of his opponents, "I'm going to win this one for my *Match*." Everyone turns to stare at me and he grins mischievously.

I roll my eyes at him, but I'm still blushing a few moments later when someone taps me on the shoulder. I turn around.

An Official waits behind me. "Cassia Reyes?" she asks.

"Yes," I answer, glancing over at Xander. He's engrossed in making his move and doesn't see what's happening.

"Could you come outside with me for a moment? It won't take long, and it's nothing to worry about. Merely procedural."

Does the Official know what happened when I tried to view the microcard?

"Of course," I say, because there's no other answer when an Official asks you for something. I look back at my friends. Their eyes are on the game in front of them and on the players moving the pieces. No one notices when I leave. Not even Xander. The crowd swallows me up and I follow the Official's white uniform out of the room.

"Let me reassure you that you have nothing to worry about," the Official tells me, smiling. Her voice sounds kind. She leads me to the small greenspace outside the center. Even though being with an Official adds to my nervousness, the open air feels good after the crowd inside.

We walk across the neatly cut grass toward a metal bench that sits directly underneath a street lamp. There's not another person in sight. "You don't even have to tell me what happened," the Official says. "I know. The face on the microcard wasn't the right one, was it?"

She *is* kind: she didn't make me say the words. I nod.

"You must be very worried. Have you told anyone what happened?"

"No," I say. She gestures for me to sit down on the bench and so I do.

"Excellent. Let me set your mind at ease." She looks directly into my eyes. "Cassia, absolutely nothing has changed. You are still Matched with Xander Carrow."

"Thank you," I say, and I'm so grateful that saying it once isn't enough. "Thank you." The confusion leaves me and I finally, finally, finally can relax. I sigh and she laughs.

"And may I congratulate you on your Match? It's caused quite a stir. People are talking about it all over the Province. Perhaps even all through the Society. It hasn't happened in many years." She pauses briefly and then continues. "I don't suppose you brought your microcard with you tonight?"

"Actually, I did." I pull it out of my pocket. "I was worried—I didn't want anyone else to see . . ."

She holds out her hand, and I drop the microcard into her outstretched palm. "Perfect. I'll take care of this." She places it inside her small Official's case. I catch a glimpse of her tablet container and notice that it is larger than standard issue. She sees my glance. "Higher-level Officials carry extra," she says. "In case of an emergency." I nod, and she continues. "But that's not something you need to worry about. Now, *this* is for you." She takes another microcard from a side pocket inside the case. "I've checked it myself. Everything is in order."

"Thank you."

Neither of us says anything for a few moments after I

slip the new microcard into my pocket. At first, I look around at the grass and the metal benches and the small concrete fountain in the center of the greenspace, which sends up silvery wet showers of water every few seconds. Then I peek over at the woman next to me, trying to catch a glimpse of the insignia on her shirt pocket. I know she is an Official, because she wears white clothing, but I am not sure which Department of Society she represents.

"I'm part of the Matching Department, authorized to deal with information malfunctions," the Official says, noticing my glance. "Fortunately, we don't have much work to do. Since the Matching is so important to the Society, it's very well regulated."

Her words remind me of a paragraph in the official Matching material: *The goal of Matching is twofold: to provide the healthiest possible future citizens for our Society and to provide the best chances for interested citizens to experience successful Family Life. It is of the utmost importance to the Society that the Matches be as optimal as possible.*

"I've never heard of a mistake like this before."

"I'm afraid it does happen now and then. Not often." She is silent for a moment, and then she asks the question that I do not want to hear: "Did you recognize the other person whose face you saw?"

Suddenly and irrationally I am tempted to lie. I want to say that I have no idea, that I have never seen that face before. I look over at the fountain again and as I watch the rise and fall of the water I know that my pause gives me away. So I answer.

"Yes."

"Can you tell me his name?"

She already knows all of this, of course, so there is nothing to do but tell the truth. "Yes. Ky Markham. That's what was so strange about the whole thing. The odds of a mistake being made, and of a mistake being made with someone else I know—"

"Are virtually nonexistent," she agrees. "That's true. It makes us wonder if the error was intentional, some kind of joke. If we find the person, we will punish them severely. It was a cruel thing to do. Not only because it was upsetting and confusing for you, but also because of Ky."

"Does he know?"

"No. He has no idea. The reason I said it was cruel to use him as part of this prank is because of what he is."

"What he is?" Ky Markham moved to our Borough back when we were ten. He is good-looking and quiet. He's very still. He is not a troublemaker. I don't see him as much as I once did; last year, he received his work position early and he no longer goes to Second School with the rest of the youth in our Borough.

The Official nods and leans a little closer, even though there is no one around to hear us. The light from the street lamp above shines down, hot, and I shift a little. "This is confidential information, but Ky Markham could never be your Match. He will never be anyone's Match."

"He's chosen to be a Single, then." I'm not sure why this information is confidential. Lots of people in our school have chosen to be single. There's even a paragraph about it in the official Matching material: *Please consider carefully whether you are a good candidate to be Matched. Remember, Singles are equally important in the Society. As you are aware, the current Leader of the Society is a Single. Both Matched and Single citizens experience full and satisfying lives. However, children are only allowed to be born to those who choose to be Matched.*

She leans closer to me. "No. He's not a Single. Ky Markham is an Aberration."

Ky Markham is an Aberration?

Aberrations live among us; they're not dangerous like Anomalies, who have to be separated from Society. Though Aberrations usually acquire their status due to an Infraction, they are protected; their identities aren't usually common knowledge. Only the Officials in the Societal Classification Department and other related fields have access to such information.

I don't ask my question out loud, but she knows what I am thinking. "I'm afraid so. It's through no fault of his own. But his father committed an Infraction. The Society couldn't overlook a factor like that, even when they allowed the

Markhams to adopt Ky. He had to retain his classification as an Aberration, and, as such, was ineligible to be entered in the Matching pool." She sighs. "We don't make the microcards until a few hours before the Banquet. It's likely the error occurred then. We're already checking to see who had access to your microcard, who could have added Ky's picture before the Banquet."

"I hope you find out who did it," I say. "You're right. It's cruel."

"We'll find out," she says, smiling at me. "I can promise you that." Then she looks down, glances at her watch. "I have to leave now. I hope that I've been able to eliminate your concern."

"Yes, thank you." I try to pull my thoughts from the boy who is an Aberration. I should be thinking about how wonderful it is that everything is back in order. But instead I think about Ky—how sorry I feel for him, how I wish I didn't have to know this about him and could have gone on thinking he had chosen to be a Single.

"I don't need to remind you to keep the information about Ky Markham confidential, do I?" she asks mildly, but I hear the iron in her voice. "The only reason I shared it with you was so that you could know without a doubt that he was never intended to be your Match."

"Of course. I won't say anything to anyone."

"Good. It's probably best that you keep this to yourself.

Of course, we could call a meeting if you would like. I could explain to your parents and Xander and his parents what happened—"

"No!" I say forcefully. "No. I don't want anyone to know, except—"

"Except who?"

I don't answer, and suddenly her hand is on my arm. She does not grip me roughly, but I can tell that she will wait out the answer to her brief question: "Who?"

"My grandfather," I admit. "He's almost eighty."

She lets go of my arm. "When is his birthday?"

"Tomorrow."

She thinks for a moment, then nods. "If you feel that you need to talk to someone about what happened, he would be the optimal one. Still. That is the only person?"

"Yes," I say. "I don't want anyone else to know. I don't mind Grandfather knowing because . . ." I leave the sentence unfinished. She knows why. At least one of the reasons why, anyway.

"I'm glad you feel that way," the Official says, nodding. "I have to admit that it makes things easier for me. Obviously, when you talk to your grandfather, you will tell him that he will be cited if he mentions this to anyone else. And that's certainly not something he wants now. He could lose his preservation privileges."

"I understand."

The Official smiles, stands up. "Is there anything else I can help you with tonight?"

I am glad the interview is over. Now that all is right again with my world, I want to take my place back inside that room full of people. It suddenly feels very lonely out here.

"No, thank you."

She gestures at the path leading back to the center. "Best wishes to you, Cassia. I'm glad I could help."

I thank her one last time and walk away. She stays behind, watching me go. Even though I know it's nonsense, I feel as if she watches me all the way to the door, all the way down the halls and back into the room and over to the table where Xander still plays the game. He looks up and holds my gaze. He noticed that I was gone. *Everything all right?* his eyes ask me, and I nod. It is now.

Everything is back to normal. Better than normal—now I can again enjoy the fact that I've been Matched with Xander.

Still, I wish she hadn't told me about Ky. I won't be able to look at him the same way again, now that I know too much about him.

There are so many of us inside the game center. It is hot and humid in the room, reminding me of the tropical ocean simulation we had in Science once, the one about the coral reefs that teemed with fish before the Warming killed them all. I taste sweat and breathe water.

Someone bumps into me as an Official makes an announcement over the main speaker. The crowd goes quiet to listen:

"Someone has dropped their tablet container. Please, stand completely still and do not speak until we locate it."

Everyone stops immediately. I hear the clatter of dice and a soft thud as someone, perhaps Xander, puts down a game piece. Then all is quiet. No one moves. A lost container is a serious matter. I look at a girl near me, and she stares back at me, wide-eyed, openmouthed, frozen in place. I think again of that ocean simulation, how the instructor paused it in the middle to explain something, and the fish projected around the room stared back at us, unblinking, until she switched the simulation back on.

We all wait for the switch to be thrown, for the instructor to tell us what comes next. My mind begins to wander, to escape this place where we all hold still. Are there other unknown Aberrations standing here in this room, swimming in this water? *Water.* I recall another memory of water, real this time, a day when Xander and I were ten.

Back then, we had more free-recreation time, and in the summers we almost always spent it at the swimming pool. Xander liked to swim in the blue-chlorinated water; I liked to sit on the pockmarked cement side of the pool and swish my feet back and forth before I went in. That's what I was doing when Xander appeared next to me, a worried look on his face.

"I've lost my tablet container," he told me quietly.

I glanced down to make sure that mine was still hooked to my swimwear. It was; its metal clip snapped securely to the strap over my left shoulder. We'd had our tablet containers for a few weeks, and at that point they contained one tablet. The first one. The blue one. The one that can save us; the one with enough nutrients to keep us going for several days if we have water, too.

There was plenty of water in the pool. That was the problem. How was Xander ever going to find the container?

"It's probably underwater," I said. "Let's get the lifeguard to clear the pool."

"No," Xander said, his jaw set. "Don't tell them. They'll cite me for losing it. Don't say anything. I'll find it." Carrying our own tablets is an important step toward our own independence; losing them is the same as admitting we aren't ready for the responsibility. Our parents carry our tablets for us until we are old enough to take them over, one by one. First the blue, when we are ten. Then, when we turn thirteen, the green one. The one that calms us if we need calming.

And when we're sixteen, the red one, the one we can only take when a high-level Official tells us to do so.

At first, I tried to help Xander, but the chlorine always hurt my eyes. I dove and dove and then, when my eyes burned so much I could barely see, I climbed back onto the cement next to the pool and tried to look beneath the sun-bright surface of the water.

None of us ever wears a watch when we are small; time is kept for us. But I still knew. I knew that he had been under the water much longer than he should. I had measured it out in heartbeats and in the slap of the waves against the side of the pool as one person, then another, then another, dove in.

Did he drown? For a moment, I was blinded by sunlight slanting off the water, white, and paralyzed by my fear, which felt white, too. But then I stood up and drew a deep breath into my lungs to scream to the world *Xander is under the water, save him, save him!* Before my scream was born, a voice I did not know asked, "Is he drowning?"

"I can't tell," I said, tearing my eyes away from the water. A boy stood next to me; tanned skin, dark hair. A new boy. That was all I had time to notice before he vanished, slipping under the surface in one quick motion.

A pause, a few more slaps of the waves against the cement, and Xander's head popped up above the water. He grinned triumphantly at me, holding the waterproof case. "Got it," he said.

"Xander," I said, relieved. "Are you all right?"

"Of course," he said, the confident light back in his eyes. "Why would you think I wouldn't be?"

"You were under so long that I thought you were drowning," I admitted. "And so did that boy—" Suddenly I panicked. *Where did the other boy go?* He had not come up for air.

"What boy?" Xander asked, puzzled.

"He went searching for you." And then I saw him, below the blue, a shadow under the water. "He's right there. Is *he* drowning?"

Just then the boy broke the surface of the water, coughing, his hair glistening. A red scrape, almost healed but still noticeable, ran along his cheek. I did my best not to stare. Not just because injuries are uncommon in a place where we are all so healthy and safe, but because he was unknown to me. A stranger.

It took the boy a few moments to catch his breath again. When he did, he looked at me but spoke to Xander, saying, "You didn't drown."

"No," agreed Xander. "*You* almost did, though."

"I know," the boy said. "I meant to save you." He corrected himself. "I mean, to *help* you."

"Don't you know how to swim?" I asked him.

"I *thought* I did," the boy said, which made both Xander and me laugh. The boy looked into my eyes and smiled. The smile seemed to surprise him; it surprised me, too, the warmth of it.

The boy looked back at Xander. "She looked worried when you didn't come back up."

"I'm not worried anymore," I said, relieved that everyone was safe. "Are you visiting someone?" I asked the boy, hoping he was staying for a long visit. I already liked him because he had wanted to help Xander.

"No," said the boy, and though he still smiled, his voice sounded quiet and still like the water had become around us. He looked right at me. "I belong here."

Now, my eyes fixed on the crowd in front of me, I feel that same feeling of relief and release as I see a familiar face, someone who, until now, I had been desperately worried about. Someone I must have thought had drowned or slipped or been pulled under and might never be seen again.

Ky Markham is here and he looks right at me.

Without thinking, I take a step toward him. That's when I feel something burst beneath my foot. The lost tablet container has broken open, and everything it is supposed to protect has spilled out on the floor and been crushed under my foot. Bluegreenred.

I stop in my tracks but the movement has been noted. Officials swarm toward me and the people near me draw breath and call out, "Over here! It's broken!"

I have to turn away when an Official takes my elbow and asks me what happened. When I look back at where Ky stood, he has disappeared. Just like he did that day into the pool. Just like his face did earlier on the port at my house.

CHAPTER 6

"There was a new boy at the pool today," I told my parents that long-ago night, after the incident while Xander and I were swimming. I was careful to leave out any mention of Xander losing his tablet container. I didn't want him to get in trouble. The omission felt like the tablet itself stuck in my throat. Every time I swallowed, I felt it catch there, threatening to choke me.

But still, I didn't tell.

My parents exchanged glances. "A *new* boy? Are you sure?" my father asked.

"I'm sure," I said. "His name is Ky Markham. Xander and I swam with him."

"He's staying with the Markhams, then," my father said.

"They've adopted him," I told my parents. "He calls Aida his mother and Patrick his father. I heard him."

My parents exchanged glances. Adoptions were and are virtually unheard of in our Province of Oria.

We heard a knock on the door. "Stay here, Cassia," my father said. "Let us see who it is."

I waited back in the kitchen, but I heard Xander's father, Mr. Carrow, at the door, his deep loud voice booming through the foyer. We aren't allowed to go into one another's residences, but I could imagine him standing there on the steps, looking like an older version of Xander. Same blond hair. Same laughing blue eyes.

"I talked with Patrick and Aida Markham," he said. "I thought you'd want to know. The boy is an orphan. He's from the Outer Provinces."

"He is?" My mother's voice held a note of concern. The Outer Provinces are on the geographic fringe of the Society where life is harder and wilder. Sometimes people refer to them as the Lesser Provinces, or the Backward Provinces, because they have so little order and knowledge there. There's a higher concentration of Aberrations there than in the general populace. And even Anomalies, some say. Though no one knows for certain where the Anomalies are. They used to be kept in safe houses, but many of those stand empty these days.

"He's here with full Society approval," Mr. Carrow said. "Patrick showed me the paperwork himself. He told me to tell anyone else who might be concerned. I knew you'd be worried, Molly, and you, too, Abran."

"Well, then," my mother said, "it sounds all right." I edged around the corner to look into the foyer, where my parents' backs were to me and Xander's father stood on the steps with the night behind him.

Then Xander's father dropped his voice, and I had to listen closely to hear what he said over the low hum of the port in the foyer.

"Molly, you should have seen Aida. And Patrick. They seemed alive again. The boy is Aida's nephew. Her sister's son."

My mother's hand went up to her hair, a gesture she always made when she was uncomfortable. Because we all remembered vividly what had happened to the Markhams.

It was a rare case of government failure. A Class One Anomaly should never have been unidentified, let alone allowed to roam the streets, to sneak into the government offices where Patrick worked and where his son was visiting him that day. We all kept quiet about it, but we all knew. Because the Markham boy was gone, murdered while he waited for his father to come back from a meeting elsewhere in the building. Because Patrick Markham himself had to spend time being healed, since the Anomaly waited in the office, quiet, and attacked Patrick, too.

"Her nephew," my mother said, her voice filled with empathy. "Of course Aida would want to raise him."

"And the government might feel like they owed it to Patrick to make an exception for him," my father said.

"Abran," my mother said reproachfully.

But Xander's father agreed. "It's logical. An exception as recompense for the accident. A son to replace the one that they shouldn't have had to lose. That's how the Officials see it."

Later, my mother came to my room to tuck me in. With her voice soft like the blankets she settled around me, she asked, "Did you hear us talking?"

"Yes," I said.

"The Markhams' nephew—son—starts school tomorrow."

"Ky," I said. "That's his name."

"Yes," she said. She bent down and her long blond hair swung over her shoulder and her freckles looked like stars scattered across her skin. She smiled at me. "You'll be nice to him, won't you?" she asked. "And help him fit in? It might be hard to be new when everyone else belongs."

"I will," I promised.

As it turned out, her advice was unnecessary. The next day at Second School, Ky said hello and introduced himself to everyone. Quiet and quick, he moved through the halls; he told everyone who he was so that no one had to ask. When the bell rang, he disappeared into the groups of students. It was shocking how quickly he vanished. He was there one minute—separate and distinct and new—and then he became part of the crowd, as though he had done it all of his life. As if he had never lived anywhere but here.

And that is how it's always been with Ky, I realize now, looking back. We have always seen him swimming along the surface. Only that first day did we see him dive deep.

"I have something to tell you," I say to Grandfather as I pull up a chair next to him. The Officials didn't keep me too long at the game center after I stepped on the tablets; I still have enough time for a visit. I'm grateful, because this is the second-to-last time that I will visit him. The thought makes me feel hollow.

"Ah," Grandfather says. "Something good?" He sits by the window, as he often does at night. He watches the sun out of the world and the stars into it and sometimes I wonder if he watches the sun come up again. Is it hard to sleep when you know you are almost at the end? Do you not want to miss a moment, even those that would otherwise seem dull and unremarkable?

In the night, the colors wash away; gray and black take over. Now and then a bright pinprick of light flashes as a street lamp lights up. The air-train tracks, dull in the daylight, look like beautiful glowing paths above the ground now that their evening lights have been turned on. As I watch, an air train rushes past, carrying people along in its white and lighted space.

"Something strange," I say, and Grandfather puts down his fork. He is eating a piece of something called pie, which I have actually never tasted, but it looks delicious. I wish that it weren't against the rules for him to share his food with me.

"Everything's fine. I'm still Matched to Xander," I say. I've learned from the Society that this is the way to give news; reassurance first, all else after. "But there was an error with my microcard. When I went to view it, Xander's face vanished. And I saw someone else."

"You saw someone *else*?"

I nod, trying not to look too hard at the food on his

dish. The flakiness of the sugared crust, which reminds me of crystals on an edge of snow. The red-stained berries smeared across the plate, ripe and surely full of taste. The words I've said cling to my mind like the pastry does to the heavy silver fork. *I saw someone else.*

"What did you feel, when you saw that other boy's face come up on the screen?" Grandfather asks kindly, putting his hand on mine. "Were you worried?"

"A little," I say. "I was confused. Because I know the second boy, too."

Grandfather's eyebrows curve in surprise. "You do?"

"It's Ky Markham," I tell him. "Patrick and Aida's son. He lives in Mapletree Borough, down the street from me."

"What explanation did the Official give you for the mistake?"

"It wasn't a mistake by the Society," I say. "The Society doesn't make mistakes."

"Of course not," Grandfather says, his tone measured and even. "People do, though."

"That's what the Official thinks must have happened. She thinks someone must have altered my microcard and put Ky's face on there."

"Why?" Grandfather wonders.

"She thinks it was some kind of cruel joke. Because," I lower my voice even further, "of Ky's status. He's an Aberration."

Grandfather pushes out of his chair, knocking his tray to the ground. I'm surprised to see how thin he's grown, but he stands straight as a tree. "There was a picture of an Aberration as *your* Match?"

"Just for a moment," I say, trying to reassure him. "But it was an error. Xander's my Match. This other boy wasn't even in the Matching pool at all."

Grandfather doesn't sit down, even though I remain in my chair hoping to calm him, to make him see that this is all right.

"Did they say why he was classified that way?"

"His father did something," I say. "It isn't Ky's fault." And it isn't. I know it, and Grandfather knows it. The Officials never would have allowed the adoption if Ky himself had been a threat.

Grandfather looks at the plate where it clattered from the tray onto the floor. I move to pick it up, but he stops me. "No," he says, his voice sharp, and then he bends creakily. As if he were made of old wood, an old tree, stiff wooden joints. He pushes the last pieces of food back onto the plate and then he looks at me with his clear eyes. Nothing stiff about *them*; they are alive, full of movement. "I don't like it," he says. "Why would someone change your microcard?"

"Grandfather," I say. "Please, sit down. It's a prank, and they'll find out who did it and take care of everything. An Official from the Matching Department said so herself." I wish I hadn't told him. Why did I think there would be comfort in the telling?

But now there is. "That poor boy," Grandfather says, his

voice sad. "He's been marked through no fault of his own. Do you know him well?"

"We're friendly, but we're not close. I see him sometimes during free-rec hours on Saturdays," I explain. "He received his permanent work position a year ago and so I don't see him much anymore."

"And what *is* his work position?"

I hesitate to tell Grandfather because it is such a dismal one. We were all surprised when Ky received such a lowly assignment, since Patrick and Aida are well respected. "He works at the nutrition disposal center."

Grandfather makes a grimace. "That's hard, unfulfilling work."

"I know," I say. I've noticed that, in spite of the gloves the workers wear, Ky's hands are permanently red from the heat of the water, the machines. But he does not complain.

"And the Official let you tell me this?" Grandfather asks.

"Yes," I say. "I asked her if I could tell one person. You."

Grandfather's eyes gleam mischievously. "Because the dead can't talk?"

"No," I say. I love Grandfather's jokes, but I can't joke back, not about this. It's coming too quickly. I will miss him too much. "I wanted to tell you because I knew you would understand."

"Ah," Grandfather says, raising his eyebrows in a wry expression. "And did I?"

Now I *am* laughing, a little. "Not as well as I'd hoped. You acted like my parents would have, if I'd told them."

"Of course I did," he says. "I want to protect you."

Not always, I think, raising my eyebrows back at him. Grandfather is the one who finally made me stop sitting at the edge of the pool.

He joined us there one summer day and asked, "What is she doing?"

"That's what she always does," Xander said.

"Can't she swim?" Grandfather asked, and I glared at him because I could speak for myself. He knew that.

"She can," Xander said. "She just doesn't like to do it."

"I don't like the jumping-in part," I informed Grandfather.

"I see," he said. "What about the diving board?"

"Especially not that."

"All right," he told me. He sat next to me on the edge. Even back then, when he was younger and stronger, I remember thinking how old he looked compared to my friends' grandparents. My grandparents were one of the last couples who chose to be Matched later in life. They were thirty-five when they Matched. My father, their one child, wasn't born until four years later. Now, no one is allowed to have a child after they turn thirty-one.

The sun shone right through his silver hair and made me see each strand even when I wasn't looking for such detail.

It made me sad, even though he made me angry. "*This* is exciting," he said, kicking his feet in the water. "I can see how you'd never want to do anything but sit." I heard the teasing in his voice and turned away.

Then he stood up and walked toward the diving board. "Sir," said the waterguard in charge of the pool. "Sir?"

"I have a recreational pass," Grandfather told her, not stopping. "I'm in excellent health." Then he climbed up the ladder to the diving board, looking stronger and stronger the higher he climbed.

He didn't look over at me before he jumped; he went right in, and before he broke through the surface of the water I was on my feet, walking across the hot wet cement to the high-dive ladder, the soles of my feet and my pride both on fire.

And I jumped.

"You're thinking of the pool, aren't you?" he asks me now.

"Yes," I say, laughing a little. "You didn't keep me safe then. You practically dared me to leap to my death," and then I cringe, because I didn't mean to say that word. I don't know why I'm afraid of it. Grandfather isn't. The Society isn't. I shouldn't be.

Grandfather doesn't seem to notice. "You were ready to jump," he says. "You just weren't sure of it yet."

We both fall silent, remembering. I try not to look at the timepiece on the wall. I have to leave soon so I can make curfew, but I don't want Grandfather to think that I am marking the minutes. Marking time until our visit is over. Marking time until his life is over. Although, if you think about it, I am marking time for my own life, too. Every minute you spend with someone gives them a part of your life and takes part of theirs.

Grandfather senses my distraction and asks me what is on my mind. I tell him, because I won't have many more chances to do so, and he reaches out and grips my hand. "I'm glad to give you part of my life," he says, and it is such a nice thing to say and he says it so kindly that I say it back. Even though he is almost eighty, even though his body seemed frail earlier, his grip feels strong, and again I feel sad.

"There's something else I wanted to tell you," I say to Grandfather. "I signed up for hiking as my summer leisure activity."

He looks pleased. "They've brought that back?" Grandfather used to hike as one of his leisure activities years ago, and he's talked about it ever since.

"It's new this summer. I've never seen it offered before."

"I wonder who the instructor is," he says, thoughtfully. Then he looks out the window. "I wonder where they'll take you to hike." I follow his gaze again. There isn't much wildness out there, though we have plenty of greenspace—parks and recreation fields. "Maybe to one of the larger recreation areas," I say.

"Maybe to the Hill," he says, the light returning to his eyes.

The Hill is the last place in the City that has been left forested and wild. I can see it now, its prickly green back rising out of the Arboretum where my mother works. It was once mostly used for Army training, but since most of the Army has been moved to the Outer Provinces, there isn't as much need for it anymore.

"Do you think so?" I ask, excited. "I've never been there before. I mean, I've been to the Arboretum lots of times, of course, but I've never had permission to go on the Hill."

"You'll love it if they let you hike the Hill," Grandfather says, his face animated. "There's something about climbing to the highest point you can see, and there's no one clearing a path for you, no simulator. Everything's real—"

"Do you really think they'll let us hike there?" I ask. His enthusiasm is contagious.

"I hope so." Grandfather gazes out the window in the direction of the Arboretum, and I wonder if the reason he spends so much time looking out lately is because he likes to remember what he carries within.

It is as though he can read my mind. "I'm nothing but an old man sitting here thinking about his memories, aren't I?"

I smile. "There's nothing wrong with doing that." In fact, at the end of a life, it's encouraged.

"That's not exactly what I'm doing," Grandfather said.

"Oh?"

"I'm *thinking*." Again, he knows my thoughts. "It's not the same as remembering. Remembering is part of thinking, but not all of it."

"What are you thinking about?"

"Many things. A poem. An idea. Your grandmother." My grandmother died early of one of the last kinds of cancer when she was sixty-two. I never knew her. The compact was hers before it was mine—a gift from her mother-in-law, Grandfather's mother.

"What do you think she would say about my Match?" I ask him. "About what happened today?"

He's quiet, and I wait. "I think," he says finally, "she would ask you if you wondered."

I want to ask him what he means, but I hear the bell ringing, announcing that the final air train for the Boroughs will be coming through soon. I have to go.

"Cassia?" Grandfather says as I stand up. "You still have the compact I gave you, don't you?"

"Yes," I say, surprised that he would ask. It's the most valuable thing I own. The most valuable thing I will ever own.

"Will you bring it to my Final Banquet tomorrow?" he asks.

Tears well in my eyes. He must want to see it again to remember my grandmother, and his mother. "Of course I will, Grandfather."

"Thank you."

My tears threaten to spill over onto his cheek as I bend down to kiss him. I hold them back; I don't cry. I wonder when I can. It won't be tomorrow night at the Final Banquet. People will be watching then. To see how Grandfather handles leaving, and to see how we manage being left.

As I walk down the hall, I hear other residents talking to themselves or to visitors behind their closed doors, and the sound of ports turned up loud because many of the elderly cannot hear well. Some rooms are silent. Perhaps some are like Grandfather, sitting in front of open windows and thinking about people who are no longer here.

She would ask you if you wondered.

I step into the elevator and push the button, feeling sad and strange and confused. What did he mean?

I *know* Grandfather's time is running out. I have known this for a long time. But why, as the elevator doors slide shut, do I suddenly feel that mine is running out as well?

My grandmother would want to know if I wondered if it wasn't a mistake after all. If Ky were meant to be my Match.

For a moment, I did. When I saw Ky's face flash in front of me so quick I couldn't even see the color of his eyes, only the dark of them as they looked back at me, I wondered, *Is it you?*

CHAPTER 7

Today is Sunday. It is Grandfather's eightieth birthday, so tonight he will die.

People used to wake up and wonder, "Will today be the end?" or lie down to sleep, not knowing if they would come back out of the dark. Now, we know which day will be the end of the light and which night will be the long, last one. The Final Banquet is a luxury. A triumph of planning, of the Society, of human life and the quality of it.

All the studies show that the best age to die is eighty. It's long enough that we can have a complete life experience, but not so long that we feel useless. That's one of the worst feelings the elderly can have. In societies before ours, they could get terrible diseases, like depression, because they didn't feel needed anymore. And there is a limit to what the Society can do, too. We can't hold off all the indignities of aging much past eighty. Matching for healthy genes can only take us so far.

Things didn't used to be this fair. In the old days, not everyone died at the same age and there were all kinds of problems and uncertainty. You could die anywhere—on the street, in a medical center as my grandmother did, even on an air train. You could die alone.

No one should die alone.

The hour is very early, faint blue and pale pink, as we arrive on the almost-empty air train and walk along the cement pathway toward the door of Grandfather's building. I want to step off the path and take off my shoes and walk with my bare feet on the cool, sharp grass, but today is not a day to deviate from what is planned. My parents and Bram and I are all quiet, thinking. None of us have work or leisure hours. Today is for Grandfather. Tomorrow, things go back to normal again and we will move on and he will be gone.

It's expected. It's fair. I remind myself of this as we climb into the elevator to go to his apartment. "You can push the button," I tell Bram, trying to joke with him. Bram and I used to fight over who got to push the buttons when we came to visit. Bram smiles and presses the 10. *For the last time*, I think to myself. After today, there will be no Grandfather to visit. We will have no reason to come back.

Most people don't know their grandparents this well. The kind of relationship I have with my other grandparents in the Farmlands is much more common. We communicate via port every few months and visit every few years. Many grandchildren watch the Final Banquet on the portscreens, too, one step removed from what's happening. I have never envied those other children; I've pitied them. Even today, I feel that way.

"How long do we have before the Committee shows up?" Bram asks my father.

"About half an hour," my father answers. "Does everyone have their gifts?"

We nod. Each of us has brought something to give Grandfather. I'm not sure what my parents chose for him, but I know Bram went to the Arboretum to get a rock from a spot as near to the Hill as possible.

Bram catches me looking at him, and he opens his palm to show me the rock again. It is round and brown and still a bit dirty. It looks a little like an egg, and when he brought it back yesterday, he told me that he'd found it under a tree in a pile of soft green pine needles that looked like a nest.

"He's going to love it," I say to Bram.

"He'll love your gift, too." Bram closes his fist around the rock again. The doors slide open and we step out into the hall.

I've made Grandfather a letter for my gift. I got up early this morning and spent time cutting and pasting and copying sentiments on the letter-making program on the port. Before I printed the letter, I found a poem from the decade in which he was born and included it as well. Not many people care about poetry after they finish school, but Grandfather always has. He's read all of the Hundred Poems many times.

One of the doors along the hall opens and an old woman peeks her head out. "You're going to the Banquet for Mr. Reyes?" she asks, and she doesn't even wait for us to answer. "It's private, isn't it?"

"It is," my father says, stopping politely to speak with her, even though I know he is eager to see his father. He can't keep himself from glancing down the hall at Grandfather's closed door.

The woman grumbles a little. "I wish it were public. I'd like to go so I can get ideas. Mine's in less than two months. You can bet it's going to be public." She laughs a little, a short, harsh sound, and then she asks, "Can you come and tell me about it afterward?"

My mother comes to the rescue, as she and my father always do for each other. "Perhaps," Mama says, smiling, and she takes my father's hand and turns her back on the woman.

We hear a disappointed sigh and then a click behind us as the woman closes her door. The nameplate on her door says Mrs. Nash, and I remember that Grandpa has talked about her before. Nosy, he said.

"Can't she wait for her own turn to come, instead of talking about it on Grandfather's day?" Bram mutters, pushing open the door to Grandfather's residence.

It already feels like a different place. More hushed. A little lonelier. I think that is because Grandfather is not sitting at the window anymore. Today, he rests in a bed in the living room as his body shuts down. Right on time.

"Could you move me over to the window?" Grandfather asks, after saying hello to all of us.

"Certainly." My father reaches for the edge of the bed and pulls it smoothly toward the early morning light. "Remember when you did this for me? When I had all those inoculations as a child?"

Grandfather smiles. "That was a different house."

"And a different view," my father agrees. "All I could see from that window was the neighbor's yard and an air-train track if I looked high enough."

"But beyond that there was sky," Grandfather says softly. "You can almost always see the sky. And what's beyond that, I wonder? And after this?"

Bram and I exchange glances. Grandfather must be wandering a little today, which is to be expected. On the day the elderly turn eighty, the decline always accelerates. Not everyone dies at exactly the same time, but it is always before midnight.

"I've invited my friends to come immediately after the Committee visits," Grandfather says. "And then after they leave I'd like to spend some one-on-one time with each of you. Starting with you, Abran."

My father nods. "Of course."

The Committee does not take long. They arrive, three men and three women in their long white lab coats, and they bring things with them, too. The Banquet clothes that Grandfather will wear. Equipment for tissue preservation. A microcard with a history of his life so he can watch it on the port.

With the exception of maybe the microcard, I think Grandfather will like our gifts better.

After a few moments, Grandfather reappears wearing his Banquet clothes. They are basically plainclothes, simple pants and a shirt and socks, but they are made of fine-quality material, and he has been able to select the color.

I feel something catch in my throat when I see that the color he has chosen for his clothing is a light green. We are so much alike. And I wonder if he realized when I was born that the days of our Banquets would be so close together, since our birthdays are only a few days apart.

We all sit politely, Grandfather in his bed and the rest of us on chairs, while the Committee completes their part of the celebration.

"Mr. Reyes, we present to you the microcard with images and records from your life," they say. "It has been compiled by one of our best historians in your honor."

"Thank you," Grandfather says, reaching out his hand.

The box containing the microcard is like the silver one we receive when we are Matched, except for the color: gold. The microcard inside has pictures of Grandfather as a small boy, a teenager, a man. He hasn't seen some of these images in years, and I imagine that he is excited to view them today. The microcard also includes a summary of his life in words, read by one of the historians. Grandfather turns the golden box over in his hands as I did with my silver box not long ago at the Match Banquet. His life cupped in his palms, as mine was.

One of the women speaks next. She seems gentler than the others, but maybe that is because she is smaller and younger than the rest. "Mr. Reyes, have you chosen the person to take possession of your microcard when today is over?"

"My son, Abran," Grandfather says.

She holds out the device for the tissue collection, which, as a final courtesy to the elderly, the Society allows to take place privately, among family. "And we are pleased to formally announce that your data indicates you have qualified for preservation. Not everyone qualifies, as you know, and it is another honor that you can add to your already long list of achievements."

Grandfather takes the device from her and thanks her again. Before she can ask him who he's trusted with the delivery of the sample, he volunteers the information. "My son, Abran, will take care of this as well."

She nods her head. "Simply swab your cheek and put the sample in here," she says, demonstrating. "Then seal it up. You need to bring the sample to the Biological Preservation Department within twenty-four hours of collection. Otherwise we cannot guarantee that preservation will be effective."

I'm glad that Grandfather has qualified to have a tissue sample frozen. Now, for him, death may not necessarily be the end. Someday, the Society might figure out a way to bring us back. They don't promise anything, but I think we all know that it will happen eventually. When has the Society ever failed in reaching a goal?

The man next to her speaks. "The food for your guests and your own final meal should arrive within the hour." He leans over to hand Grandfather a printed menu card. "Are there any last-minute modifications you would like to make?"

Grandfather looks at the card and shakes his head. "Everything looks in order."

"Enjoy your Final Banquet, then," the man says, pocketing the card.

"Thank you." There is a wry twist to Grandfather's mouth as he says this, as though he knows something they don't.

As the Committee leaves, they all shake Grandfather's hand and say, "Congratulations." And I swear that I can read Grandfather's mind as he meets their gaze with his sharp eyes. *Are you congratulating me on my life, or on my death?*

"Let's get *this* over with," Grandfather says with a spark in his eye, looking at the tissue collection device, and we all laugh at his tone. Grandfather swabs his own cheek, puts the sample in the clear glass tube, and seals it shut. Some of the solemnity leaves the room now that the Committee has gone.

"Everything's going very well," Grandfather says, handing the tube to my father. "I am having a perfect death so far."

My father winces, an expression of pain crossing his face. I know he, like me, would prefer that Grandfather not use that word, but neither of us would think of correcting Grandfather today. The pain on my father's face makes him look younger, almost like a child for a moment. Perhaps he remembers his mother's death—so unusual, so difficult compared to a Final Banquet like this.

After today, he will be no one's child.

Even though I don't want to, I think of the murdered Markham boy. No celebration. No tissue preparation, no good-byes. *That hardly ever occurs,* I remind myself. *The odds of that happening are almost a million to one.*

"We have some gifts for you," Bram says to Grandfather. "Can we give them to you now?"

"*Bram,*" my father says reproachfully. "Perhaps he wants to get the microcard ready for viewing. He has guests on the way."

"I do want to do that," Grandfather says. "I'm looking forward to seeing my life pass before my eyes. And I'm looking forward to the food."

"What did you choose?" Bram asks, eager. The selections for Grandfather and his guests are the same, but it is an actual law that we must eat the food from the trays and he must eat the food on *his* plate. We're not allowed to share.

"All desserts," Grandfather says with a grin. "Cake. Pudding. Cookies. And something else. But let me see your gift before we do any of that, Bram."

Bram beams. "Close your eyes."

Grandfather obeys and holds out his hand. Bram places the rock gently into Grandfather's palm. A few particles of earth fall on the blanket covering Grandfather, and my mother reaches to brush them away. But at the last second, she pulls her hand back and smiles. Grandfather won't mind the dirt.

"A rock," Grandfather says, opening his eyes and looking down. He smiles at Bram. "I have a feeling I know where you found it."

Bram grins and ducks his head. My grandfather holds on tight to the rock. "Who's next, then?" he asks, almost merrily.

"I'd like to give my gift later, during the good-byes," my father says quietly.

"That won't leave me very much time to enjoy it," Grandfather teases.

Suddenly self-conscious about my letter—I don't want him to read it in front of everyone—I say, "Me too."

There is a knock on the door: some of Grandfather's friends. A few minutes after we let them in, more arrive. And more. And then the nutrition personnel, with all of Grandfather's desserts—his last meal—and the separate trays for his guests.

Grandfather lifts the cover from his plate and a heavenly, warm-fruit smell fills the room.

"I thought you might like some pie," Grandfather says, looking at me. He saw me, then, the other day, and I smile at him. At his signal, I lift the covers from the guest trays and we all gather around to eat. I serve everyone else first and then I pick up my piece of pie, flaky and warm and fruit-filled, and lift a forkful of the pastry to my mouth.

I wonder if death will always taste this good.

~

After all the guests have put down their forks and sighed in satiation, they talk with Grandfather, who leans back on a pile of thick white pillows. Bram eats on, stuffing himself with bites of everything. Grandfather smiles at him from across the room, amused.

"It's *so good*," Bram says around a mouthful of pie, and Grandfather laughs outright, a sound so warm and familiar that I smile, too, and put my hand down. I was about to touch Bram's arm, tell him to quit feasting. But if Grandfather doesn't mind, why should I?

My father doesn't eat anything. He puts a piece of pie on a round, white plate and then holds it in his hands, juice seeping out onto the china without him noticing. A little drop of it falls to the floor when he stands up to say good-bye to Grandfather's guests after the viewing of the microcard. "Thank you for coming," Papa says, and my mother bends down behind him to dab up the drop with her napkin. Someone else will move in after Grandfather leaves, and they won't want to see the signs of another person's Banquet. But that's not why my mother did it, I realize. She wanted to spare my father any worry, any tiny bit at all.

She takes the plate from my father as the door shuts behind the last guest. "Family time now," she says, and my grandfather nods.

"Thank goodness," he says. "I have things to say to each of you."

So far, except for that one moment when he talked about what might come next, Grandfather has been behaving as usual. I've heard that some of the elderly have surprised everyone at the end, by choosing not to die with dignity. They cry and get upset and go crazy. All it does is make their families sad. There is nothing they can do about it. It's the way things are.

By some unspoken agreement, my mother and Bram and I go into the kitchen to let my father speak with Grandfather first. Bram, drowsy and stuffed with food, puts his head down on the table and falls asleep, snoring gently. My mother smoothes his curly brown hair with her hand, and I imagine that Bram dreams of more desserts, a plate heaped with them. My eyes feel heavy, too, but I don't want to miss any part of Grandfather's last day.

After my father, Bram has a turn, and then my mother goes in to speak with Grandfather. The gift she has for him is a leaf from his favorite tree at the Arboretum. She picked it yesterday, so the edges have curled and become brown, but there is still green in the middle. She told me, while we waited and Bram slept, that Grandfather had asked if he could have his final celebration at the Arboretum, out in the blue-sky air. Of course, his request was denied.

My turn at last. As I go into the room I notice that the windows are open. It is not a cool afternoon, and the breeze feels urgent and hot as it blows through the apartment. Soon, though, it will be night and things will be cooler.

"I wanted to feel the air moving," Grandfather says to me as I sit in the chair next to his bed.

I hand him the gift. He thanks me and reads through it. "These are lovely words," Grandfather says. "Fine sentiments."

I should feel pleased, but I can tell there is something more coming.

"But none of these words are your own, Cassia," Grandfather says gently.

Tears sting my eyes and I look down at my hands. My hands that, like almost everyone else in our Society, cannot write, that merely know how to use the words of others. Words that have disappointed my grandfather. I wish I had brought a rock like Bram. Or nothing at all. Even coming here empty-handed would be better than disappointing Grandfather.

"You have words of your own, Cassia," Grandfather says to me. "I have heard some of them, and they are beautiful. And you have already given me a gift by visiting so often. I still love this letter because it is from you. I don't want to hurt your feelings. I want you to trust your own words. Do you understand?"

I look up and meet his eyes, and nod, because I know that's what he'll want me to do, and I can give that gift to him even if my letter is a failure. And then I think of something else. Since that day on the air train, I've kept the cottonwood seed in the pocket of my plainclothes. I pull it out now and give it to him.

"Ah," he says, lifting it up to look at it more closely. "Thank you, my dear. Look. It's trailing clouds of glory."

Now I wonder if Grandfather *is* starting to slip away already. I don't know what he means. I glance at the door, wondering if I should get one of my parents.

"I'm an old hypocrite, too," he says, his eyes mischievous again. "I told you to use your own words, and now I'm going to ask you for someone else's. Let me see your compact."

Surprised, I hold it out to him. He takes it and taps it sharply against his palm, twists something. The base of the compact opens up and I gasp in shock as a paper falls out. I can see right away that it is old—heavy and thick and creamy, not slick and white like the curls of paper that come out of the ports or the scribes.

Grandfather unfolds the paper carefully, gently. I try not to look too closely, in case he does not want me to see, but with a glance I can tell that the words are old, too. The type is not one in use anymore; the letters are small and black and cramped together.

His fingers tremble; whether it is from the end of his life drawing close or because of what he holds in his hand, I do not know. I want to help him, but I can tell that this is something he must do himself.

It doesn't take long for him to read the paper, and when he's finished, he closes his eyes. An emotion crosses his face that I cannot read. Something deep.

Then he opens his bright, beautiful eyes and looks straight

at me while he folds the paper back up. "Cassia. This is for you. It's even more precious than the compact."

"But it's so—" I stop before I can say the word *dangerous*.

There is no time. I hear my father and mother and brother speaking in the hall.

Grandfather looks at me with love in his eyes, and holds the paper out to me. A challenge, an offering, a gift. After a moment, I reach for it. My fingers close around the paper and he lets go.

He gives me back the compact, too; the paper fits neatly inside. As I snap the artifact shut, Grandfather leans toward me.

"Cassia," he whispers. "I am giving you something you won't understand, yet. But I think you will someday. You, more than the rest. And, remember. It's all right to wonder."

He holds on for a long time. It is an hour before midnight in a deep blue night when Grandfather looks at us and says the best words of all with which to end a life. "I love you. I love you. I love you. I love you."

We all say it back to him. Each of us means it and he smiles. He leans back on his pillows and closes his eyes.

Everything inside him has worked perfectly. He has lived a good life. It ends as it is supposed to end, at exactly the right time. I am holding his hand when he dies.

CHAPTER 8

"None of the showings are new," our friend Sera complains. "They've been the same for the past two months." Saturday night again; the same conversation as the week before.

"It's better than the other two choices," Em says. "Isn't it?" She glances over at me, waiting for my opinion. I nod. The choices are the same as usual: game center, showing, music. It's been less than a week since Grandfather's death, and I feel strange. He is gone, and now I know that there are stolen words inside my compact. It feels strange to know something others don't and to have something I shouldn't.

"So another vote from Cassia for the showing," Em says, keeping track. She winds a strand of black hair around her finger, looks at Xander. "What about you?"

I'm sure Xander wants to go back to the game center, but I don't. Our last excursion there didn't end so well, what with my stepping on the tablets and having to meet with an Official.

Xander knows what I'm thinking. "It wasn't your fault," he says. "You weren't the one who dropped them. It's not as though they cited you or anything."

"I know. But still."

We don't really discuss the music. Most youth aren't crazy about sitting with a few other people in the hall and listening to the Hundred Songs piped in from some other place—or maybe even some other time. I don't think I've ever heard of any work positions related to music. Maybe that makes sense. Maybe songs only need to be sung once, recorded, and passed along.

"No, let's do the showing," Xander says. "You know, that one about the Society? With all the aerial views?"

"I haven't seen that one yet," Ky Markham says behind me.

Ky. I turn to look at him, our eyes meeting for the first time since the night I stepped on the tablets. I haven't seen him since then. I should say I haven't seen him *in person*; all week long, his face has appeared in my mind the way it appeared on the screen, surprising me with its clarity and then disappearing suddenly. Leaving me wondering what it means. Why I keep thinking of him instead of moving on.

Perhaps it's because of what Grandfather said, at the end. By telling me it was all right to wonder. Somehow, though, I don't think he meant Ky. I think it might be something bigger. Something to do with the poetry.

"That settles it, then. We'll watch that one," Sera says.

"How could you miss an entire showing?" Piper's question is a good one. We never miss showings when they're new. This one has been around for several months, which means there should have been plenty of opportunities for Ky to see it. "Didn't you go with us when we went?"

"No," Ky says. "I worked late that night, I think." His tone is mild, but there is, and always has been, something a little deeper and more resonant about his voice. It has a slightly different timbre than most voices. It's the kind of thing you forget until you hear it again and remember *Oh yes. His voice has music.*

We all fall silent, as we always do when Ky talks about his work. We don't know what to say to him when he mentions it. I know now that he probably wasn't surprised with his assignment at the nutrition disposal center. He's always known he was an Aberration. He's been walking around with secrets for much longer than I have.

But the Society *wants* him to keep his secrets. I don't know what they would do if they found out about mine.

Ky looks away from Piper and back to me, and it occurs to me that I've been wrong about his eyes. I thought they were brown but I see now that they are dark blue, brought out by the color of his plainclothes. Blue is the most common eye color in Oria Province, but there is something different about his eyes and I'm not sure what it is. More depth? I wonder what he sees when he looks at me. If he seems to have depth to me, do I seem shallow and transparent to him?

I wish I had a microcard about Ky, I think. *Maybe, since I didn't really need one for Xander, I could ask for another one instead.* The thought makes me smile.

Ky still looks at me and I wonder for a moment if he is going to ask me what I am thinking about. But, of course, he doesn't. He doesn't learn by asking questions. He is an Aberration from the Outer Provinces and yet he has managed to blend in here. He learns by watching.

So I take my cue from him. I ask no questions and I keep my secrets.

When we sit down in the theater, Piper goes in first. Then Sera, Em, Xander, me, and last of all, Ky. The bigscreen hasn't rolled down and the lights aren't dimmed yet, so we have a few minutes to talk. "Are you all right?" Xander asks me quietly, his words a whisper near my ear. "It's not the tablets, is it? Is it your Grandfather?"

He knows me so well. "Yes," I say, and he reaches for my hand, gives it a squeeze. It's strange to me how our old childhood gestures come back, ones that dropped away as we stayed friends but grew older. Holding his hand still feels like friendship, like something I've known for years—but also different, now that it means more. Now that it means a Match.

Xander waits, to see if I have more to say, but I don't. *I can't tell Xander about Ky because Ky's sitting right here next to me*, I think, *and I can't tell Xander about the paper because this place is too crowded*. These are the reasons I give myself for not confiding in Xander as I usually do.

They do not feel as true as they should.

Em says something to Xander and he turns to answer. I stare straight ahead for a moment, thinking about how strange it is that I have started keeping secrets from Xander just as we have been Matched.

"It's been a few weeks since I've been able to spend Saturday night with all of you," Ky says. I glance over at him as the lights begin to dim, softening his face and, somehow, lessening the space between us. His next words hold a trace of bitterness—only a trace, but more than I've ever heard from him. "Having my vocation keeps me busy. I'm glad you all don't seem to mind."

"It's no trouble," I say. "We're your friends." But even as I say it, I wonder if we are. I don't know him the way I know the others.

"Friends." Ky says the word softly, and I wonder if he is thinking of the friends he must have had in the Outer Provinces.

The theater goes dark. I know without looking that Ky isn't turned toward me anymore and that Xander is. I look forward, straight into the black.

I always enjoy these few seconds in the theater before a showing, when all is dark and I am waiting. I always feel a drop in my stomach—wondering if, when the lights of the showing come on, I might find myself completely alone. Or wondering if the lights won't come up at all. I feel like I can't be sure; not in that first moment. I don't know why I like it.

But of course the lights come on the screen and the showing begins and I am not alone. Xander sits on one side of me, Ky on the other, and in front of me the screen shows the beginnings of the Society.

The cinematography is excellent; swooping low across the blue ocean, the green of the coast, over snow-crowned mountains, and on into the golden fields of the Farmlands, over the white dome of our very own City Hall (the audience cheers when it comes into view). Across more rolling green and gold toward another City, and another, and another. In each Province of the Society, people are likely cheering as they see their City—even if they have seen this showing before. When you see our Society like this, it's hard not to feel proud. Which, of course, is the point.

Ky takes a deep breath and I glance over at him. What I see surprises me. His eyes are wide and he has forgotten to keep his face still and calm. Instead, it is alight with wonder. He seems to think that he is really flying. He doesn't even notice me watching.

After that soaring beginning, however, the showing is basic. We go through how things used to be before the Society came into being and before everything worked according to statistics and predictions. Ky's face settles back into its usual smooth expression; I keep sneaking glances over during different parts of the showing to see if he is reacting again. But he's not.

When they get to the part about the implementation of Matching, Xander turns to look at me. In the pale light from the screen, I see his smile and I smile back. Xander's hand tightens on mine and I forget about Ky.

Until the end.

At the end, the showing takes us back to how things were before the Society. How things would be again if the Society fell. I don't know what set they used for this, but it is almost laughable. They have gone over the top with the dramatic, barren redlands; the shabby little houses; the few sullen, hard, sad-looking actors walking around the dangerous, almost-empty streets. Then, as if out of nowhere, sinister black aircraft appear in the sky and the people run screaming away. The Anthem of the Society plays in the background, ornate higher notes crying across a strong bass line that pounds the feelings home.

The scene is overdone. It's ludicrous, especially after the quiet scene at Grandfather's that I witnessed on Sunday. This isn't what death looks like. One of the actors falls to the ground dramatically. Garish red bloodstains cover his clothing. I hear Xander give a little snort of laughter next to me, and I know that he feels the same way I do. Feeling bad that I've ignored Ky for so long, I turn to him to share the joke.

He is crying. Without a sound.

A tear slips down his cheek and he brushes it away so quickly I almost don't know if it was there, but it was. It was. And now another tear, gone as quickly as the first. His eyes are so full that I wonder how he can see. But he does not look away from the screen.

I am not used to seeing someone suffer. I turn away.

When the movie ends, reprising the sweeping travelogue from the beginning, Ky takes a deep breath. I can tell that it aches. I don't glance over at him again until the lights go back up in the theater. When they do, he is calm and composed and back to the Ky I know. Or the one I thought I knew.

No one else has noticed. Ky does not know that I have seen him.

I say nothing. I ask no questions. I turn away. This is who I am. *But not who Grandfather thought you could be.* The thought comes into my mind like a sideways glance, like a flash of blue next to me. Ky. Is he watching me? Waiting for me to meet his gaze?

I wait one moment too long before I turn back. When I do, Ky is not looking at me anymore. If he ever was.

CHAPTER 9

Two days later, I stand with a group of other students in front of the main building of the Arboretum. An early morning mist lifts around us, shapes of people and trees appearing, it seems, out of nowhere.

"Have you ever done this before?" the girl next to me asks. I don't know her at all, so she must be from another Borough, a different Second School.

"Not really," I say, distracted by the fact that one of the figures appearing out of the mist has the shape of Ky Markham. He moves quiet and strong. Careful. When he sees me, he lifts his hand to wave. Apparently he has signed up for hiking as his summer leisure activity, too. After a second's pause, during which I smile and wave back at Ky, I add, "No. I've been walking. Never hiking."

"*No one* has done this before," says Lon, an annoying boy that I know from Second School. "It hasn't been offered in years."

"My grandfather knew how," I say.

Lon won't shut up. "*Knew*? As in past tense? Is he dead?"

Before I can answer, an Officer in Army green clears his throat as he comes to stand in front of us. He's older with crisp-short white hair and olive skin. His coloring and bearing remind me of Grandfather.

"Welcome," the Officer says in a voice as clipped and sharp as his hair. He does not sound welcoming, and I realize that the similarities to Grandfather do not go far. I have to stop looking for Grandfather. He won't materialize from the trees, no matter how much I wish it could happen. "I'm your instructor. You will address me as Sir."

Lon can't stop himself. "Do we get to go on the Hill?"

The Officer fixes him with a gaze and Lon wilts.

"No one," the Officer says, "speaks without my permission. Is that understood?"

We all nod.

"We're not going to waste any time. Let's get started."

He points behind him to one of the thickly forested Arboretum hills. Not the Hill, not the big one, but one of the smaller foothills that are usually off-limits unless you're an Arboretum employee. These small hills are not that high, but my mother tells me that they are still a good climb through underbrush and growth.

"Get to the top of it," he says, turning on his heel. "I'll be waiting."

Is he serious? No tips? No training before we start?

The Officer disappears into the undergrowth.

Apparently he *is* serious. I feel a small smile lifting the corners of my mouth, and I shake my head to get rid of it. I am the first to follow the Officer into the trees. They are thick summer green and when I push my way through them, they smell like Grandfather. Perhaps he is in the trees after all. And I think, *If I ever dared to open that paper, this would be the place.*

I hear other people moving through the trees around me and behind me. The forest, even this type of semicultivated forest, is a noisy place, especially with all of us tromping through it. Bushes smack, sticks crunch, and someone swears nearby. Probably Lon. I move faster. I have to fight against some of the bushes, but I make good progress.

My sorting mind wishes I could identify the birdcalls around me and name the plants and flowers I see. My mother likely knows most of them, but I won't ever have that kind of specialized knowledge unless working in the Arboretum becomes my vocation.

The climb gets harder and steeper but not impossible. The little hill is still part of the Arboretum proper, so it isn't truly wild. My shoes become dirty, the soles covered in pine needles and leaves. I stop for a moment and look for a place to scrape off some of the mud so I can move faster. But, here in the Arboretum, the fallen trees and branches are all removed immediately after they fall. I have to settle for scraping my feet, one at a time, along the bark-bumped side of a tree.

My feet feel lighter when I start walking again and I pick up speed. I see a smooth, round rock that looks like a polished egg, like the gift Bram gave to Grandfather. I leave it there, small and brown in the grass, and I move even faster, pushing the branches out of my way and ignoring the scratches on my hands. Even when a pine branch snaps back and I feel the sharp slap of needles and sinewy branch on my face, I don't stop.

I'm going to be the first one to the top of this hill and I'm glad. There is a lightness to the trees ahead of me, and I know it is because there is sky and sun behind them instead of more forest. I'm almost there. *Look at me, Grandfather*, I think to myself, but of course he can't hear me.

Look at me.

I veer suddenly and duck into the bushes. I fight my way through until I crouch alone in the middle of a thick patch of tangled leaves where I hope I will be well concealed. Dark brown plainclothes make good camouflage.

My hands shake as I pull out the paper. Was this what I planned all along when I tucked the compact inside the pocket of my plainclothes this morning? Did I know somehow that I'd find the right moment here in the woods?

I don't know where else to read it. If I read it at home someone might find me. The same is true of the air train and school and work. It's not quiet in this forest, crowded with vegetation and thick, muggy morning air wet against my skin. Bugs hum and birds sing. My arm brushes against a leaf and a drop of dew falls onto the paper with a sound like ripe fruit dropping to the ground.

What did Grandfather give me?

I hold the weight of this secret in my palm and then I open it.

I was right; the words *are* old. But even though I don't recognize the type, I recognize the format.

Grandfather gave me poetry.

Of course. My great-grandmother. The Hundred Poems. I know without having to check on the school ports that this poem is not one of them. She took a great risk hiding this paper, and my grandfather and grandmother took a great risk keeping it. What poems could be worth losing everything for?

The very first line stops me in my tracks and brings tears to my eyes and I don't know why except that this one line speaks to me as nothing else ever has.

Do not go gentle into that good night.

I read on, through words I do not understand and ones that I do.

I know why it spoke to Grandfather:

Do not go gentle into that good night,
Old age should burn and rave at close of day;
Rage, rage, against the dying of the light.

And as I read on, I know why it speaks to *me*:

Though wise men at their end know dark is right,
Because their words had forked no lightning they
Do not go gentle into that good night.

My words have forked no lightning. Grandfather even told me this, before he died, when I gave him that letter that I didn't truly write. Nothing I have written or done has made any difference in this world, and suddenly I know what it means to rage, and to crave.

I read the whole poem and eat it up, drink it up. I read about meteors and a green bay and fierce tears and even though I don't understand all of it—the language is too old—I understand enough. I understand why my grandfather loved this poem because I love it too. All of it. The rage and the light.

The line under the title of the poem says *Dylan Thomas, 1914–1953*.

There is another poem on the other side of the paper. It's called "Crossing the Bar," and it was written by someone who lived even further in the past than Dylan Thomas—*Lord Alfred Tennyson. 1809–1892.*

So long ago, I think. So long ago they lived and died.

And they, like Grandfather, will never come back.

Greedy, I read the second poem, too. I read the words of both poems over again several times, until I hear the sharp snap of a stick near me. Quickly, I fold up the paper and put it away. I have lingered too long. I have to go; to make up the time I've lost.

I have to run.

I don't hold back; this isn't the tracker, so I can push myself hard, through the branches and up the hill. The words of the Thomas poem are so wild and beautiful that I keep repeating them silently to myself as I run. Over and over I think *do not go gentle, do not go gentle, do not go gentle.* It isn't until I'm almost at the top of the hill that realization hits me: There's a reason they didn't keep this poem.

This poem tells you to fight.

One more branch stings my face as I break through the clearing, but I don't stop—I push out into the open. I look around for the Officer. He's not there, but someone else is already at the top. Ky Markham.

To my surprise, we are alone on top of the hill. No Officer. No other hikers.

Ky's more relaxed than I have ever seen him, leaning back on his elbows with his face tipped toward the sun and his eyes closed. He looks different and unguarded. Looking at him, I realize that his eyes are where I notice most the distance he keeps. Because when he hears me, he opens them and looks at me, and it almost happens. I almost catch a glimpse of something real before I see again what he wants me to see.

The Officer appears out of the trees next to me. He moves quietly, and I wonder what he's observed in the woods. Did he see me? He looks down at the datapod in his hand and then back up at me. "Cassia Reyes?" he asks. Apparently I was predicted to finish second. My stop must not have been as long as I thought.

"Yes."

"Sit there and wait," the Officer says, pointing toward the grassy clearing at the top of the hill. "Enjoy the view. According to this, it's going to be a few minutes before anyone else gets up here." He gestures to the datapod and then disappears back into the trees.

I pause for a moment before I walk toward Ky, trying to calm down. My heart pounds, fast, from the running. And from the sound in the trees.

"Hello," Ky says, when I get closer.

"Hello." I sit on the grass next to him. "I didn't know you were doing hiking, too."

"My mother thought it would be a good choice." I notice how easily he uses the word "mother" to describe his aunt Aida. I think about how he has slipped into his life here, how he became who everyone expected him to be in Mapletree Borough. Despite being new and different, he did not stand out for long.

In fact, I've never seen him finish first in anything before, and I speak before I think. "You beat us all today," I say, as if that fact weren't obvious.

"Yes," he says, looking at me. "Exactly as predicted. I grew up in the Outer Provinces and have had the most experience with activities like this." He speaks formally, as if reciting data, but I notice a sheen of sweat across his face; and the way he's stretching his legs out in front of him looks familiar. Ky's been running, too, and he must be fast. Do they have trackers in the Outer Provinces? If not, what did he run to out there? Were there also things he had to run *from*?

Before I can stop myself, I ask Ky something that I should not ask: "What happened to your mother?"

His eyes flash to me, surprised. He knows I don't mean Aida, and I know that no one else has ever asked him that question. I don't know what made me do it now; perhaps Grandfather's death and what I've read in the woods have left me on edge and vulnerable. Perhaps I don't want to dwell on who might have seen me back in the trees.

I should apologize. But I don't and it's not because I feel like being mean. It's because I think he might want to tell me.

But I am mistaken. "You shouldn't ask me that question," he says. He doesn't look at me, so all I can see is one side of him. His profile, his dark hair wet with the mist and the water that fell from the trees as he passed through them. He smells like forest, and I lift my hands to my face to smell them—to see if I do, too. It might be my imagination, but it seems to me that my fingers smell like ink and paper.

Ky's right. I know better than to ask a question like that. But then he asks me something that *he* shouldn't ask. "Who did *you* lose?"

"What do you mean?"

"I can tell," he says simply. He's looking at me now. His eyes are still blue.

The sun feels hot on the back of my neck and the top of my hair. I close my eyes the way Ky did earlier and tip my head back so that I can feel the heat on my eyelids and across the bridge of my nose.

Neither of us says anything. I don't keep my eyes closed for long, but when I open them the sunlight still blinds me for a moment. In that moment, I know I want to tell Ky. "My grandfather died last week."

"Was it unexpected?"

"No," I say, but really, in some ways, it was. I did not expect Grandfather to say the things he said. But I did expect his death. "No," I say again. "It was his eightieth birthday."

"That's right," Ky says thoughtfully, almost to himself. "People here die on their eightieth birthday."

"Yes. Isn't it like that where you came from?" I'm surprised that the words escaped my mouth—not two seconds ago he reminded me not to ask about his past. This time, though, he answers me.

"Eighty is . . . harder to achieve," he says.

I hope that the surprise doesn't show on my face. Are there different death ages in different places?

People call and feet crunch from the edge of the forest. The Officer steps out of the bushes again and asks people their names as they break into the clearing.

I shift my position to stand up and I swear I hear the compact in my pocket chink against my tablet container. Ky turns to look at me and I hold my breath. I wonder if he can tell that there are words in my head, words I am struggling to remember and memorize. Because I know that I can never open the paper again. I have to get rid of it. Sitting here next to Ky, drinking in the sun with my skin, my mind is clear—

and I let myself realize what that sound in the woods meant earlier. That sharp, stick-snapping sound.

Someone saw me.

Ky takes a breath, leans in closer. "I saw you," he says, his voice soft and deep like water falling in the distance. He is careful with his words, speaking them so they can't be overheard. "In the woods."

Then. For the first time I can remember, he touches me. His hand on my arm, fast and hot and gone before I know it. "You have to be careful. Something like that—"

"I know." I want to touch him back, to put my hand on his arm too, but I don't. "I'm going to destroy it."

His face stays calm but I hear the urgency in his tone. "Can you do it without getting caught?"

"I think so."

"I could help you." He glances over at the Officer as he says this, casually, and I realize something that I haven't noticed until now because he's so good at hiding it. Ky always acts as though someone watches him. And, apparently, he watches back.

"How did you beat me to the top?" I ask suddenly. "If you saw me in the woods?"

Ky looks surprised by the question. "I ran."

"I ran too," I say.

"I must be faster," he says, and for a moment I see a hint of teasing, almost a smile. Then it's gone, and he's serious again, urgent. "*Do* you want me to help you?"

"No. No, I can do it." Then, because I don't want him to think I'm an idiot, a risk-taker for the sake of risk-taking, I say more than I should. "My grandfather gave it to me. I shouldn't have kept it as long as I did. But . . . the words are so beautiful."

"Can you remember them without it?"

"For now." I have the mind of a sorter, after all. "But I know I won't be able to keep them forever."

"And you want to?"

He thinks I'm stupid. "They are so beautiful," I repeat lamely.

The Officer calls out; more people come through the trees; someone calls to Ky, someone calls to me. We separate, say good-bye, walk to different places on the top of the little hill.

Everyone looks out into the distance at something. Ky and his friends face the dome of City Hall, talking about something; the Officer looks out at the Hill. The group I stand with gazes off toward the Arboretum's meal hall and chatters about our lunch, about getting back to Second School, whether or not the air trains will be on time. Someone laughs, because the air trains are always on time.

A line from the poem comes to my mind: *there on the sad height.*

I tilt my head back again and look at the sun through my closed eyelids. It is stronger than I am; it burns red against the black.

The questions in my mind seem to make a humming sound, like that of the bugs in the woods earlier. *What happened to you in the Outer Provinces? What Infraction did your father commit that made you an Aberration? Do you think I'm crazy for wanting to keep the poems? What is it about your voice that makes me want to hear you speak?*

Are you supposed to be my Match?

Later, I realize that the one question that didn't even cross my mind was the most urgent one of all: *Will you keep my secret?*

CHAPTER 10

The pattern in my neighborhood has shifted this evening; something is wrong. People wait at the air-train stop with faces closed, not talking to each other. They climb on without the usual greetings to those of us climbing off. A small white air car, an Official vehicle, sits sidled up next to a blue-shuttered house on our street. My house.

Hurrying down the metal stairs from the air-train stop, I look for more shifts in the pattern as I walk. The sidewalks tell me nothing. They are clean and white as always. The houses near mine, shut tight, tell me a little more—if this is a storm, it will be waited out behind closed doors.

The air-car's landing gear is delicately splayed out, resting on the grass. Behind the plain white curtains in the window, I see figures move. I hurry up the steps and hesitate at the door. Should I knock?

I tell myself to stay calm, stay clear. For some reason I picture the blue of Ky's eyes and I can think better, realizing that reading the situation correctly is part of getting through it safely. *This could be anything. They could be checking the food distribution system, house to house. That happened once, in a Borough near here. I heard about it.*

This might have nothing to do with me.

Are they telling my parents about Ky's face on the microcard? Do they know what Grandfather gave me? I haven't had a chance to destroy the poems yet. The paper is still in my pocket. Did someone besides Ky see me reading it in the woods? Was it the Officer's shoe that snapped the stick?

This might have everything to do with me.

I don't know what happens when people break the rules, because people here in the Borough don't break them. There are minor citations issued from time to time, like when Bram is late. But those are small things, small errors. Not large errors, or errors committed with purpose. *Infractions.*

I'm not going to knock. This is my house. Taking a deep breath, I twist the knob and open the door.

Someone waits for me inside.

"You're back," Bram says, relief in his tone.

My fingers tighten around the piece of paper in my pocket, and I glance in the direction of the kitchen. Maybe I can make it to the incineration tube and stuff the poems down into the fire below. The tube will register a foreign substance; the thick paper is completely different from the paper goods—napkins, port printings, delivery envelopes—that we are allowed to dispose of in our residences. But that might still be safer than keeping it. They can't reconstruct the words themselves after I've burned them.

I catch a glimpse of a Biomedical Official in a long white

lab coat moving through the hall into the kitchen. I let go of the poems, take my hand out of my pocket. Empty.

"What's wrong?" I ask Bram. "Where are Papa and Mama?"

"They're here," Bram says, voice shaking. "In their room. The Officials are searching Papa."

"Why?" My father doesn't have the poems. He never even knew about them. But does that matter? Ky's classification is because of his father's Infraction. Will my mistake change my whole family?

Perhaps the compact is the safest place for the poems after all. My grandparents kept it hidden there for years. "I'll be right back," I say to Bram, and I slip into my room, slide the compact out of my closet. *Twist.* I open the base, put the paper in.

"Did someone come in?" an Official in the hall asks Bram.

"My sister," Bram says, sounding terrified.

"Where did she go?"

Twist, again. The compact doesn't close right. A corner of the paper sticks out.

"She's in her room, changing clothes. She got all dirty from hiking." Bram's voice sounds steadier now. He's covering for me, without even knowing why. And he's doing a good job of it, too.

I hear footsteps in the hall and I open the compact back up, slide the corner in.

I twist, a muted snap takes place. *At last.* With one hand,

I unzip my plainclothes; with the other, I put the compact back on the shelf. I turn my head as the door opens, surprise and outrage on my face. "I'm changing!" I exclaim.

The Official nods at me, seeing the smudge of dirt on my clothes. "Please come into the foyer when you're finished," he says. "Quickly."

My hands sweat a little as I pull off the clothes that smell of forest and put them in the laundry receptacle. Then, in my other plainclothes, stripped of everything that might look or smell like poetry, I leave my room.

"Papa never turned in Grandfather's tissue sample," Bram says in a whisper once I come back into the foyer. "He lost it. That's why they're here." For a moment, curiosity overrides his panic. "Why'd you have to change your clothes so fast? You weren't *that* dirty."

"I *was* dirty," I whisper back. "Shh. Listen." I hear murmurs of voices in my parents' room, and then my mother's voice, raised. And I can't believe what Bram told me. My father *lost* Grandfather's sample?

Sorrow cuts through the fear inside me. This is bad, very bad, that my father has made such an enormous mistake. But not only because it might mean trouble for him, and for us. Because it means that Grandfather is really gone. They can't bring him back without the sample.

Suddenly I hope the Officials find something in our house after all.

"Wait here," I tell Bram, and I go into the kitchen. A Biomedical Official stands near the waste receptacle waving a device up and down, back and forth, over and over. He takes a step and begins the motions again in a new spot in the kitchen. I see the words printed along the side of the object he holds. *Biological Detection Instrument.*

I relax slightly. Of course. They have something to detect the bar code engraved on the tube Grandfather used. They don't need to tear the house apart. Perhaps they won't find the paper after all. And perhaps they *will* find the sample.

How could Papa lose something so important? How could he lose his own father?

In spite of my instructions, Bram follows me into the kitchen. He touches my arm and we turn back toward the hallway. "Mama's still arguing in there," he says, gesturing to our parents' room. I grab Bram's hand and hold it tight. The Officials don't *need* to search my father; they have the Detection Instruments to tell them where to look. But I guess they have to make their point: My father should have been more careful with something so important.

"Are they searching Mama, too?" I ask Bram. Are we all going to share in our father's humiliation?

"I don't think so," Bram says. "She just wanted to be in there with Papa."

The bedroom door opens and Bram and I jump back out of the way of the Officials. Their white lab coats make them seem tall and pure. One of them can tell we are frightened, and he gives us a small smile intended to reassure. It doesn't work. He can't give back the lost sample or my father's dignity. The damage is done.

My father walks behind the Officials, pale and unhappy. In contrast, my mother looks flushed and angry. She follows my father and the Officials into the front room, and Bram and I stand in the doorway to watch what happens.

They didn't find the sample. My heart sinks. My father stands in the middle of the room while the Biomedical Team berates him. "How could you do this?"

He shakes his head. "I don't know. It's inexcusable." His words sound flat, as if he has repeated them so many times that he has given up any hope of the Officials believing him. He stands up straight, the way he always does, but his face looks tired and old.

"You recognize that there is no way to bring him back now," they say.

My father nods, his face full of misery. Even though I am angry with him for losing the sample, I can tell that he feels awful. Of course he does. *This is Grandfather.* In spite of my anger, I wish I could take Papa's hand but there are too many Officials around him.

And I'm full of hypocrisy. I did something against the rules today, too, and what I did was intentional.

"This may result in some sanctions for you at work," one of the Officials says to my father, in a tone so mean I wonder if she will get cited herself. No one is supposed to speak this way. Even when an error occurs, things aren't supposed to get personal. "How can they expect you to handle the restoration and disposal of artifacts if you can't even keep track of *one* tissue sample? Especially knowing how important it was?"

One of the other Officials says quietly, "You ruined the sample belonging to your own *father*. And then you didn't report the loss."

My father passes his hand over his eyes. "I was afraid," he says. He knows the seriousness of the situation. He doesn't need them to tell him. Cremation occurs within hours of death. There's no way to get another sample. It's gone. He's gone. Grandfather is really gone.

My mother presses her lips tightly together and her eyes flash, but her anger is not for my father. She is mad at the Officials for making him feel worse than he already does.

Even though there is nothing to say, the Officials do not leave. A few moments of cold silence pass during which no one says anything and we all think about how nothing can save Grandfather now.

A chime sounds in the kitchen; our dinner has arrived. My mother walks out of the room. I hear the sounds of her taking the food delivery and placing it on the table. When she walks back into the room, her shoes make stabbing, serious sounds on the wood floor. She means business.

"It's mealtime," she says, looking at the Officials. "I'm afraid they haven't sent any extra portions."

The Officials bristle a little. Is she trying to dismiss them?

It's hard to tell. Her face seems open, her tone regretful but firm. And she's so lovely, blond hair winding down her back, flushed cheeks. None of that is supposed to matter. But somehow, it does.

And besides. Even the Officials don't dare disrupt mealtime too much. "We'll report this," the tallest one says. "I'm sure that a citation of the highest order will be issued, with the next error resulting in a complete Infraction."

My father nods; my mother glances back at the kitchen, to remind them that the food is here and getting cold, possibly losing nutrients. The Officials nod curtly at us and, one by one, they leave, walking through the foyer, past the port, out the only door in the house.

After they depart our whole family sighs with relief. My father turns to us. "I'm sorry," he says. "I'm sorry." He looks at my mother and waits for her to speak.

"Don't worry about it," she says bravely. She knows that my father now has a mistake logged against him in the permanent database. She knows that it means Grandfather is gone. But she loves my father. She loves him too much, I sometimes think. I think it now. Because if *she* isn't angry with him, how can *I* be?

When we sit down to dinner my mother embraces him and leans her head on his shoulder for a moment before she hands him his foilware. He reaches up to touch her hair, her cheek.

Watching them, I think to myself that someday something like this might happen to me and to Xander. Our lives will be so intertwined that what one of us does will affect the other down to the ends, like the tree my mother transplanted once at the Arboretum. She showed it to me when I came to visit her. It was a little thing, a baby tree, but still it tangled with things around it and required care to move. And when she finally pulled it out, its roots still clung to the earth from its old home.

Did Ky do that, when he came here? Did he bring anything with him? It would have been difficult; they would have searched him so carefully, he had to adapt so quickly. Still, I don't see how he couldn't bring *something*. Secret, maybe, inside, intangible. Something to nourish him. Something of home.

Feet pounding, fists clenched, I hit the tracker running.

I wish I could run outside, away from the sadness and shame in my house. Sweat trickles down the front of my gymgear, through my hair, across my face. I brush it away and glance back down at the tracker screen.

There's a rise in the curve on the tracker screen: a simulated hill. *Good.* I've reached the peak of the workout, the most difficult part, the fastest part. The tracker spins below me, a machine named for the circular tracks where people used to compete. And named for what it does—tracking information about the person running on it. If you run too far, you might be a masochist, an anorexic, or another type, and you will have to see an Official of Psychology for diagnosis. If it's determined that you are running hard because you genuinely like it then you can have an athletic permit. I have one.

My legs ache a little; I look straight ahead and will myself to see Grandfather's face within my mind, to hold it there. If there's really no chance for him to ever come back, then I am the one who has to keep him alive.

The incline increases, and I keep pace, wishing for the feeling of climbing the hill earlier that day when we were hiking. Outside. Branches and bushes and mud and sunlight on the top of a hill with a boy who knows more than he will say.

The tracker beeps. Five minutes left before the workout ends, before I've run the distance and time I should in order to keep up my optimal heart rate and maintain my optimal body mass index. I have to be healthy. It's part of what makes us great, what keeps our life span long.

All of the things that were shown in early studies to be good for longevity—happy marriages, healthy bodies—are ours to have. We live long, good lives. We die on our eightieth birthdays, surrounded by our families, before dementia sets in. Cancer, heart disease, and most debilitating illnesses are almost entirely eradicated. This is as close to perfect as any society has ever managed to get.

My parents talk upstairs. My brother does his schoolwork and I run to nowhere. Everyone in this house does what he or she is supposed to do. It's going to be all right. My feet hit smack-slap on the belt of the tracker and I pound the worry out of me step by step. Step by step by step by step by step.

I'm tired, I don't know if I can go any farther, when the tracker beeps and slows, slows, slows to a stop. Perfect timing, programmed by the Society. I bend my head down, gasping for breath, sucking in air. There is nothing to see at the top of this hill.

Bram sits on the edge of my bed, waiting for me. He holds something. At first I think it is my compact and I take a step forward, worried—*Has he found the poetry?*—but then I realize that it is Grandfather's watch. Bram's artifact.

"I sent a port message to the Officials a few minutes ago," Bram says. His round eyes look up at me, tired and sad.

"Why did you do that?" I ask in shock. Why would he want to see or talk to an Official after what happened today?

Bram holds up the watch. "I thought that maybe they could get enough tissue from this. Since Grandfather touched it so many times."

Hope shoots through my veins like adrenaline. I pull a towel from the hook in my closet and wipe it across my face. "What did they say? Did they respond?"

"They sent back a message saying it wouldn't be enough. It wouldn't work." He rubs the shiny surface of the watch with his sleeve to clean away the smudges where his fingers were. He looks at the face of the clock as if it can tell him something.

But it can't. Bram doesn't even know how to tell time yet. And besides, Grandfather's watch hasn't worked in decades.

It's nothing but a beautiful artifact. Heavy, made of silver and glass. Nothing like the thin plastic strips we wear now.

"Do I look like Grandfather?" Bram asks hopefully. He slides the watch onto his arm. It is loose around his thin wrist. Skinny, brown-eyed, straight-backed, small—he *does* look a little like Grandfather in that moment.

"You do." I wonder if there is anything of Grandfather to see in me. I liked hiking today. I like reading the Hundred Poems. Those things that were a part of him are a part of me. I think about the other grandparents I have, out in the Farmlands, and about Ky Markham and the Outer Provinces and about all the things I do not know and places I will never see.

Bram smiles at my response and looks down proudly at the watch.

"Bram, you can't take that to school, you know. You could get in trouble."

"I know."

"You saw what happened to Papa when the Officials got after him. You don't want them getting mad at you for breaking the rules about artifacts."

"I won't," he says. "I know better than that. I don't want to lose it." He reaches for my silver box from the Match Banquet. "Can I keep it in here? It seems like a good place. You know, special." He shrugs in embarrassment.

"All right," I say, a little nervously. I watch him open the silver box and put the artifact carefully inside next to the microcard. He doesn't even glance at the compact sitting on the shelf and for that I am grateful.

Later that night when it is dark and Bram has gone to bed, I open the compact and take the paper out. I do not look at it; instead, I slip it into the pocket of my plainclothes for the next day. Tomorrow, I will try to find a trash incinerator away from home to drop it in. I don't want anyone to catch me doing it here. It's too dangerous now.

I lie down and look up at the ceiling, trying again to think of Grandfather's face. I can't bring it back. Impatient, I roll over, and something hard presses into my side. My tablet container. I must have dropped it when I changed my plainclothes earlier. It isn't like me to be so careless.

I sit up. The light from the street lamps outside comes in foggy through the window, enough to see the tablets as I twist open the container and spill them onto the bed. For a moment, as my eyes adjust, they all seem to be the same color. But then I can see which is which. The mysterious red tablet. The blue one that will help us survive in case of an emergency, because even the Society can't control nature all of the time.

And the green one.

Most people I know take the green tablet now and then. Before a big test. The night of the Match Banquet. Any time you might need calming. You can take it up to once a week without the Officials taking special note of it.

But I've never taken the green tablet.

Because of Grandfather.

I was so proud to show him when I started carrying it. "Look," I told him, unscrewing the lid of the silver container. "I've got blue *and* green now. All I need is the red one and I'll be an adult."

"Ah," Grandfather said, looking properly impressed. "You are growing up, that's for certain." He paused for a moment. We were walking outside, in the greenspace near his apartment. "Have you taken the green one yet?"

"Not yet," I said. "But I have to give a presentation on one of the Hundred Paintings in my Culture class next week. I might take it then. I don't like speaking in front of everyone."

"Which painting?" he asked.

"Number nineteen," I tell him, and he looks thoughtful, trying to remember which one that is. He doesn't—didn't— know the Hundred Paintings as well as the Hundred Poems. But still, he knew it after enough thought. "The one by Thomas Moran," he guesses, and I nod. "I like the colors in that one," he said.

"I like the sky," I told him. "It's so dramatic. All the clouds up above, and in the canyon." The painting felt a little dangerous—streaming gray clouds, jagged red rocks—and I liked that, too.

"Yes," he said. "It's a beautiful painting."

"Like this," I said, even though the greenspace was

beautiful in an entirely different way. Flowers bloomed everywhere, in colors we were not allowed to wear: pinks, yellows, reds, almost startling in their boldness. They drew the eye; they scented the air.

"Greenspace, green tablet," Grandfather said, and then he looked at me and smiled. "Green eyes on a green girl."

"That sounds like poetry," I said, and he laughed.

"Thank you." He paused for a moment. "I wouldn't take that tablet, Cassia. Not for a report. And perhaps not ever. You are strong enough to go without it."

Now, I lie down on my side, curl my hand around the green tablet. I don't think I'll take it, not even tonight. *Grandfather thinks I'm strong enough to go without it.* I close my eyes and think of Grandfather's poetry.

Green tablet. Green space. Green eyes. Green girl.

When I fall asleep, I dream that Grandfather has given me a bouquet of roses. "Take these instead of the tablet," he tells me. So I do. I pull the petals off each rose. To my surprise each petal has a word written on it, a word from one of the poems. They're not in the right order, and this puzzles me, but I put them in my mouth and taste them. They taste bitter, the way I imagine the green tablet would taste. But I know Grandfather is right; I have to keep the words inside if I want to keep them with me.

When I wake in the morning, the green tablet is still in my hand, and the words are still in my mouth.

CHAPTER 11

Breakfast sounds from the kitchen carry down the hall to my room. The chime, announcing the arrival of the food delivery sliding through its slot. A crash—Bram knocking something over. Chairs scrape, voices murmur as my mother and father talk with Bram. Soon, the smell of the food comes in underneath my door, or maybe it drifts through the thin walls of our house, permeating everything. The smell is a familiar one, a smell of vitamins and something metallic, perhaps the foilware.

"Cassia?" my mother says outside my door. "You're late for breakfast."

I know. I want to be late to breakfast. I don't want to see my father today. I don't want to talk about what happened yesterday, but I don't want to not-talk about it either, to sit at the table with our portions of food and pretend that Grandfather isn't gone for good.

"I'm coming," I say, and I pull myself out of bed. Out in the hall I hear an announcement on the port, and I think I catch the word *hiking*.

When I walk into the kitchen, my father has already left for work. Bram pulls on his raingear, grinning wildly. How can he forget about last night so quickly? "It's supposed to rain today," he informs me. "No hiking for you. They said so on the port."

My mother gives Bram his hat and he jams it onto his head. "Good-bye!" he says, and he heads for the air train, early for once because he likes the rain.

"So," my mother says. "It looks like you'll have a little free time. What do you think you'll do?"

I know immediately. Most of the other hikers will use their time hanging out in the common area inside the school, or finishing assignments in the school's research library. I have something else in mind, a visit to a different library. "I think I might go visit Papa."

My mother's eyes soften; she smiles. "I'm sure he'd like that, since you missed him this morning. He won't be able to stop work long, though."

"I know. I just want to say hello." *And destroy something dangerous, something I'm not supposed to have. Something more likely to be found at an old library than anywhere else, if they truly do record the composition of everything burned in the incineration tubes.*

I pick up one of the dry triangles of toast tucked inside my foilware, thinking of the way the two poems looked on the paper. I remember many of the words, but not all of them, and I *want* all of them. Every last one. Is there any way I can sneak one more glance before I destroy the paper? Is there any way to make the words last?

If only we still knew how to write instead of just type things into our scribes. Then I could write them down again someday. Then I might be able to have them when I am old.

Looking out the window, I watch Bram waiting at the air-train stop. It's not raining yet, but he jumps up and down on the metal steps to the platform. I smile to myself and hope no one tells him to stop, because I know exactly what he's doing. In the absence of real thunder, he's making his own.

Ky is the only one walking toward the air-train platform when I go outside. The train to Second School has left and this next one goes into the City. He must have to report to work when his leisure activities get canceled; no free hour or two for him. Watching Ky walk, his shoulders straight, his head up, it strikes me how lonely he must be. He's spent so long blending into the crowd, and now they've separated him out again.

Ky hears me coming up behind him and turns around. "Cassia," he says, sounding surprised. "Did you miss your train?"

"No." I stop a few feet away, to give him his space if he wants it. "I'm taking this one. I'm going to visit my father. You know, since hiking was canceled."

Ky lives in our Borough, so of course he knows the Officials visited us last night. He won't say anything, though—no one will. It's not their business unless the Society says that it is.

I take another step toward the air-train stop, toward Ky.

I expect him to move, to start up the stairs to the platform, but he doesn't. In fact, he takes a step closer to me. The tree-spiked Hill of the Arboretum rises in the distance behind him, and I wonder if we will ever hike there. The thunderstorm, still a few miles away, rolls and rumbles gray and heavy across the sky. Ky looks up. "Rain," he says, almost under his breath, and then he looks back at me. "Are you going to his office in the City?"

"No. I'm going past that. He's working on a site out at the edge of Brookway Borough."

"Can you make it out there and back in time for school?"

"I think so. I've done it before when he was working out that way."

Against the clouds, Ky's eyes seem lighter, reflecting the gray around them, and I have an unsettling thought: perhaps his eyes have *no* color. They reflect what he wears, who the Officials tell him to be. When he wore brown, his eyes looked brown. Now that he wears blue, they look blue.

"What are you thinking about?" he asks me.

I tell him the truth. "The color of your eyes."

My answer catches Ky off guard; but after a second he smiles. I love his smile; in it, I see a hint of the boy he was that day at the pool. Were his eyes blue then? I can't remember. I wish I'd looked more closely.

"What are *you* thinking about?" I ask. I expect the shutters to close in as they always do: Ky will give me some expected answer, like "I was thinking about what I need to do at work today" or "The activities for free-rec on Saturday night."

But he doesn't. "Home," he says simply, still looking at me.

The two of us hold each other's gazes for a long, unembarrassed moment and I feel that Ky knows. I'm not sure *what* he knows—whether he knows me, or just something about me.

Ky says nothing more. He looks at me with those changeable eyes, those eyes that I thought were the color of earth but instead are the color of sky, and I look back. I think we have done more seeing the last two days than in all the years we have known each other.

The female announcer's voice cuts through the silence: "Air train approaching."

Neither of us speaks as we hurry up the metal steps to the platform together, racing the clouds in the distance. For now, we win, reaching the top as the air train slides to a stop in front of us. Together we climb on, joining groups of others in dark blue plainclothes and a few Officials here and there.

There aren't two seats together. I find a seat first, and Ky sits across from me. He leans forward, resting his elbows on his knees. Someone, another worker, calls out a greeting to him and Ky calls back. The train is crowded and people pass between us, but I can watch him now and then in the gaps they leave. And it strikes me that this might be part of the reason I am going to see my father today; not just to destroy the paper, but to ride on this train with Ky.

We reach his stop first. He climbs off without looking back.

From the raised air-train platform, the rubble of the old library appears to be covered in enormous black spiders. The huge black incinerators spread their leglike tubes out across the bricks and over the edges into the basement of the library. The rest of the building has all been torn away.

I climb down the stairs and walk toward the library. I'm out of place at this work site. But not forbidden. Still, it would be better if no one saw me yet. I edge close enough to see down into the hole. The workers, most dressed in blue plain-clothes, suck up piles of papers with the incineration tubes. My father told us that right when they thought they had gone through everything, they found steel boxes of books buried down in the basement. Almost as though someone tried to hide and preserve the books against the future. My father and the other Restoration specialists have been through the boxes and they haven't found anything special, so they will inciner-ate all of it.

One figure wears white. An Official. My father. All workers have protective helmets, so I can't see his face, but the confidence is back in his walk. He moves purposefully, in his element, giving directions and pointing out where he wants the tubes to go next.

Sometimes I forget that my father is an Official. I rarely see him on-duty, in his uniform, which he changes into at work. The sight of him in his uniform simultaneously comforts me—they didn't take away his ranking after last night, at least not yet—and sets me on edge. It is strange to see people in different ways.

Another thought crosses my mind: before he turned seventy and was required to quit work, *Grandfather* was an Official. *But it's different with Papa and Grandfather*, I tell myself. Neither of them are, or were, high-level Officials in places like the Match Department or the Safety Department. Those are the ones that do most of the Official-type things, like implement rules. We're thinkers, not enforcers: learners, not doers.

Most of the time. My great-grandmother, an Official herself, did steal that poem.

My father glances once at the sky, aware of the impending thunderstorm. Speed is important, but they have to be methodical. "We can't just set things on fire," he's told me. "The tubes are like the incineration devices at home. They record the amount and type of the matter destroyed." There are a few piles of books left and, as I watch, the workers move from one to another, following his orders. It's faster to incinerate individual pages instead of books, so they slice the books open, gutting them along the spines, preparing them for the tubes.

My father looks at the sky again and gestures in a "hurry up" motion to the other workers. I need to get back to school, but I keep watching.

I'm not the only one. As I glance up, over across the chasm of spiders and books, I see another figure in white. An Official. Watching, too. Checking on my father.

The site personnel drag the incineration tube to a newly readied pile. The books' backs are broken; their bones, thin and delicate, fall out. The workers shove them toward the incineration tube; they step on them. The bones crackle under their boots like leaves. It reminds me of fall, when the City brings around the incineration equipment to our neighborhoods and we shovel the fallen maple leaves into the tubes. My mother always laments the waste, since decayed leaves can be good fertilizer, just as my father laments the waste of the paper that could be recycled when he has to incinerate a library. But the higher Officials say some things are not worth saving. Sometimes it's faster and more efficient to destroy.

One leaf escapes. Caught on a swirl of wind from the impending thunderstorm, it rises up, almost reaching my feet as I stand near the edge of this small canyon that was once a library. It hovers there, so close I can almost see the words written on it, and then the wind dies down for a moment and it falls back.

I glance up. Neither Official watches me. Not my father, not the other. My father is intent on the books he's destroying; the other Official is intent on my father. It's time.

I reach into my pocket and pull out the paper Grandfather gave me. I let go of it.

It dances on the air for a moment before it falls, too. A fresh gust of wind almost saves it, but a worker catches sight of it and lifts a tube up to suck the paper from the air, to suck the words from the sky.

I'm sorry, Grandfather.

I stand and watch until all the bones are shoved into the incineration tubes, until all the words have been turned into ash and nothing.

I lingered too long at the library work site and I'm almost late for class. Xander waits for me near the main doors of Second School.

He pushes one of them open, holding its weight with his shoulder. "Is everything all right?" he asks quietly as I stop there in the doorway.

"Hi, Xander," someone calls out to him. He nods in their direction, but doesn't look away.

For a moment, I think that I should tell Xander everything. Not just about what happened last night with the Officials, which is what has him worried, but *everything*. I should tell him about Ky's face on the screen. I should tell him about Ky in the woods, how he saw the poem. I should tell Xander about the poem itself and the way it felt to let it go. Instead, I shake my head. I don't want to talk right now.

Xander changes the subject, his eyes lighting up. "I almost forgot. I have something to tell you. There's a new Saturday activity coming up."

"Really?" I ask, grateful to him for understanding, for not pressing further. "Is there a new showing?"

"No, even better. We can replant the flower beds in front of First School and eat dinner outside. Like a—what's the word?—like a picnic. There's going to be ice cream afterward, too."

The enthusiasm in Xander's voice makes me smile a little. "Xander, that's nothing but a glorified work project. They want some free labor and they're bribing us with ice cream."

He grins at me. "I know, but it's good to have a break. Keeps me fresh for the games the next time. So you want to plant, too, right? I know the spots will fill up fast, so I signed you up already in case you did."

A tiny bit of annoyance that he did this without talking to me first flashes through me, but it vanishes almost instantly when I notice that his smile seems a little awkward. He knows he's crossed a line—he never would have done something like this before we were Matched—and the fact that he worries about it makes it all right. Besides, even though it *is* a glorified work project, I would have signed up in a heartbeat myself. Xander knows that. He knows me and he looks out for me.

"That's fine," I tell Xander. "Thanks." He lets go of the door and we walk into the hall together. In the back of my mind I find myself wondering what Ky will do that night. They don't tell you about free-rec options at work. By the time he gets home and finds out about it, the spots will likely be full because of the newness of the activity and because of the ice cream. We could sign him up, though. I could walk over to one of the ports here at the school and . . .

Time's up. The chime rings over the speakers in the hall.

Xander and I duck through the classroom door, slide into our desks and take out our readers and scribes. Piper usually sits next to us in Applicable Sciences, but I don't see her. "Where's Piper?"

"I meant to tell you. She got her final work position today."

"She did? What is it?"

But the chime rings again and I have to face front and wait to find out until after class. Piper has her vocation! A few people get them early, like Ky, but the rest of us receive them at some point during the year after our seventeenth birthday. One by one we get picked off until everyone is gone and there's no one left in our year at Second School.

I hope Xander and Em don't get called for a long time. It wouldn't be the same here without them, especially without Xander. I glance over at him. He gazes at the instructor as though this is all he wants to do in the world. His fingers tap on the scribe; he jiggles one foot impatiently, always ready to know more. It's hard to keep up with him—he's so smart, he learns so fast. What if he moves on soon to his vocation and leaves me behind?

Things are happening so quickly. Getting to my seventeenth birthday felt like steps taken slowly down a path where I saw each pebble, noticed each leaf, and felt pleasantly bored and anticipatory at the same time. Now it feels as if I am running down the path, flat out and breathing hard. It feels like I'll arrive at my Contract date in no time at all. Will things ever slow down again?

I look away from Xander. *Even if Xander gets his vocation first, we're still Matched*, I remind myself. He's not going to leave me behind. He doesn't know that I saw Ky's face that day on the screen.

If I told Xander, would he understand? I think he would. I don't think it would jeopardize our Match, or our friendship. All the same, those are two things I don't want to risk losing.

I look back up at the instructor. The window behind her is dark, the sky filled with heavy low clouds. I wonder what they'd look like from the top of the big Hill. Can you climb high enough to get above the clouds, look down on the rain from a place in the sun?

Without meaning to, I envision Ky on the hill, face turned to the warmth. I close my eyes for a moment, imagining I am up there too.

The thunderstorm finally hits in the middle of class. I picture the rain in that greenspace where I met with the Official, making the fountain overflow and pounding the bench where I sat. I imagine I can hear the drops slap as they hit the metal, sigh as they reach the grass and dirt. It is dark as evening outside. The water beats on the roof and streams through the rain gutters. The one window in our classroom

Ally Condie

is sheeted and shaded in rain and we can't see out for the flood.

A line from that other poem, the Tennyson one, comes to mind suddenly: *The flood may bear me far.*

If I had kept the poems from Grandfather, I'd be riding on a flood that I couldn't stop. I did what I had to do; I did the right thing. But it is as though the rain outside pours on me, too, eroding my relief and leaving only regret: The poems are gone, and I can never get them back.

132

CHAPTER 12

At work that evening, we have an interesting sort for a change. Even Norah becomes animated as she describes it to me at her desk. "We're looking at different physical traits for a Matching pool," she says. "Eye color. Hair color. Height and weight."

"Is the Match Department going to use our sorts?" I ask.

She laughs. "Of course not. It's for practice. This is to see if you pick up patterns in the Matchees' data that the Officials have already noticed."

Of course.

"There's something else," Norah adds. She lowers her voice, not because this is a secret but because she doesn't want to distract the others from their work. "The Officials told me that they're going to administer your next test personally."

This is a good sign. This means that they want to see for themselves if I can work under pressure. This means that they may be considering me for one of the more interesting sorting-related vocations.

"Do you know when?"

She does, I can see, but she's not supposed to tell me. "Sometime soon," she says again, vaguely, and then she gives me one of her rare smiles. She turns back to her screen and I go to my station to get started.

This is good, I think. I might get an optimal vocation assignment if I can impress the Officials enough. Everything is going well again. I won't think about Grandfather and the lost sample and the burned poems or my father and the Officials searching him. Or that Ky won't ever get to be Matched to anyone or work anywhere besides the nutrition disposal center. I won't think about any of it. It's time to clear my mind and sort.

It is actually rather startling when you sort eye colors, how limited the possibilities truly are: such a small, finite number of options. Blue, brown, green, gray, hazel—these are all of the options for eye color, even with many ethnicities represented in the population. Long ago there were genetic mutations, like albinos, but those don't exist anymore. Hair color is similarly limited: black, brown, blond, red.

So few options, and yet an infinite number of variations. For example, plenty of boys in this database have blue eyes and dark hair like Ky, but I am positive that not one of them looks as he does. And even if someone did, if one of those boys looked exactly like him or if he had a twin somehow, no one else could have the combination of movement and restraint, of honesty and secrecy, that Ky has. His face keeps appearing in my mind, but I know that it's not the Society's mistake anymore. It's mine. I'm the one who keeps thinking of him when I should be thinking of Xander.

The tiny printer next to me beeps, and I jump.

I made a mistake and I didn't notice my error within an acceptable time frame. A little slip of paper curls out onto the table next to me and I pick it up. "ERROR AT LINE 3568." I hardly ever make errors, so this will cause interest. I go back to the line where the mistake was made and correct it. If this happens next week while the Officials are watching—

It won't happen. I won't let it happen. But before I lose myself in the sorting again, I allow myself one brief moment to think of Ky's eyes, of his hand on my arm.

"Someone said a girl your age came to the work site today," my father says. He came to meet me at the air-train stop, something he does now and then with Bram or me so that we can have a little one-on-one time before we get home. "Was it you?"

I nod. "They canceled hiking because of the rain, so I thought I'd come see you before school. Since I didn't see you this morning. But you were busy and I didn't have much time. I'm sorry I couldn't stay."

"You should come again, if you want to," he says. "I'm back in the office all next week. That's a much shorter ride."

"I know. Maybe I will." My answers sound a little distant, and I hope he can't tell that I'm still slightly angry with him for losing the sample. I know it's irrational and that he feels horrible, but I'm still upset. I miss my grandfather. I held on to that tube, to the hope that he might come back.

My father stops and looks at me. "Cassia. Did you have something you wanted to ask me? Or tell me? Is that why you came to the site?"

His kind face, so like Grandfather's, looks worried. I have to tell him. "Grandfather gave me a paper," I say, and my father turns instantly pale. "It was inside my compact. There were old words on it—"

"*Shhh,*" my father says. "Wait."

A couple walks toward us. We smile and say hello and separate around them on the sidewalk. When they are far enough away my father stops. We stand in front of our house now, but I can tell that he doesn't want to continue this conversation inside. I understand. I have something I want to ask him and I want the answer before we go where the port hums and waits in the foyer. I'm worried we won't have a chance to talk about this again.

"What did you do with it?" he asks.

"I destroyed it. Today, at the work site. It seemed like the safest place."

I think I see a flash of disappointment cross my father's face but then he nods. "Good. It's best that way. Especially right now."

I know he's referring to the visit from the Officials, and

before I can stop myself I ask, "How could you lose the sample?"

My father covers his face with his hands, a gesture so sudden and anguished that I take a step back.

"I didn't lose it." He takes a deep breath, and I don't want him to finish but I can't find the words to stop him. "I destroyed it. That day. He made me promise that I would. He wanted to die on his own terms."

The word "die" makes me cringe, but my father isn't finished. "He didn't want them to be able to bring him back. He wanted to choose what happened to him."

"But you had a choice, too," I whisper, angry. "You didn't have to do it. And now he's *gone*."

Gone. Like the Thomas poem. I was right to destroy the poem. What did Grandfather think I could or would do with it? My family doesn't rebel. *He* didn't, aside from the small act of keeping the poem. And there's no reason *to* rebel. Look what the Society gives us. Good lives. A chance at immortality. The only way it can be ruined is if we ruin it ourselves. Like my father did, because my grandfather asked him to.

Even as I turn away from my father and run inside, eyes burning with tears, part of me understands him and why he chose to do what Grandfather asked. Isn't that what I'm doing, too, every time I think the words of the poem or try to be strong without the green tablet?

It's hard to know which ways to be strong. Was it weak

to let go of the paper, watch it drift to its death as silent and white and full of promise as a cottonwood seed? Is it weak to feel the way I do when I think of Ky Markham? To know exactly the spot on my skin where he touched me?

Whatever I've been feeling for Ky must stop. Now. I am Matched with Xander. It does not matter that Ky has been places I've never been or that he wept during the showing when he thought no one could see. It does not matter that he knows about the beautiful words I read in the woods. Following the rules, staying safe. Those are the things that matter. Those are the ways I have to be strong.

I will try to forget that Ky said "home" when he looked into my eyes.

CHAPTER 13

"Cassia Reyes," I say, holding out my scancard. The worker records the number on the side of the foilware dinner with her datapod and gives the meal to me.

The datapod beeps again as Xander takes his food and stands beside me. "Do you see Em anywhere? Or Piper or Ky?" he asks.

Blankets patchwork the play yard on the side of First School. It's a real picnic—food eaten outdoors on the grass. The workers rush around the yard, trying to get the right meals into the right hands. It's a bit of a hassle and I can see why they don't do this very often. It's much easier to have food sent to people's homes, schools, workplaces.

"I don't think Piper and Ky signed up in time," I say. "Because of work."

Someone waves at us from a blanket in the middle of the yard. "There's Em," I tell Xander, pointing, and together we weave our way through the blankets on the grass and say hello to our classmates and friends. Everyone is in a good mood, giddy with the novelty of the whole activity. Looking down, trying not to step on anyone's blanket or in anyone's food, I walk right into Xander, who has stopped. He turns to grin at me over his shoulder. "You almost made me drop my dinner," he says, and I tease him back, giving him a little shove. He flops down on the blanket next to Em and leans over to look in her foilware container. "What did they send us?"

"Meat-and-veggie casserole," Em says, making a face.

"Remember the ice cream," I say.

I'm almost finished eating when someone calls out to Xander from across the grass. "I'll be right back," he tells us before he stands up and makes his way through the crowd. I can track his progress through the mass of people; they turn to watch him pass, call out his name.

Em leans over and says to me, "I think something's wrong with me. I took the green tablet this morning. *Already*. I meant to save it for later this week. You know."

I almost ask Em what she means and then I feel like a terrible friend, because how could I forget? Her Match Banquet. She meant to save the tablet for that night, because she's getting nervous.

"Oh, Em," I say, putting my arm around her, hugging her. She and I have been drifting apart lately, but not by choice. This happens, as you get closer to your work assignments and vocations. But I miss her. Nights like this, especially. Summery nights, when I remember how it was to be younger and have more time. When Em and I used to spend so many of our free-rec hours together. We had more of them, then.

"It'll be a wonderful night," I tell her. "I promise. Everything's so beautiful. It's exactly like they tell us it will be."

"Really?" Em asks.

"Of course. Which dress did you pick?" They redesign the dresses every three years, so Em has the same pool to choose from that I did.

"One of the yellow ones. Number fourteen. Do you remember it?"

So much has happened since I stood in the Matching Office and picked out my dress. "I don't think I do," I say, searching my mind.

Em's voice becomes animated as she describes the dress. "It's very light yellow and it's the one with the butterfly sleeves . . ."

I remember now. "Oh, Em, I loved that dress. You'll be beautiful." She will, too. Yellow is the perfect color for Em; it will look lovely against her creamy skin, her black hair, and dark eyes. It will make her look like sunshine, the spring kind.

"I'm so nervous."

"I know. It's hard not to be."

"Everything's different now that you've been Matched with Xander," Em tells me. "I've been, you know, wondering."

"But my Match with Xander doesn't make it any more likely—"

"I know. We all know that. But now we can't help but wonder." Em looks into her foilware container, at her nearly untouched dinner.

A chime sounds from the loudspeakers and we all automatically begin to gather our things. Time to work. Em sighs and stands up. Traces of worry still line her face, and I remember how it felt when I waited for my Match.

"Em," I say impulsively. "I have a compact you can borrow, if you want, for your Banquet. It's golden. It would look perfect with your dress. I'll bring it over tomorrow morning."

Em's eyes widen. "You have an artifact? And you'd lend it to *me*?"

"Of course. You're one of my best friends."

Red-blossomed newrose plants sit in black plastic tubs, waiting for us to plant them into the ground in front of First School. First School always looks so cheerful. I can picture the inside of the school with its bright yellow walls, green tile floors, and blue classroom doors. It's easy to feel safe here. I always did when I was young. *I feel safe here now*, I tell myself. *There's no poem left. Papa's problems are over. I'm safe here, and everywhere else.*

Except, perhaps, on the little hill where, in spite of my decision to stay safe, I often find myself glancing over at Ky, wondering. Wishing we could talk again, but not daring to take the risk of saying anything to him besides the common things, the things we always say.

I look over my shoulder for Ky, but I still don't see him.

"What kind of flowers are these?" Xander asks as we dig. The soil is thick and black. It comes apart in clumps as we lift it.

"Newroses," I tell Xander. "You probably have some growing in your yard. We have them in ours."

I don't tell him that they're not my mother's favorite. She thinks the ones we have in the City in all the gardens and public spaces are too hybridized, too far from their original selves. The oldroses took a lot of care to grow; each blossom was a triumph. But these are hardy, showy, bred for durability. "We don't have newroses in the Farmlands," my mother says. "We have other flowers, wildflowers."

When I was little, she used to tell me stories about those different flowers that grew wild in the Farmlands. The stories didn't have a plot; they weren't even really stories as much as they were descriptions, but they were beautiful and they lulled me to sleep. "Queen Anne's lace," my mother would say in a slow, soft voice. "Wild carrot. You can eat the root when it's young enough. The flower is white and lacy. Lovely. Like stars."

"Who's Queen Anne?" I'd ask, drowsy.

"I can't remember. I think she's in the Hundred History Lessons somewhere. But shhhh. That's not important. What's important is that you see the lace in front of you, too many little flowers to count, but you try anyway . . ."

Xander hands me a newrose plant and I pull it from its small plastic tub and put it in the ground. The strong, stringy roots have grown in circles around the inside of the pot, for lack of anywhere else to go. I spread them out as I put the newrose plant into the ground. Looking at the soil makes me think of the dirt my shoes collect while we hike. And thinking of hiking makes me think of Ky. Again.

I wonder where he is. As Xander and I plant the flowers and talk, I picture Ky working while the rest of us play, or listening to the music piped into the almost-empty auditorium. I imagine him walking through the crowds at the recreation building and taking his turn playing a game that he will likely lose. I see him sitting in the theater watching the showing, tears in his eyes. *No.* I banish the images from my mind. I won't do this anymore. The choice is made.

I never had a choice to begin with.

Xander knows I'm not listening to him as closely as I should. He glances to make sure no one can hear us and then he says softly, "Cassia. Are you still worried about your father?"

My father. "I don't know," I say. It's the truth. I don't know how I feel about him right now. Already the anger is giving way—almost against my will—to more understanding, more empathy. If Grandfather had looked at *me* with his fiery eyes and asked me to do him one last favor, would *I* have been able to tell him no?

The evening slides in slowly, darkening the sky by degrees. There's a trace of light left when the chime rings again and we stand up to survey our work. A small breeze drifts across the grounds and the flower beds ripple red in the dusk.

"I wish we could do this every Saturday," I say. It feels like we have created something beautiful. My hands are stained red from some of the crushed petals; and they smell of earth and newrose, a sharp-flower smell that I like in spite of my mother's comments about the oldrose perfume being more subtle, more delicate. What's wrong with being durable? What's wrong being something, someone, that lasts?

Standing there looking at my work, however, I realize that all my family has ever done is sort. Never create. My father sorts old artifacts like my grandfather did; my great-grandmother sorted poems. My Farmlander grandparents plant seeds and tend crops, but everything they grow has been assigned by the Officials. Just like the things my mother grows at the Arboretum.

Just like we did here.

So I didn't create anything after all. I did what I was told and followed the rules and something beautiful happened. Exactly as the Officials have promised.

"There's the ice cream," Xander says. The workers wheel the freezer carts along the sidewalk near the flower beds. Xander grabs me by one hand and Em by the other and pulls us into the nearest line.

It takes the workers much less time to hand out our foil cups of ice cream than it took them to pass out dinner because the ice cream is all the same. Our meals have our specialized vitamins and enrichments and have to be given to the right person. The ice cream is a nothing food.

Someone calls out to Em and she goes over to sit by them. Xander and I find a place a little apart from everyone else. We lean our backs against the sturdy cement-block walls of the school and stretch out our legs. Xander's are long and his shoes are worn. He must be due for some new ones soon.

He digs his spoon into the single white scoop and sighs. "I'd plant acres of flowers for this."

I agree. Cold and sweet and wonderful, the ice cream slides across my tongue and down my throat and into my stomach, where I swear I can feel it long after it melts. My fingers smell like soil and my lips taste like sugar and I'm so awake right now I wonder if I'll be able to sleep tonight.

Xander holds out his last spoonful toward me.

"No, it's yours," I say, but he insists. He is smiling and generous and it seems ungracious to push his hand away, so I don't.

I take the spoon from him and pop the last bite into my mouth. It's the kind of thing you could never do at a real meal—share food—but it's acceptable tonight. The Officials wandering around supervising don't even bat an eye. "Thanks," I say, and then Xander's act of kindness inexplicably makes me feel a little like crying, so I have to joke instead. "We shared a spoon. That's practically kissing."

Xander rolls his eyes. "If you think that, you've never been kissed before."

"Of course I've been kissed before." We are teenagers, after all. Until we're Matched, we all have crushes and flirt and play kissing games. But that's all they are—games—because we know we'll be Matched someday. Or we'll stay Single and the games will never end.

"Was there anything in the guidelines about kissing? Anything I should remember?" I ask, teasing Xander.

I see an answering look of mischief in his eyes as he leans a little closer. "There are no rules about kissing, Cassia. We're Matched."

I have looked at Xander's face many times, but never like this. Never in the almost-dark, never with a feeling in my stomach and heart that is two parts excitement and one part nervousness. I glance around but no one looks at us, and even if they did, all they would see is two shadowy figures sitting rather close as the evening dims.

So I lean closer, too.

And if I needed any more confirmation that the Society knows what they're doing, that this is the Match for me, the taste of Xander's kiss would convince me. It feels right, sweeter than I expected.

A chime rings across the schoolyard as Xander and I pull back, looking at each other. "We still have an hour of free-rec time left," Xander says, glancing down at his watch, his face open, unembarrassed.

"I wish we could stay," I say, and I mean it. The air feels so warm on my face out here. It's real air, not chilled or warmed for my convenience. And Xander's kiss, my first real kiss, makes me press my lips together, try to taste it again.

"They won't let us," he says, and I see that it's true. They're already gathering the cups, telling us to finish up our free-rec hours someplace else because the light is leaving here.

Em detaches from her other group of friends and walks

over to us, graceful. "They're going to see the end of the showing," she says, "but I'm tired of that. What are you going to do?" The moment she asks the question, her eyes widen a little, remembering. That Xander and I are Matched. She had forgotten, for a moment, and now she worries she'll be out of place.

But Xander's voice is warm, easy, friendly. "Not enough time for a game," he says. "There's a music hall near here, one stop over. Should we go there?"

Em looks relieved, glances at me to make sure it's all right. I smile at her. Of course it is. She's still our friend.

As we walk to the air-train stop, I think about how there were once more of us. Then Ky got his work assignment, then Piper. I don't know where Sera is tonight. Em is here, but there will come a time when she leaves, too, when it's just Xander and me.

It's been a long time, months even, since I've been to a music hall. To my surprise, this one is filled with blue-clothed people. With workers, young and old, who have finished their late shift. I suppose this happens often; with only a little time left, where else do they have to go? They must stop here on their way back out from the City. Some of them sleep, I see to my surprise, heads tipped back, tired. No one seems to mind. Some talk.

Ky's here.

I find him almost immediately in the sea of blue, almost

before I knew I was looking. Ky sees us, too. He waves but doesn't stand.

We slide into the nearest seats, Em, Xander, me. Em asks Xander about *his* experience at the Match Banquet, searching again for assurance, and he starts telling her a funny story about not knowing how to put his cuff links on that night, or how to tie his cravat. I try to keep from noticing Ky, but somehow I still see when he stands up and edges his way toward us. I smile a little when he takes the seat next to me. "I didn't know you liked music so much."

"I come here a lot," Ky says. "Most of the workers do, as I'm sure you've noticed."

"Doesn't it get boring?" The high clear voice of the woman who sings this song winds above us. "We've heard the Hundred Songs so many times."

"They're different, sometimes," Ky says.

"Really?"

"They're different when you're different."

I'm not sure what he means, but I'm distracted suddenly by Xander pulling on my arm. "Em," he whispers, and I look at Em. She's shaking, breathing fast. Xander stands up and trades seats with her, guiding her, shielding her with his body so that she's on the inside of our group instead of on the edge.

I lean, too, instinctively helping to hide her, and soon Ky presses next to me, blocking her, too. It's the second time we've touched, and although I'm worried about Em, I can't help but notice it, can't help but want to lean into him a little in spite of the fact that I still feel Xander's kiss on my lips.

We've closed around Em now, hiding her. Whatever's happening, the less people who see it, the better. For Em's sake. For ours. I glance up. The Official in charge of the music hall hasn't noticed us yet. So many people are here, and most of them workers, requiring a closer eye than students. We have a little time.

"Let's get your green tablet," Xander says to Em gently. "It's an anxiety attack. I've seen people at the medical center who have them. All they have to do is take their green tablet, but they're so scared they forget." Even though his voice sounds confident, he bites his lip. He seems worried for Em, and he's not supposed to say too much about his job to others who don't share his vocation.

"You can't," I whisper. "She took it earlier today. She hasn't had time to get another one yet." I don't say the rest of it. *And she'll get in trouble for taking two in one day.*

Xander and Ky exchange glances. I've never seen Xander hesitate like this—can't he do something? I know he can. Once, a child on our street fell and blood was everywhere. Xander knew what to do—he didn't even flinch—until the full-time medics arrived and took the boy to the medical center to fix him up.

Ky doesn't move either. *How can you?* I think, angry. *Help her!*

But even while he holds still, his eyes hold Xander's. Ky's lips move. *"Yours,"* he whispers, looking at Xander.

For a split second, Xander doesn't understand; and then at the same moment he does, I do, too.

But here is the difference between us. Xander doesn't hesitate once he knows what Ky means. "Of course," Xander whispers, and he reaches for his tablet container. Now that he knows what to do, he's fast, he's smooth, he's Xander.

He puts his own green tablet in Em's mouth. I don't think she knows what's happening; she's shaking so much, she's so afraid. She swallows reflexively; I doubt she tastes anything as it goes down.

Almost immediately, her body relaxes. "Thank you," she says to us, closing her eyes. "I'm sorry. I've been worrying too much about the Banquet. I'm sorry."

"It's fine," I whisper, looking at Xander and then at Ky.

Between the two of them, they've pulled it off. For a moment, I wonder why Ky didn't give Em his tablet, but then I remember. He's an Aberration. And Aberrations aren't allowed to carry tablets of their own.

Does Xander know now? Did Ky just give himself away?

But I don't think Xander guessed. Why would he? It makes as much sense for him to give Em the tablet as it would for Ky. More, even. Xander has known Em longer. He settles back in his seat, watching Em as he takes her pulse, his hand around her delicate wrist. He looks up at Ky and me and nods. "Everything's fine now," he says. "She's going to be fine."

I put my arm around Em, and close my eyes, too, listening to the music. The song the woman was singing has ended, and now it's the Anthem of the Society, bass notes rumbling, choir coming in for the final verse. Their voices sound triumphant; they sing as one. Like us. We closed around Em in a circle to protect her from the eyes of the Officials; and none of us will tell about the green tablet.

I am glad that all is well, glad that I promised to let Em borrow the compact for her Banquet. For what is the point of having something lovely if you never share it?

It would be like having a poem, a beautiful wild poem that no one else has, and burning it.

After a moment, I open my eyes and glance over at Ky. He doesn't look back, but I know he knows I'm watching. The music is soft, slow. His chest rises and falls. His lashes are black, impossibly long, the exact color of his hair.

Ky is right. I will never hear this song the same way again.

CHAPTER 14

At work the next day, we all notice immediately when the Officials enter the room. Like dominos falling at a game table, head after head turns toward the door of the sorting center. The Officials in their white uniforms are here for me. Everyone knows it and I know it, so I don't wait for them. I push my chair back and stand up, my eyes meeting theirs across the dividers that separate our slots.

It's time for my test. They nod for me to follow.

So I do, heart pounding but head held high, to a small gray room with a single chair and several small tables.

As I sit down, Norah appears in the doorway. She seems slightly anxious but gives me a reassuring smile before she looks at the Officials. "Do you need anything?"

"No, thank you," says an Official with gray hair, who looks significantly older than the other two. "We've brought everything we require."

None of the three Officials makes small talk as they set things in order. The Official who spoke first seems to be in charge. The others, both women, are efficient and smooth. They hook up a datatag behind my ear and one inside the neck of my shirt. I don't say anything, not even when the gel they use stings my skin.

The two women step back and the older Official slides a small screen across the table toward me. "Are you ready?"

"Yes," I say, hoping my voice sounds level and clear. I straighten my shoulders and sit up a little taller. If I act as though I'm not afraid maybe they will believe me. Although the datatags they've attached to me might tell a different story, thanks to my racing pulse.

"Then you may begin."

The first sort is a numbers one, a simple one, a warmup. They are fair. They want me to get my legs under me before they move into the hard sorts.

As I sort the numbers on the screen, making order out of chaos and detecting patterns, my heartbeat evens out. I stop trying to hold onto so many other things—the memory of Xander's kiss, what my father has done, curiosity about Ky, worry about Em in the music hall, confusion about myself and how I am meant to be and who I am meant to love. I let it all go like a child with a handful of balloons on her First Day at First School. They float away from me, bright and dancing on the breeze, but I don't look up and I don't try to grab them back. Only when I hold onto nothing can I be the best, only then can I be what they expect me to be.

"Excellent," the oldest Official says as he inputs the scores. "Quite excellent. Thank you, Cassia."

The female Officials remove my datatags. They meet my eyes and smile at me because now they can't be accused of showing any partiality. The test is finished. And it seems that I have passed, at least.

"It's been a pleasure," the gray-haired Official says, reaching across the small table toward me. I stand up and shake his hand and then the hands of the other two Officials. I wonder if they can feel the current of energy that runs through me: The blood in my veins is made of adrenaline and relief. "That was an exceptional demonstration of sorting ability."

"Thank you, sir."

On their way out the door, he turns back to me one last time and says, "We have our eyes on you now, young lady."

He shuts the metal door behind him. It makes a thick, solid sound, a sound of finality. As I listen to the nothing that follows I suddenly realize why Ky likes to blend in. It is a strange feeling, knowing for certain that the Officials watch me more closely. It is as though I stood in the way when that door swung shut and I find myself pinned now by the weight of their observation—a concrete thing, real and heavy.

The night of Em's Match Banquet I go to bed early and fall asleep quickly. It is my night to wear the datatags and I hope the information they gather from my dreams shows the sleep patterns of a completely normal seventeen-year-old girl.

But in my dream I'm sorting for the Officials again. The screen comes up with Em's picture and I'm supposed to sort her into a Matching pool. I freeze. My hands stop. My brain stops.

"Is there a problem?" the gray-haired Official asks.

"I can't tell where I should sort her," I say.

He looks at Em's face on the screen and smiles. "Ah. That's not a problem. She has your compact, doesn't she?"

"Yes."

"She'll carry her tablets to the Banquet in it, as you did. Simply tell her to take the red one and everything will be fine."

Suddenly I'm at the Banquet, pushing through girls in dresses and boys in suits and parents in plainclothes. I turn them, shove them, do whatever I have to do to see their faces, because everyone here wears yellow and it all blurs together, I can't sort, I can't see.

I spin another girl around.

Not Em.

I accidentally knock a tray full of cake out of a waiter's hand, trying to catch up to a girl with a graceful walk. The tray falls on the floor and the cake breaks apart, like soil falling from roots.

Not Em.

The crowd thins, and a girl in a yellow dress stands alone in front of a blank screen.

Em.

She's about to cry.

"It's all right!" I call out to her, pushing my way through more people. "Take the tablet and everything will be fine!"

Em's eyes brighten; she pulls out my compact. She lifts the green tablet and puts it in her mouth, fast.

"No!" I cry out, too late. "The—"

She puts the blue tablet in her mouth next.

"—red one!" I finish, pushing through one last cluster of people to stand in front of her.

"I don't have one," she says, turning around, her back toward the screen now. She shows me the open compact, empty. Her eyes are sad. "I don't have a red tablet."

"You can have mine," I say, eager to share with her, eager to help her this time. I won't sit idly by. I pull out my container, twist the top, put the red tablet right into her hand.

"Oh, thank you, Cassia," she says. She lifts it to her mouth. I see her swallow.

Everyone in the room has stopped milling about. They all look at us now, eyes on Em. What will the red tablet do? None of us knows, except me. I smile. I know it will save her.

Behind Em the screen flashes on with her Match—right in time for him to see Em fall down, dead. Her body makes a heavy sound when it falls, in contrast to the lightness of her eyes fluttering shut, of her dress fluttering in folds around her, of her hands fluttering open like the wings of something small.

I wake up sweating and freezing at the same time, and it takes me a minute to calm myself down. Even though the Officials have laughed at the notion that the red tablet is a death tablet, the rumors still persist. That explains why I dreamed about it killing Em.

Just because I dreamed it doesn't mean it's true.

The sleep tags feel sticky on my skin, and I wish I didn't have to wear them tonight. At least the nightmare isn't a recurring one, so I can't be accused of obsessing over something. Besides, I don't think they can tell exactly *what* I dreamed. Just that I did. And a teenage girl having an occasional nightmare can't be uncommon. No one will flag that particular piece of data when it loads to my file.

But the gray-haired Official said that they had their eyes on me.

I stare up into the dark with an ache in my chest that makes it hard to breathe. But not hard to think.

Ever since the day of Grandfather's Final Banquet last month, I've gone back and forth between wishing he had never given me that paper and being glad that he did. Because at least I have the words to describe what I feel is happening inside of me: the dying of the light.

If I couldn't name it, would I even know what it is? Would I even feel it at all?

I pick up the microcard that the Official gave me in the greenspace and tiptoe toward the port. I need to see Xander's face; I need reassurance that everything is in order.

I stop short. My mother stands at the portscreen talking to someone. Who would contact her so late at night?

My father sees me from the front room, where he sits on the divan waiting for my mother to finish. He gestures for me to come in and sit next to him. When I do, he glances at the microcard in my hands and smiles and teases like any father would. "Seeing Xander at school isn't enough? You want to catch another glimpse of him before you go to sleep?"

He puts his arm around me and gives me a hug. "I understand. I was the same way with your mother. That was back when they let us print out a picture from the ports right away instead of making us wait until after our first meeting."

"What did your parents think of Mama being a Farmlander?"

My father pauses. "Well, they were both a little concerned, to be honest. They never thought I'd Match with someone who didn't live in a City. But it didn't take them long to decide they were happy about it." He gets that smile on his face, the one he always gets when he talks about falling in love. "It only took that first meeting to change their minds. You should have seen your mother then."

"Why did you meet in the City instead of in the Farmlands?" I ask. Usually, it's customary for the first meeting to be held close to the girl's home. There's always an Official from the Match Department present to make sure things go smoothly.

"She insisted on coming here even though it was a long

train ride. She wanted to see the City as soon as possible. My parents and the Official and I all went to the station to meet her."

He pauses and I know he is picturing the meeting in his mind, imagining my mother stepping off that air train.

"And?" I know I sound impatient, but I have to remind him that he's not back in the past. He's here in the present and I need to know everything I can about the Match that made me.

"When she stepped off the train, your grandmother said to me, 'She still has the sun on her face.'" My father pauses and smiles. "She did, too. I'd never seen anyone look so warm and alive. My parents never voiced a concern about her again. I think we all fell in love with her that day."

Neither of us notice my mother standing in the doorway until she clears her throat. "And I with all of you." She seems a little sad, and I wonder if she's thinking of Grandfather or Grandmother or both. She and my father are now the last two people left who remember that day, except for maybe the Official who oversaw their meeting.

"Who called so late on the port?" I ask.

"Someone from work," my mother says. Looking weary, she sits down next to my father and leans her head on his shoulder as he puts his arm around him. "I have to leave on a trip tomorrow."

"Why?"

My mother yawns, her blue eyes opening wide. Her face is still sun-kissed from all her work outdoors. She looks a little older than usual and for the first time I see a bit of gray interwoven in her thick blond hair, some shadows in the sunlight. "It's late, Cassia. You should be asleep. *I* should be asleep. I'll tell you and Bram all about it in the morning."

I don't protest. I close my hand over the microcard and say, "All right." Before I leave for my room my mother leans over to give me a kiss good night.

Once I'm back in my room I listen through the walls again. Something about my mother leaving right now alarms me. Why now? Where is she going? How long will she be gone? She rarely goes on trips for work.

"So?" my father says in the other room. He's trying to keep his voice quiet. "Is everything all right? I can't think of the last time we've had a call so late at night."

"I can't tell. Something seems to be going on, but I don't know what it is. They're pulling a few of us from other Arboretums to come look at a crop at the Arboretum in Grandia Province." Her voice has the singsong quality that it gets when it's very late and she's very tired. I remember it from the nights when she used to tell me those flower stories and I feel reassured. If she doesn't think something is wrong, then everything must be fine. My mother is one of the smartest people I know.

"How long will you be gone?" my father asks.

"A week at the most. Do you think Cassia and Bram will be all right? It's rather a long trip."

"They'll understand." There's a pause. "Cassia still seems upset. About the sample."

"I know. I worry about that." My mother sighs, a soft sound that somehow I still hear through the wall. "It was an honest mistake. I hope she sees that soon."

Mistake? It wasn't a mistake, I think. And then I realize: *She doesn't know. He hasn't told her. My father has a secret from my mother.*

And I have a horrible thought.

So their Match isn't perfect after all.

The moment I think it, I wish it back. If their Match isn't perfect, then what are the chances that mine will be?

The next morning, another thunderstorm tumbles the leaves on the maple trees and showers rain on the newroses. I'm eating my breakfast, oatmeal again, steaming in its foilware dish when I hear the port announce: *Cassia Reyes, your leisure activity, hiking, has been canceled for the day due to inclement weather. Please report to Second School for extra study hours instead.*

No hiking. Which means no Ky.

The walk to the air train is a wet one, and muggy. The rain adds to the water in the air; trapping the humidity. My coppery hair begins to tangle and curl, as it does sometimes in weather like this. I look up at the sky but only see the mass of clouds, no break anywhere.

No one else is on my air train, not Em, not Xander, not Ky. They probably caught other trains, or are still getting ready, but I have a sense of something missed, something missing. Some*one* missing.

Maybe it is me.

Once I'm at school, I go upstairs to the research library, where there are several ports. I want to find out about Dylan Thomas and Alfred Lord Tennyson and if they have any poems that *did* make the selection. I don't think they did, but I have to make sure.

My fingers hover over the screen on the port as I hesitate. The fastest way to find out would be to type in their names, but then there would be a record of someone searching for them and the search could be traced back to me. It's much safer to go through the lists of poets in the Hundred Poems database instead. If I'm looking through poet after poet after poet, that will seem more like an assignment for class and less like a search for something specific.

It takes a long time to go through each name, but I finally get to the Ts. I find one poem by Tennyson and I want to read it but I don't have time. There is no Thomas. There is a Thoreau. I touch that name; one poem of his, *The Moon*, has been saved. I wonder if he wrote anything else. If he did, it is gone now.

Why did Grandfather give me those poems? Did he want me to find some meaning in them? Does he not want me to go gentle? What does that even mean? Am I supposed to fight against authority? I might as well ask if he wants me to commit suicide. Because that's what it would be. I wouldn't actually die, but if I tried to break the rules they'd take away everything I value. A Match. A family of my own. A good vocation. I would have nothing. I don't think Grandfather would want that for me.

I can't figure it out. I've thought and thought about it and turned the words over in my head. I wish I could see the words again on paper and puzzle it out. For some reason, I feel like everything would be different if I could see them outside of myself, not only in my mind.

I've realized one thing, though. Even though I've done the right thing—burned the words and tried to forget them—it doesn't work. These words won't go away.

I'm relieved the minute I see Em sitting in the meal hall. She practically glows, and when she sees me, she lifts her arm to wave. The Banquet went well, then. She didn't panic. She made it through. She isn't dead.

I hurry through the line, sliding into the seat next to her. "So," I ask, even though I already know the answer, "how was the Banquet?" Her radiance shines on everyone in the room. Everyone at our table smiles.

"It was *perfect*."

"It's not Lon, then?" I say, making a feeble joke. Lon was Matched a few months ago.

Em laughs. "No. His name is Dalen. He's from Acadia Province." Acadia is one of the more heavily forested provinces to the east, miles away from our rolling hills and rivered valleys here in Oria. They have stone in Acadia, and sea. Things we don't have much of here.

"*And . . .*" I lean forward. So do the rest of our friends gathered at the table, all of us eager for details about the boy Em will marry.

"When he stood up, I thought, 'He can't be for me.' He's tall and he smiled at me right through the screen. He didn't even look a little bit nervous."

"So he's handsome?"

"Of course." Em smiles. "And he didn't seem too disappointed in me, either, thank goodness."

"How could he be?" Em shines so radiantly today in her drab brown plainclothes that I imagine she was impossible to look away from last night in her yellow dress. "So, he's handsome. But what exactly does he look like?" I'm embarrassed to hear a hint of jealousy in my voice, plain and clear. No one gathered around me to find out what Xander was like. There was no mystery because they already knew.

Em is kind enough to ignore it. "Actually, a little like Xander . . ." she begins, and then she breaks off.

I follow her gaze to where Xander stands a few feet away from us, holding his foilware on a tray and looking stricken.

Did he hear the jealousy in my voice when Em described her Match?

What is wrong with me?

I try to cover it up. "We're talking about Em's Match. He looks like you."

Xander recovers quickly. "So he's *unbelievably* handsome." He sits down next to me but he doesn't look in my direction. I'm embarrassed. He definitely heard me.

"Of course," Em laughs. "I don't know why I was so worried!" She blushes a little, probably remembering the night in the music hall, and looks at Xander. "It all turned out perfectly—the way you said it would."

"I wish they still let you print out a picture right away," I say. "I want to see what he looks like."

Em describes her Match and tells us facts about Dalen that she learned from her microcard, but I'm too distracted to hear much. I worry that I've hurt Xander and I want him to look at me or take my hand, but he does neither of those things.

Em grabs my arm on our way out of the meal hall. "Thank you so much for letting me borrow the compact. I think it helped to have something to hold onto, you know?"

I nod, agreeing.

"Ky gave it back to you this morning, didn't he?"

"*No.*" My heart drops. Where is my compact? Why doesn't Em have it?

"He didn't?" Em's face pales.

"No," I say. "Why does he have it?"

"I saw him on the air train after the Match Banquet. He was coming home late from work. I wanted you to have the compact back as soon as possible." Em takes a deep breath. "I knew you'd see Ky at hiking before you'd see me here, and I couldn't bring it straight back to your house because I was worried I'd be late for curfew."

"Hiking was canceled this morning because of the weather."

"It was?" Hiking is the one summer leisure activity that absolutely can't be done in inclement weather. Even swimming can be done in the indoor pool. Em looks sick. "I should have realized that. But why didn't he find some way to get it to you? He knew how important it was. I made sure to tell him."

Good question. But I don't want this to ruin Em's big moment. I don't want her to worry. "I'm sure he gave it to Aida to give to my mother or father," I say, trying to sound lighthearted. "Or he'll give it to me tomorrow at hiking."

"Don't worry," Xander says, looking directly at me now. He reaches out with his words to cross the small divides that keep coming between us. "You can trust Ky."

CHAPTER 15

As I walk to the air-train stop the next morning, things feel crisp, less weighted. The cool of the night accomplished what the rain yesterday did not; the air feels fresh. New. The sun blinking through the last of the clouds dares the birds to sing, and they do. It dares me to let the light in, and I do. Who wouldn't rage against the death of something so beautiful?

I'm not the only one who feels it. At hiking, Ky finds me standing at the front of the group, just as the Officer begins speaking. Ky presses the compact into my hand. I feel the touch of his fingers and I think he leaves them there, on mine, the smallest bit longer than necessary.

I put the compact into my pocket.

Why here? I wonder, still tingling. *Why not give it to me at home?*

I'm glad I lent it to Em, but I'm glad I have it back, too. The compact is the one link that I have left to my grandparents and I vow never to let it out of my hands again.

I think maybe Ky will wait for me to go in the woods, but he doesn't. When the Officer blows the whistle, Ky takes off without a backward glance, and all at once my new-bright feeling dissolves a little bit.

You have your compact back, I remind myself. *Something returned.*

Ky disappears completely into the trees ahead of me.

Something lost.

Three minutes later, alone in the woods, I realize that Ky didn't give me back my compact. It's something else—I can tell the moment I pull it out of my pocket to make sure it looks all right. The object is similar: gold, a case you can snap open and shut, but it's definitely not my artifact.

There are letters—N,E,S,W—and an arrow on the inside. It spins and spins and keeps pointing back to me.

I didn't think that Aberrations could have access to artifacts, but Ky obviously does. Did he give it to me on purpose? By accident? Should I try to give it back or wait until he says something to me?

There are far too many secrets in these woods, I decide. I find myself smiling, polished bright again, ready for the sun.

"Sir? Sir? Lon's fallen. We think he's injured."

The Officer swears under his breath and looks at Ky and me, who are the only two up on the top of the hill except for this boy. "You two stay up here and keep track of who comes when, all right?" The Officer gives me the datapod and, before I can say anything, he disappears back into the forest with the boy.

I think about telling Ky that we need to exchange artifacts, but before I say the words, something stops me. For some reason I want to hold on to the mysterious spinning arrow in its gold case. Just for another day or two.

"What are you doing?" I ask him instead. His hand moves, making shapes and curves and lines in the grass that seem familiar.

His blue eyes flash up to me. "I'm writing."

Of course. That's why the marks look familiar. He is writing in an old-fashioned, curved kind of writing, like the script on my compact. I've seen samples of it before but I don't know how to do it. No one does. All we can do is type. We could try to imitate the figures, but with what? We don't have any of the old tools.

But I realize as I watch Ky that you can make your own tools.

"How did you learn to do this?" I don't dare sit down next to him—someone could come through the trees at any moment and need me to enter them in the datapod—so I stand as close as I dare. He grimaces and I realize I am standing right in the middle of his words. I take a step back.

Ky smiles but doesn't answer; he keeps on writing.

This is the difference between us. I live to sort; he knows how to create. He can write words whenever he wants. He can swirl them in the grass, write them in the sand, carve them in a tree.

"No one knows I can do this," Ky says. "Now I have a secret of yours and you have one of mine."

"Just one?" I say, thinking of the spinning arrow in the gold case.

Ky smiles again.

Some of the rain from last night pooled in the heavy, drooping petals of the wildflowers here. I dip my finger in the water and try to write along the slick green surface of one of the broad leaves. It feels difficult, awkward. My hands are used to tapping a screen, not to sweeping and swirling in controlled movements. I haven't held a paintbrush in years, not since my days in First School. Because the water is clear, I can't really see my letters but I still know that they aren't formed correctly.

Ky dips his finger into another droplet and writes a glistening C on the leaf. He makes the curve smoothly, gracefully.

"Will you teach me?" I ask.

"I'm not supposed to do that."

"We're not supposed to be doing any of this," I remind him. Sounds drift up from the tangled trees and undergrowth below us. Someone is coming. I feel desperate to make him promise to teach me before anyone gets here and this moment vanishes. "We're not supposed to know poems or writing or . . ." I stop myself. I ask again. "Will you teach me?"

Ky doesn't answer.

We're not alone anymore.

Several people have reached the top, and from the wails I can hear through the forest, the Officer and Lon's group are not far behind. I have to enter these names into the datapod, so I step away from Ky. I look back once at where he sits with his arms folded, looking out over the hills.

It turns out that Lon will survive. Once the Officer cures the melodrama accompanying the injury, they find that all Lon has is a slightly twisted ankle. Still, the Officer warns us to take it slow on our way back to the bottom of the hill.

I want to walk down with Ky, but he attaches himself to the Officer and makes himself useful in getting Lon back down the mountain. I wonder why the Officer bothered hauling Lon to the top at all until I hear him muttering something to Ky about "making quota so they don't get after me." It surprises me, even though I know Officers must report to people, too.

I walk with a girl named Livy who is getting better and better at hiking as the days go on and who acts enthusiastic about everything. She talks and talks, and I imagine Ky's hand making that sweeping curve of the C for my name and my heart beats faster.

We're late getting back; I have to rush to the train bound for the Borough, and Ky has to rush to the one that will take him to the City for work. I've given up on talking to him again today when I feel someone brush past me. At the same time I hear a word so soft and quiet I wonder if he said it up on the hill and the wind has just now carried it down to me.

The word is *yes*.

CHAPTER 16

I'm getting good at C. When I arrive at hiking I practically sprint to the top of the hill. After I check in with the Officer, I hurry to my spot next to Ky. Before he can say anything, I pick up a stick and draw a C right there in the mud next to him.

"What's next?" I ask, and he laughs a little.

"You know, you don't need me. You could teach yourself," he says. "You could look at the letters on your scribe or your reader."

"They're not the same," I tell him. "They don't connect like yours do. I've seen your kind of writing before, but I don't know what it's called."

"Cursive," he says softly. "It's harder to read, but it's beautiful. It's one of the old ways of writing."

"That's what I want to learn." I don't want to copy the blocky, flat symbols of the letters we use now. I like the curves and sweeps of the ones Ky knows.

Ky glances over at the Officer, who stares fiercely into the trees as though daring someone else to fall and get hurt today. We don't have long before the others arrive.

"What's next?" I ask again.

"*A*," says Ky, showing me how to make a small letter *a*, embraced by a little swoop at the beginning and at the end, to attach it to what comes before and after. "Because it's the next letter in your name." He reaches and takes hold of the stick above my hand.

Up, around, down.

Guiding, gentle, his hand presses against mine on the downward strokes, releases a little on the upward ones. I bite my lip in concentration; or maybe it's that I don't dare to breathe until the *a* is finished, which it is, all too soon.

The letter looks perfect. I exhale, a little shakily. I want to look up at him, but instead I look down at our hands, right next to each other. In this light, his don't look so red. They look brown, strong. Purposeful.

Someone is coming through the trees. We both let go at the same time.

Livy bursts into the clearing. She's never been third before, and she's almost beside herself with excitement. While she chatters at the Officer, Ky and I stand up and casually trample what we've written into oblivion.

"Why am I learning to write the letters in my name first?"

"Because even if that's all you learn to write you'll still have something," he says, bending his head down to look at me, making sure I know what he's saying, what he's about to ask. "Was there anything else you wanted to learn to write instead?"

I nod and his eyes brighten with understanding.

"The words from that paper," he whispers, his eyes moving to Livy and the Officer.

"Yes."

"Do you still remember them?"

I nod again.

"Tell me a little every day," he says, "and I'll remember it for you. Then there will be two of us who know."

Even though the time is short before Livy or the Officer or someone else comes over to talk to us, I pause for a moment. If I tell Ky these words, I step into an even more dangerous place than I was before. It will put Ky in danger. And I will have to trust him.

Can I do it? I look out at the view from the top of the hill. The sky does not have an answer for me. The dome of City Hall in the distance certainly doesn't. I remember thinking of the angels from the stories when I went to my Match Banquet. I don't see any angels and they don't fly down on their cotton-soft wings to whisper in my ear. Can I trust this boy who writes in the earth?

Someplace deep within me—Is it my heart? Or perhaps my soul, the mythical part of humans that the angels cared about?—tells me that I can.

I lean closer to Ky. Neither of us looks at the other; we both gaze straight ahead to make sure that no one will suspect anything if they glance our way. That's when I whisper the words to him, my heart so full it's about to burst because I'm saying them, really saying them out loud to another person: "*Do not go gentle into that good night. Rage, rage, against the dying of the light.*"

Ky closes his eyes.

When he opens them again he slips something rough and papery into my hand. "Look at this for practice," Ky says. "Destroy it when you're done."

I can hardly wait for Second School and sorting to end so that I can look at what Ky has given me. I wait until I'm at home in the kitchen, eating my dinner alone because my work hours were long tonight. I hear my father and Bram playing a game on the port in the foyer and I feel safe enough to reach into my pocket and pull out Ky's gift.

A napkin. My first reaction is disappointment. Why this? It's a normal napkin, the kind we get from the meal halls at Second School or the Arboretum or anywhere else. Brown and pulpy. Smeared and used. I have the impulse to incinerate it right away.

But.

When I open it up there are words inside. Gorgeous words. Cursive words. They were beautiful up on the green hill with the sound of wind in trees and they are beautiful here in my gray-and-blue kitchen with the grumbling of the incinerator in the background. Dark, curling, swirling words curve across the brown paper. Where dampness has touched them the words are slightly blurred.

And it's not just words. He's drawn things, too. The surface is covered with lines and meaning. Not a picture, not a poem, not the lyrics to a song, although my sorting mind notices the pattern of all these things. But I can't classify them. This is nothing I have seen before.

I realize that I don't even know what you would use to make marks like this. All of the words I practice are written in the air or traced in the dirt. There used to be tools for writing but I don't know what they were. Even our paintbrushes in school were tethered to artscreens, our pictures wiped away almost immediately after we finished them. Somehow, Ky must know a secret, older than Grandfather and his mother and people before them. How to make. Create.

Two lives, he's written.

Two lives, I whisper to myself. The words hush and hang in the room, too soft for the port to hear above the other sounds in the house. Almost too soft for me to hear above my heart beating fast. Faster than it ever has in the woods or on the tracker.

I should go to my room, to the relative privacy of that little place with my bed, my window. My closet where plainclothes hang, dead and still. But I can't stop staring. It's hard, at first, for me to figure out what the picture is meant to be; but then I realize it's him. Ky. Drawn twice, once on each side of the fold of the napkin. The line of his jaw gives it away; the shape of his eyes, the spareness and strength of his body. The spaces left empty; his hands and the nothing they hold, though they are cupped, tipped skyward, in both pictures.

That's where the similarity between the pictures ends. In the first picture, he looks up at something in the sky, and he looks younger, his face is open. The figure there seems to think his hands might still be filled. In the second, he is older, his face narrower, and he looks down at the ground.

Along the bottom he has written *Which one is the true one, I don't ask, they don't tell.*

Two lives. I think I understand this—his life before he came here, and his life after. But what does he mean by the line of song or poetry or plea at the end?

"Cassia?" my father calls from the doorway, behind me. I scoop the napkin up with my foilware from dinner and take it all toward the incinerator and the recycling bin.

"Yes?"

Even if he sees it, it's a napkin, I tell myself, looking at the brown square on my tray. *We incinerate them after every meal, and it's even the right kind of paper, not like the one Grandfather gave me. The incineration tube won't register the difference. Ky is keeping you safe.* I lift my eyes to my father.

"It's a message for you on the port," my father says. He doesn't look down at what I carry; he's focused on my face, to see what I'm thinking. Maybe it's there that the real danger lies. I smile, try to look unconcerned.

"Is it from Em?" I slide my foilware into the recycling bin. Only the napkin left.

"No," my father says. "An Official from the Match Department."

"Oh." Just like that, I push the napkin down the incineration tube. "I'll be right there," I say to my father. I feel the faintest hint of heat from the fire below as Ky's story burns, and I wonder if I will ever have the strength to hold onto something. Grandfather's poems. Ky's story. Or if I will always be someone who destroys.

Ky told you to destroy it, I tell myself. *The man who wrote the poem is gone, but Ky is not. We have to keep it that way. Keep him safe.*

I follow my father into the foyer. Bram glares at me on his way out of the foyer because this message has interrupted his game. Hoping to hide my nervousness, I give him a playful shove as I walk toward the port.

The Official on the screen is not one I've seen before. He's a cheerful, burly looking man, not at all the cerebral, ascetic type I imagine hovering over datascreens in the Match Department. "Hello, Cassia," he says. The collar of his white uniform seems tight around his neck, and he has laugh lines near his eyes.

"Hello." I want to look down and see if my hands are stained from the drawings, the words, but I keep my eyes on the Official.

"It's been over a month since your Match."

"Yes, sir."

"Other Matchees are arranging their first port-to-port

communications now. I've spent the day putting those together for your peers. Of course, it would be rather ludicrous for you and Xander to have a formal port-to-port communication." The Official laughs cheerfully. "Don't you think?"

"I agree, sir."

"The other Officials on the Matching Committee and I decided it makes the most sense for the two of you to have an outing together instead. Supervised, of course, by an Official, as are communications for the other Matchees."

"Of course." Out of the corner of my eye I see my father standing in the door of his room, watching me. Watching over me. I'm glad he's there. Even though the idea of spending time with Xander isn't at all new or scary, the idea of an Official at our meeting feels a little strange.

I hope it isn't the Official from the greenspace, I think suddenly.

"Excellent. You'll be eating outside of your home tomorrow night. Xander and the Official assigned to your Match will pick you up at your regular mealtime."

"I'll be ready."

The Official signs off and the port beeps, indicating that we have another call waiting. "We're popular this evening," I say to my father, glad of the distraction so we don't have to talk about my outing with Xander. My father already looks hopeful and hurries to stand next to me. It is my mother.

"Cassia, can I speak with your father alone for a few

minutes?" she asks me after we exchange hellos. "I don't have much time to talk tonight. I have some things I need to tell him." She looks tired, and she still wears her uniform and insignia from work.

"Of course," I say.

A knock sounds at the door and I go to answer it. It's Xander. "We still have a few minutes before curfew," he says. "Do you want to come talk on the steps with me?"

"Of course." I close the door behind me and go outside. The porch light shines bright above us and we are in full view of the world—or at least the world of Mapletree Borough—as we sit down on the cement steps side by side. It feels good to be with Xander, in a different way than it feels good to be with Ky.

Still. Being with Ky, being with Xander—both things feel like standing in the light. Different types of light, but neither feels dark.

"It sounds like the two of us have an outing tomorrow night," Xander says.

"The three of us," I say, and when he looks puzzled, I add, "Don't forget the Official."

Xander groans. "Right. How could I forget?"

"I wish we could go alone."

"Me too." Neither of us says anything for a moment. The wind sails along our street, ruffling the leaves on the maple trees. In the evening light the leaves look silver-gray; their colors are gone, sucked away for now by the night. I think of the night I sat with Grandfather and thought the same thing; I think of the old disease of color blindness, eliminated generations ago, and how the world might have looked to those people.

"Do you ever daydream?" Xander asks me.

"All the time."

"Did you ever daydream about your Match? Before the Banquet, I mean?"

"Sometimes," I say. I stop watching the play of the wind on the leaves of the maple tree and glance at Xander.

I should have looked at Xander before I answered. It's too late now. Now I can tell by his eyes that my answer wasn't what he hoped, that by saying what I did I closed a door instead of opening it. Perhaps Xander dreamed about me and wanted to know if I dreamed about him. Perhaps he has moments of uncertainty, as I do, and needs me to tell him that I feel sure about the Match.

This is the problem with being an uncommon Match. We know each other too well. We feel the uncertainties in our touch, see them in each other's eyes. We don't work them out on our own miles away from each other the way the other Matches do. They don't see the day-to-day. We do.

Still, we *are* a Match, and a deep understanding runs through us even in the midst of a misunderstanding. Xander reaches for my hand and I lace my fingers through his. This is the known. This is good. When I think about sitting on a porch with him on other nights in this life we've been given, I can picture it easily and happily.

I want Xander to kiss me again. It's late evening and there's even a newrose smell in the air the way there was for our first kiss. I want him to kiss me again so that I know that what I feel for him is real, if it is more or less real than Ky's hand brushing mine on top of the little hill.

Down the street, the last air train from the City sighs into the station. A few moments later we see the figures of late workers hurrying down the sidewalks to get back to their houses by curfew.

Xander stands up. "I'd better get back. See you tomorrow at school."

"See you tomorrow," I say. He squeezes my hand and joins the others on the sidewalk walking toward home.

I don't go inside. I watch the figures and wave to a few of them. I know who I'm waiting for. Just when I think I won't see him, Ky pauses in front of my house. Almost before he's stopped, I walk down the steps and over to talk to him.

"I've been meaning to do this for the last few days," Ky says. At first I think he's reaching for my hand and my heart pauses, but then I see that he's holding out something. One of the brown paper envelopes that people who work in offices sometimes use. He must have gotten it from his father. I realize right away that my compact might be inside, so I reach to take the envelope from him. Our hands do not touch and I find myself wishing that they had.

What is wrong with me?

"I have your . . ." I pause because I don't know what to call the case that holds the spinning arrow.

"I know." Ky smiles at me. The moon, hanging heavy and low in the sky near the horizon, is a harvest-yellow slice like the melon we get to eat during the Autumn Holiday. The moon's light brightens Ky's face a little but his smile does even more.

"It's inside." I gesture behind me, at the steps and the lighted porch. "If you want to stay here, I can run in and get it."

"That's all right," Ky says. "It can wait. You can give it to me later." His voice sounds quiet, almost shy. "I want you to have a chance to look at it."

I wonder what color his eyes are right now. Do they reflect the black of the night or the light of the moon?

I move closer to try to see, but as I do, the almost-curfew bell rings down the street and we both jump. "I'll see you tomorrow," Ky says as he turns to leave.

"See you then."

I have five more minutes before I have to be inside, so I stay out and do not move. I watch him all the way down the street and then I look up at the moon in the sky and close my eyes. In my mind, I see the words I read earlier:

Two lives.

Ever since the day of the mistake with my Match, I've never known which life is my true one. Even with the reassurances of the Official that day in the greenspace, I think a part of me hasn't felt at peace. It was as though I saw for the first time that life could branch into different paths, take different directions.

Back inside the house, I tip my compact out of the envelope and take Ky's artifact from its hiding place deep in the pocket of one of my extra sets of plainclothes. When I place them side by side, it's easy to tell the difference between the two golden circles. The surface of Ky's artifact is plain, scratched. The compact shines brighter, and its engraved letters catch my eye.

On a whim, I pick up my artifact, twist the base, look inside. I know Ky saw me reading the poems in the forest. Did he also see me open the compact?

What if Ky left a message for me?

Nothing.

I put the compact away on its shelf.

I decide to keep the envelope, to put Ky's artifact inside before I put it back in the pocket of my extra plainclothes for safekeeping. But before I do, I open the case and watch the spinning arrow. It settles on a point, but I still spin, wondering where to go.

CHAPTER 17

The climb is almost too easy.

I slap branches out of the way, leap over rocks and push through bushes. My feet have worn a path on this hill and I know where to go and how to get there. I wish for a bigger challenge and for something harder to scale. I wish for the Hill with its fallen trees and ungroomed forest. Right now, I think, if they put me on the Hill I could run straight up it. And when I reached the top there would be a new view and maybe, if he came with me and we stood there together, I would learn even more about Ky.

I can't wait to see him and ask him about his story. Will he have more for me?

I burst through the trees and grin at the Officer.

"Got some competition for your spot today," he says as he records my climbing time on the datapod.

What does he mean? I turn to see Ky. A girl sits next to him, bright golden hair streaming down her back. Livy.

Ky laughs at something she says. He makes no move, no gesture to indicate that he wants me to come sit by him. He doesn't even look at me. Livy's taken my place. I take a step forward to get it back.

Livy holds out a stick to Ky. He doesn't even hesitate. He takes hold of it right above her hand, and I see him helping her make swirling motions in the dirt.

Is he teaching her to write?

My one step forward becomes many steps back as I turn and walk away from it all. From the glint of sunlight on her hair; from their hands, almost-touching, writing letters in the dirt; from Ky's eyes looking away from me; from the spot in the sun with wind and whispered words that are supposed to be mine.

How can I talk to Ky with her sitting right there? How can I learn how to write? How can I get more of his words?

The answer is simple: I can't.

Back down at the bottom of the hill the Officer gives us a speech. "Tomorrow will be different," he tells us. "Stay at the Arboretum air-train stop when you arrive and wait for me so I can lead you to the new site. We're finished with this hill."

"Finally," Ky says behind me in a voice so quiet only I can hear. "I was beginning to feel like Sisyphus."

I don't know who Sisyphus is. I want to turn around and ask Ky, but I don't. He taught Livy to write. Is he telling her his story, too? Did I trick myself into thinking I was special to him? Perhaps many girls know Ky's story and have fallen for the gift of writing their names.

Even as I think these things I know they are wrong, but I can't clear my mind of the sight of his hand guiding hers.

The Officer blows his whistle to dismiss us. I walk away, staying slightly separate from everyone else. I've walked a few steps when I hear Ky behind me.

"Anything you want to tell me?" he asks softly. I know what he's asking. He wants to hear more of the poem.

I shake my head *no*, turn my face away. He didn't have any words for me. Why should I give him any of mine?

I wish my mother weren't gone. The timing of this trip is strange—summer is the busiest season at the Arboretum, so many plants to tend—and I miss her for selfish reasons, too. How am I supposed to get ready for my first official outing with Xander without her?

I put on a clean pair of plainclothes, wishing that I still had the green dress. If I did, I would wear it again to remind both Xander and me of what everything was like just over a month ago.

When I come out into the foyer, my father and my brother wait for me. "You look beautiful," my father says.

"You look all right," Bram says.

"Thanks," I tell him, rolling my eyes. Bram says this every time I go somewhere. Even on the night of the Match Banquet, he said the same thing. I like to think he said it with more sincerity, though.

"Your mother's going to try to call tonight. She wants to hear all about the evening," my father says.

"I hope she can." The idea of talking with my mother comforts me.

The dinner chime sounds in the kitchen. "Time to eat," my father says, putting his arm around me. "Would you rather we waited here with you or got out of the way?"

Bram is already halfway to the kitchen. I smile at my father. "You should go eat with Bram. I'll be fine."

My father gives me a kiss on the cheek. "I'll be back as soon as the doorbell rings." He's a little wary about the Official, too. I imagine my father coming to the door and saying politely, "I'm sorry, sir. Cassia won't be able to go tonight." I imagine him smiling at Xander so that Xander knows he's not the one my father's worried about. And then I picture my father closing the door gently but firmly and keeping me safe inside this house. Inside these walls where I have been safe for so long.

But this house isn't safe anymore, I remind myself. *This house is where I first saw Ky's face on a microcard. Where they searched my father.*

Is there a safe place anywhere in this Borough? In this City, this Province, this world?

I resist the urge to repeat the words of Ky's story to myself while I wait. He is already in my mind far too much and I don't want him coming along tonight.

The doorbell rings. Xander. And the Official.

I don't think I'm ready to do this and I don't know why.

Or rather, I do know why, but I can't look at it too closely right now or I know it will change everything. Everything.

Outside the door, Xander waits for me. It strikes me that this symbolizes what is wrong here. No one can ever really come in, and when it's time to let them, we don't know how.

I take a deep breath and open the door.

"Where are we going?" I ask on the air train. The three of us sit side by side—me, Xander, and our bored-looking Official, who is youngish and wears the most perfectly ironed uniform I've ever seen.

The Official answers. "Your meals have been sent to a private dining hall. We'll eat dinner there and then I'll escort you both back to your homes." He rarely makes eye contact with us, choosing instead to look past us, out the windows. I don't know whether he intends to make us feel at ease or uncomfortable. So far he's doing the latter.

A private dining hall? I look over at Xander. He raises his eyebrows at me and mouths the words "Why bother?" and gestures to the Official. I try not to laugh. Xander's right. Why go to all the trouble of eating at a private dining hall when this outing is anything but private?

I start to feel sorry for all the Matchees who have to have their first conversations monitored by the Officials over the ports. At least Xander and I have had thousands of conversations before.

The dining hall is a small building one air-train stop over, a place where Singles sometimes go, where our parents can arrange to have meals in the evening now and then if they'd like to get away. "It looks nice," I say in a lame attempt at conversation as we approach the hall. A small greenspace surrounds the redbrick box of a building. In the greenspace, I catch sight of a flower bed full of the ever-present newroses and also some kind of ethereal wildflower.

And then a memory so specific and so clear that it's hard to believe I haven't thought of it until now comes to mind. I remember a night when I was much younger and my parents returned from an evening out. Grandfather had come to stay with Bram and me, and I heard my parents talking with him before my father went to Bram's room and my mother came into mine. A soft pink-and-yellow bloom fell out of her hair when she leaned over to pull up my blankets. She tucked it quickly back behind her ear out of sight, and I was too sleepy to ask how she came by the blossom. At the time, it confused me as I drifted off to sleep: How did she get the flower when picking them is forbidden? I forgot the question in my dreams and never asked it upon waking.

Now I know the answer: My father sometimes bends the rules for those he loves. For my mother. For Grandfather. My father is a little like Xander, the night that he bent the rules to help Em.

Xander takes my arm, bringing me back into the present. When he does, I can't help myself; I glance over at the Official. He doesn't say anything.

The inside of the dining hall looks nicer than a regular meal hall, too. "Look," Xander says. Flickering lights in the center of each table simulate an old romantic system of lighting, candles.

People look at us as we pass among the tables. We're clearly the youngest patrons there. Most are our parents' age or young couples several years older than Xander and me, couples newly Contracted. I see a few people who are probably Singles out on recreational dates, but not many. The Boroughs in this area are primarily family boroughs, full of parents and contracted couples and youth under the age of twenty-one.

Xander notices the staring and stares back, his arm still linked with mine. Under his breath he whispers to me, "At least everyone at school is pretty much over our Match by now. I hate the watching."

"I do, too." Thankfully, the Official doesn't gawk at us. He leads the way through the tables and finds one marked with our names near the back. The waiter arrives with our food almost as soon as we sit down.

The simulated candlelight flickers across the round black metal table in front of me. No tablecloths, and the food is regulation food—we'll eat the same thing here that we'd eat at home. That's why it's necessary to book in advance; so the nutrition personnel can get your meal to the right spot. Obviously dining here doesn't compare at all to the Match Banquet at City Hall, but it's the second-nicest place I've ever eaten in my life.

"The food's good and hot," Xander says as the steam escapes from his foilware container. He peels back the lid and peers inside. "Look at my portion. They want me to bulk up so they keep giving me more and more."

I glance over at Xander's portion of noodles with sauce. It *is* enormous. "Can you eat all of that?"

"Are you joking? Of course I can." Xander acts offended.

I peel back the foilware and look at my portion. Next to Xander's, it seems minuscule. Maybe I'm making this up, but my portions seem to be smaller lately. I'm not sure why. The hiking and running on the tracker keep me fit. If anything, I should be getting more food, not less.

It must be my imagination.

The Official, looking even less interested than before, twists the noodles from his container on a fork and looks around the room at the other patrons. His food is exactly the same as ours. I guess the myths about certain departments' Officials eating better than anyone else aren't true. Not when they eat in public, anyway.

"How's hiking going?" Xander asks me, popping a bite of noodles into his mouth.

"I like it," I answer honestly. *Except for today.*

"Even more than swimming?" Xander teases me. "Not that you ever did much of that, I guess. Sitting there on the edge."

"I swam," I tell him, teasing back. "Sometimes. Anyway. I do like it more than being at the pool."

"That's not possible," Xander says. "Swimming is the best. I heard that all you've been doing at hiking is climbing that same little hill over and over."

"All you do at swimming is swim around the same little pool over and over."

"That's different. Water's always moving. It's never the same."

Xander's comment reminds me of what Ky said in the music hall about the songs. "I guess that's true. But the hill is always moving, too. The wind moves things, and the plants grow and change . . ." I fall silent. Our neatly pressed Official tilts his head, listening to our conversation. That's why he's here, isn't it?

I move my food around and the motion makes me think of writing with Ky. One of the noodles is curved like a *C*. *Don't*. I have to stop thinking about Ky.

Some of my food stubbornly refuses to wrap around my fork. I twirl the utensil around and around and finally give up and shove some noodles into my mouth, the ends sticking out. I have to slurp them in.

Embarrassing. For some reason my eyes fill with tears. I put down my fork and Xander reaches over to straighten it. As he does, he looks straight into my eyes, and I can see the question there as though he speaks it out loud: *What's wrong?*

Shaking my head slightly, I smile back at him. *Nothing.*

I glance over at our Official. He's momentarily distracted,

listening to something on his earpiece. Of course. He is still on duty.

"Xander, why didn't you—you know—kiss me the other night?" I ask suddenly, since the Official isn't listening right at this moment. I should be embarrassed, but I'm not. I want to know.

"There were too many people watching." Xander sounds surprised. "I know the Officials don't care, since we're Matched, but, you know." He inclines his head slightly toward the Official next to us. "It's not the same when you're being watched."

"How could you tell?"

"Haven't you noticed all the Officials on our street lately?"

"Watching my house?"

Xander raises his eyebrows. "Why would they be watching your house?"

Because I read things I shouldn't read and learn things I'm not meant to know and I might be falling in love with someone else. What I say is, "My father . . ." I let my voice trail off.

Xander flushes. "Of course. I should have realized . . . It's not that, at least I don't think so. These are basic-level Officials, police officers. They've been patrolling a lot more lately and not just in our Borough. In all the Boroughs."

Our street was full of Officials that night and I didn't even know. Ky must have known. Maybe that's why he wouldn't come up the porch steps. Maybe that's why he never touches me. He's afraid of being caught.

Or maybe it's even more simple than that. Maybe he never *wants* to touch me. Perhaps to Ky I am only a friend. A friend who finally wants to know his story, nothing more.

And at first that's who I was. I wanted to know more about this boy who lives among us, but who never truly speaks. More about what happened before. I wanted to know more about my mistaken Match. But now I feel like finding out about him is one of the ways I find out about myself. I did not expect to love his words. I did not expect to find myself in them.

Is falling in love with someone's story the same thing as falling in love with the person himself?

CHAPTER 18

Another air car sits on our street, this time in front of Em's house. "What's going on?" I ask Xander, whose eyes widen with fear. The Official with us looks interested but not surprised. I resist the urge to grab his shirtfront tight, wrinkling it in my hands. I hold back from hissing, "Why do you watch us? What do you know?"

The door to Em's house opens and three Officials come out. Our Official turns to Xander and me and says, almost abruptly, "I hope you both had an enjoyable evening. I'll file the report with the Matching Committee first thing tomorrow."

"Thank you," I say automatically as he turns back to the air-train stop, although I don't know why. I don't feel grateful.

The Officials at Em's house walk across her yard and go to the house next door. They hold a container, something Society-issued, and they're not smiling. In fact, if I had to say how they looked, I would say they looked *sad*. I don't like it. "Should we go see if Em is all right?" I ask, and as I do, she opens her front door and looks out. She sees Xander and me and hurries across the yard to meet us.

"Cassia, it's all my fault. It's all my fault!" Em's voice shakes, and tears mark her face.

"What's your fault, Em? What happened?" I glance next door to make sure the Officials aren't watching us, but they've already disappeared inside. Em's neighbors opened the door before the Officials had to knock, as though they were expected.

"What's this about?" Xander's voice sounds harsh and I send him a look, trying to tell him to be patient.

Em's face grows even paler and she grabs my arm. Her voice is hushed. "The Officials are collecting all the artifacts."

"What?"

Em's lips tremble. "They said that I'd been seen with an artifact at the Match Banquet, and they'd come to collect it. I told them it wasn't mine, I'd borrowed it from you and given it back." She swallows and I remember the night of the green tablet. I put my arm around her and glance at Xander. Em keeps speaking, her voice shaky. "I shouldn't have told them. But I was so scared! Now they're going to take it from you. They're going house to house."

House to house. They'll be at mine soon. I want to comfort Em, but I have to try to save my artifact, futile as the effort might be. *I have to go home.* I give Em a hug. "Em, it's not your fault. Even if you hadn't told them, they knew I had an artifact. It's registered, and I took it to my Banquet."

Then I remember something, and fear washes over me.

Ky's artifact. I still have it tucked away in my closet. The Officials might know about my artifact, but they don't know about Ky's. It could get us both in trouble.

How can I hide it?

"I have to go home," I say, out loud this time. I pull my arm away from Em's shoulders and turn toward my house. How long do I have before the Officials get there? Five minutes? Ten?

Em starts crying harder, but I don't have time to reassure her again. I walk as quickly as I can without drawing attention. A few steps later and Xander is next to me, linking his arm in mine as if we have been on a normal outing and are on our way home.

"Cassia," he says. I don't look at him. I can't stop thinking about all that could be lost in a few short moments. Ky is already an Aberration. If they find out that he has an artifact, will he become an Anomaly?

I could cover up for him. I could say that it's mine and I found it when we hiked in the woods. Would they believe me?

"Cassia," Xander says again. "I can hide it for you. Say you've lost it. Make your story convincing."

"I can't let you do that for me."

"You can. I'll wait for you outside while you grab the compact. It's small enough to fit in your hand, right?" I nod. "When you come back out, act like you're crazy about me, like you hate saying good-bye. Throw your arms around me. Drop it down my shirt. I'll take care of it after that."

I've never seen this side of Xander before, I think, and then I instantly realize that I have. When he plays the games he's like this. Cool and calm and full of strategy and daring. And in the games at least, his risks almost always pay off.

"Xander, this isn't a game."

"I know that." His face looks grim. "I'll be careful."

"Are you sure?" I shouldn't let him do this. It's weak to consider it. But still: He can take my compact for me. He would save it for me. He would risk this for me.

"I'm sure."

Once I close the front door behind me, I run down the hall to my room as fast as I can. No one from my family sees me, for which I'm grateful. With shaking hands I tear open my closet door and push the sets of plainclothes along the rack until I find the pair where I've hidden Ky's artifact inside the pocket. I open the brown paper envelope and tip it so that the arrow in its case slides out. I shove the envelope into my pocket; I grab the compact from the shelf and look at the two items in my hands.

Golden and beautiful. In spite of myself, I'm tempted to give Xander my compact instead of Ky's spinning arrow, but I put the compact onto my bed and close my hand over Ky's artifact. Saving my compact would be selfish. It would only save a *thing*. But saving Ky's artifact saves both of us from questioning and him from becoming an Anomaly. And how can I let them take the last piece of his old life?

This is safer for Xander, too. They don't know Ky's artifact exists, so hopefully they won't miss it. My compact will be accounted for and taken away, as expected, so they won't look for it or wonder if I've given it to someone else.

I run back down the hall and open the front door.

"Xander, wait!" I call out to him, trying to make my voice light. "Aren't you going to kiss me good night?"

Xander turns, his face open and natural. I don't think anyone else could see the glint of cunning in his eyes, but I know him so well.

I skip down the steps and he holds out his arms to me. We embrace, his hands at the small of my back and my arms around his neck. I place my hand just under the collar of his plainclothes and open my fingers. The artifact slides down his back and my palm lies flat against his warm skin. We look each other straight in the eyes for a moment and then I lean close to his ear.

"Don't open it," I whisper to Xander. "Don't keep it in your house. Bury it or hide it somewhere. It's not what you think."

Xander nods.

"Thank you," I say, and then I kiss him right on the lips and I mean that kiss. Even though I know I'm falling for Ky it is impossible not to love Xander for everything he is and everything he does.

"Cassia!" Bram calls from the steps.

Bram. He's going to lose something today, too. I think

of Grandfather's watch and anger rises in me. *Do they have to take everything?*

Xander breaks away from our embrace. He has to hurry to hide the artifact before they get to his house. "Good-bye," he says with a smile.

"Good-bye," I call back.

"Cassia!" Bram calls again, fear in his voice. I glance back down the street, but I don't see any Officials yet. They must still be in one of the houses between mine and Em's.

"Hi, Bram," I say, attempting to sound casual. It's better for us all if he doesn't suspect what Xander and I have done. "Where's—"

"They're taking the artifacts," Bram says, voice shaking. "They called Papa in to help with the collection."

Of course. I should have realized. They need someone like him to help determine if the artifacts are real or false. Another fear strikes me. Was he supposed to take *our* artifacts? Did he pretend mine was lost? Did he lie for Bram or me? How many stupid mistakes is he willing to make for those he loves?

"Oh no," I say, trying to act as though all of this is new to me. Hopefully Bram won't find out that Em told me earlier. "Did he take ours with him?"

"No," Bram says. "They won't let anyone collect from their own families."

"Did he know this was going to happen?"

"No. When the call came over the port he was shocked.

But he had to report right away. He told me to listen to the Officials and not to worry."

I want to put my arm around Bram and comfort him because he is about to lose something, something important. So I do. I hold onto my brother and for the first time in years he hugs me back, tight, the way he did when he was a little boy and I was the big sister he admired more than anyone else in the world. I wish I could have saved his watch, but it was the wrong color, silver instead of gold. And the Officials know about it. *There was nothing I could do*, I tell myself, trying to believe it.

We hold on for a few seconds and then I pull away and look Bram in the eyes. "Go get it," I say to him. "Go look at it for the last few minutes you have and remember it. Remember it."

Bram doesn't pretend to hide the tears in his eyes now.

"Bram," I say, and I hug him again. "Bram. Something bad could have happened to the watch even without this. You could have lost it. You could have broken it. But this way you can look at it one last time. It's never really lost to you as long as you remember it."

"Can't I try to hide it?" Bram asks. He blinks and a tear escapes. He brushes it away angrily. "Will you help me?"

"No, Bram," I say gently. "I wish we could, but it's too dangerous." What I risk has a limit. I won't risk Bram.

When the Officials arrive at our house and come in the door they find Bram and me sitting on the divan side by side. Bram holds silver; I hold gold; we both look up. But then Bram's gaze flickers back to the polished silver surface in his hands and I glance down at the gold one in mine.

My face looks back at me, distorted by the curve of the compact's surface, the way it was at the Match Banquet. Then, the question I asked myself was: *Do I look pretty?*

Now the question I ask is: *Do I look strong?*

As I look at my eyes and the set of my jaw, it seems to me that the answer is *yes*.

A short, balding Official speaks first. "The Government has decided that artifacts promote inequality among members of Society," he says. "We request that everyone turn in their artifacts for catalog and display at the Museum in each City."

"Our records indicate that there are two legal artifacts in this residence," a tall Official adds. Does he stress the word *legal*, or is it my imagination? "One silver watch, one gold compact."

I don't say anything and neither does Bram.

"Are these the artifacts?" the bald Official asks, looking at the items we hold. He seems weary. This must be a terrible job. I imagine my father taking artifacts from people—old people like Grandfather, children like Bram—and I feel sick.

I nod. "Do you want them now?"

"You may retain them for a few more minutes. We are required to do a quick search of the house."

Bram and I both sit quietly while they go through our house. It doesn't take long.

"Nothing valuable here," one of them says quietly to another in the hallway.

My heart is on fire and I have to keep my mouth shut tight so that I don't try to burn these Officials with the flames. *That's what you think,* I say to myself. *You think there's nothing here because we're not putting up a fight. But there are words in our heads that no one else knows. And my grandfather died on his terms, not yours. We have things of value but you can never find them because you don't even know how to look.*

They walk back into the room and I stand up. Bram does, too. The Officials wave detection instruments around us to make sure we haven't concealed anything on our persons. Of course, they find nothing.

The female Official comes forward and I see a pale band of skin on her finger, where a ring must have been. She lost something today, too. I hold out the compact, thinking about how my artifact has traveled from a time before the Society, from one family member to another, to me. And now I have to let it go.

The Official takes my compact; she takes the watch from Bram. "You can come see them in the Museum. Any time you like."

"It's not the same," he says, and then he straightens his shoulders. And oh, I see Grandfather, I do. My heart swells with the thought that perhaps he isn't completely gone after all. "You can take it," Bram says, "but it will always be mine."

Bram goes to his room. The heaviness in his step and the way he closes the door tells me that he wants to be alone.

I feel like punching something but I shove my hands into my pockets instead. There I find the brown paper envelope: a crumpled shell that once contained something valuable and beautiful. It's only an envelope, not an artifact; it didn't even register on the Officials' detection instruments. I pull it out and tear it in half, angrily. I want to rip it up and shred it to pieces. The jagged line along the envelope pleases me. It feels good to destroy. I get ready to make another wound. I look down for another place to tear.

My breath catches in my throat when I see what I almost ruined.

Another part of Ky's story. There's something else the Officials have missed.

Drowning, drinking the words at the top say, the letters strong and beautiful, like he is. I think of his hand writing them, his skin brushing the napkin. I bite my lip and look at the picture below.

Two Kys again, the younger one, and the one now, both of them with hands still cupped. The background in the first one is a spare, bare landscape, the bones of rocks rising behind

MATCHED

Ky. In the second picture, he's here in the Borough. I see a maple tree behind him. Rain falls in both pictures, but in the first one his mouth is open, his head tipped back, he drinks from the sky. In the second one his head is down, his eyes panicked, the rain thick around him, streaming off him like a waterfall. There is too much rain here. He could drown.

When it rains, I remember are the words written at the bottom.

I look out the window where the burning evening sun sets in a clear sky. There is no trace of clouds, but I promise myself that when it rains I will remember too. This paper, these pictures and words. This piece of him.

CHAPTER 19

The air train into the City the next morning is almost silent. No one wants to talk about what happened in the Borough last night. Those who gave up their artifacts are hushed with the loss; those who never had any to begin with are quiet out of respect. Or, perhaps, out of satisfaction, because now everything has been equalized.

Before he gets off at his stop for swimming, Xander leans over to kiss my cheek and says softly, "Under the newroses in front of Ky's house."

He steps off the air train and disappears with the other students while I ride on toward the Arboretum. Questions crowd my mind: *How did Xander hide the artifact in the Markhams' flower bed unseen? Does he know it belongs to Ky or is it coincidence that he picked the Markhams' house as the hiding place?*

Does he know what I'm starting to feel for Ky?

Whatever Xander knows or guesses, one thing is certain: He couldn't have picked a better hiding place. We're all charged with keeping our yards neat and clean. If Ky digs in his own yard, no one will suspect anything. I just have to tell him where to look.

Like everyone else, Ky stares out the window as we glide toward the Arboretum. Did he see Xander's kiss? Did he care? He does not meet my eyes.

"We're pairing off for this next round of hiking," the Officer says once we reach the bottom of the Hill. "You are each partnered with another hiker according to ability assessed by analyzing the data I collected from your earlier hikes. That means Ky is paired with Cassia; Livy is paired with Tay . . ."

Livy's face falls and I try to keep mine expressionless.

The Officer finishes reading his list. "You have a different goal on the Hill," he says. "You won't ever see the top here. The Society has asked us to use our hiking time to mark obstacles on the Hill." He gestures to the bags piled next to him. They hold strips of red cloth. "Every pair takes a bag. Tie the markers on branches near fallen trees, in front of particularly bad thickets, etc. Later, a survey crew will come through. They're going to clear and pave a path on the Hill."

They're going to pave the Hill. At least Grandfather doesn't have to see it.

"What if we run out of cloths?" Lon whines. "They haven't cleared the Hill in years. There'll be obstacles everywhere! We might as well mark every tree we see."

"If you run out of cloths, use rocks to make cairns," the Officer says. He turns to Ky. "Do you know how to make a cairn?"

There's the briefest of hesitations before Ky answers. "Yes."

"Show them."

Ky gathers a few rocks from the ground around us and stacks them, largest first, in a small pile. His hands are quick and sure, the way they are when he's teaching me to write. The tower looks precarious but does not fall.

"See? It's simple," the Officer says. "I'll blow my whistle later and that means you need to start making your way back. You blow your whistles if you get lost." He gives us each a standard-issue metal whistle. "It shouldn't be hard. Just head back down the mountain the way you came."

The Officer's thinly veiled disgust for us used to amuse me. Today, I understand it. I feel disgust when I think of how we climb our little hills when the Officials say the word. How we hand over our most precious items at their bidding. How we never, ever fight.

We are barely out of view of the others when Ky turns to me and I turn to him and for a moment I think he is going to touch me. I sense, more than see, his hand move slightly and then drop back down. I feel a disappointment deeper than the disappointment I felt this morning when I opened my closet and did not see the compact resting there.

"Are you all right?" he asks. "Last night, when they searched the houses—I didn't know until after I came home."

"I'm fine."

"My artifact . . ."

Is that all he cares about? I whisper fiercely, *"It's in your flower bed. Buried under the newroses. Dig it up and then you'll have it back."*

"I don't care about the artifact," he says, and although he still does not touch me, I am warmed at the fire in his eyes. "I couldn't sleep all night, worrying that I'd gotten you in trouble. I care about *you.*"

Those words are quiet here under the trees but they sing loudly in my heart, louder than all the Hundred Songs caroled all at once. And his eyes are shadowed underneath, from thinking about me. I want to reach up and touch that skin under his eyes, the one place I've seen any vulnerability in him, make him feel better. And then I could run my fingers there, across his cheekbones, down to his lips, to the place where his jaw meets his neck, where his neck meets his shoulder line. *I like the places where one part meets another*, I think, *eyes to cheek, wrist to hands*. Somewhat shocked at my own thoughts, I take a step back.

"How did you—"

"Someone helped me."

"Xander," he says.

How does he know? "Xander," I agree.

Neither of us speaks for a moment; I stand back, seeing him whole. Then he turns and begins to walk through the trees again. It is slow going; the underbrush grows so tangled here that it's more of a climb than a hike. Trees that fell have not been cleared away and lie like giant bones across the forest floor.

"Yesterday . . ." I begin. I have to ask, as inconsequential as the question now seems. "Were you teaching Livy how to write?"

Ky stops again and looks at me. His eyes seem almost green under the canopy of the trees. "Of course not," he says. "She wanted to know what we were doing. She saw us writing. We weren't careful enough."

I feel stupid and relieved. "Oh."

"I told her I'd been showing you how to draw the trees." He picks up a stick next to me and starts moving it around to make a pattern that does look remarkably like leaves. Then he places the stick down as the trunk of the tree. I keep looking at his hands after he has finished, not sure what else to do.

"No one draws once they're out of First School."

"I know," he says. "But at least it's not expressly forbidden."

I reach into the bag I carry for a piece of red cloth and tie it on a fallen tree near Ky. I keep my eyes down, looking now at my fingers as they twist the fabric into a knot. "I'm sorry. About the way I acted yesterday." When I straighten up, Ky has already moved on.

"Don't be," Ky says, pulling a tangle of climbing green vines away from a shrub so that we can pass through. He throws the vines at me and I catch them in surprise. "It's good to see you jealous once in a while." He smiles, sun in the woods.

I try not to smile in return. "Who said I was jealous?"

"No one," he says. "I could tell. I've been watching people for a long time."

"Why did you let me hold onto it, anyway?" I ask him. "The case with the arrow. It's beautiful. But I wasn't sure—"

"No one but my parents know that I have it," he says. "When Em gave me the compact to give back to you, I noticed how much alike they were. I wanted you to see it."

His voice sounds lonely all of a sudden, and I can almost hear another sentence, the one that instinct still keeps him from saying: *I wanted you to see me.* Because isn't this what it's all about, the golden case with the arrow, the bits of story offered here and there? Ky wants someone to see him.

He wants me *to see him.*

My hands ache to reach for him. But I can't bring myself to betray Xander in that way after everything he has done. After he saved us both—Ky and me—just last night.

But there is something I can continue to give Ky that is purely mine, that doesn't belong to Xander. The poem.

I only mean to tell him a few more lines, but once I start telling him it's hard to hold back, and I say the whole thing. The words go together. Some things are created to be together.

"The words aren't peaceful," Ky says.

"I know."

"Then why do they make me feel calm?" Ky asks in wonder. "I don't understand."

In silence, we push our way through more undergrowth, the poem heavy in our minds.

Finally, I know what it is I want to say. "I think it's because when we hear it we know we're not the only ones who ever felt this way."

"Tell it to me again," Ky asks softly. His breath catches; his voice is husky.

All the rest of the time, until we hear the Officer's whistle, we move up the Hill repeating the poem back to each other like a song. A song that just the two of us know.

Before we leave the forest, Ky finishes teaching me to write my name in the soft dirt underneath one of the fallen trees. We crouch down, red cloths in hand, acting as though we are tying them on in case anyone comes by and sees us. It takes me a little while to learn *s* but I like the way it looks—like something leaning into the wind. The clean line and dot of *i* is easy to master, and I already know how to write *a*.

I write each letter in my name and connect them together, Ky's hand near mine to guide me. We don't quite touch, but I feel the warmth of his hand, the length of his body crouched behind me as I write. *Cassia.*

"My name," I say, leaning back and looking at the letters. They are wavery, less sure than the letters Ky writes. Someone passing by might not even recognize mine as letters at all. Still, *I* can tell what they say. "What next?"

"Now," Ky says, "we go back to the beginning. You know *a*. Tomorrow we'll do *b*. Once you know them all, you can write your own poems."

"But who would read them?" I ask, laughing.

"I would," he says. He gives me another folded napkin. There, between greasy thumbprints and traces of food, is more of Ky for me to see.

I put the napkin in my pocket and I think of Ky writing out his story with his red hands, seared from the heat of the job he does. I think of him risking everything each time he slips one napkin into his pocket. All these years he's been so careful, but now he's willing to take a chance. Because he's found someone who wants to know. Someone he wants to tell.

"Thank you," I say. "For teaching me how to write."

"Thank *you*," he answers. There is a light in his eyes and I am the one who put it there. "For saving my artifact and for the poem."

There's more to say, but we're learning how to speak. Together we step out of the trees. Not touching. Not yet.

CHAPTER 20

I walk home from the air-train stop with Em after school and sorting. Once the others who came with us have gone ahead or fallen behind, Em puts her hand on my arm. "I'm so sorry," she says quietly.

"Em, don't worry about it anymore. I'm not angry." I look her in the eye so that she knows I mean it but her eyes are still sad. So many times in my life I've felt as though looking at Em is like seeing another variation of myself, but I don't feel that way now. Too much has changed recently. Still, Em is my best girlfriend. Growing apart doesn't change the fact that for a long time we grew side by side; our roots will always be tangled. I'm glad for that. "You don't have to keep apologizing," I tell her. "I'm happy I lent it to you. At least we both got to enjoy it before they took it away."

"I still don't understand," Em says softly. "They have plenty of displays in the Museum. It doesn't make any sense."

I've never heard anything so close to insubordination come out of Em's mouth before, and I grin at her. Maybe we aren't becoming so different after all.

"What are we doing tonight?" I ask, changing the subject.

Em seems relieved about the shift in topic. "I talked to Xander today and he wants to go to the game center tonight. What do you think?"

What I really think is that I'd like to go back to the top of the first little hill. The thought of being in that center with its stuffiness and crowds when we could be sitting and talking under a clean night sky seems like more than I can take. But I can do it. I can do whatever I need to in order to keep things normal. I have Ky's words to read. And perhaps, if I'm lucky, I'll see Ky himself later. I hope he comes with us.

Em interrupts my thoughts by saying, "Look. Your mother's waiting for you."

Em's right. My mother sits on the steps of the house with her face turned in our direction. When she sees me looking at her, she stands up, waves, and starts walking toward us. I wave back and Em and I pick up the pace a little.

"She's back," I say out loud, and it isn't until I hear the surprise in my voice that I recognize that part of me worried that she would stay away forever.

"Was she gone?" Em asks, and I realize that my mother's absence is likely one of those things that we aren't supposed to mention outside of our family. Not that the Officials said that explicitly; it's simply the kind of thing we've learned to keep to ourselves.

"Back early from work," I clarify. It's not even a lie.

Em says good-bye and goes into her house. Her maple tree isn't going to make it, I think, noticing that even in the middle of summer the tree only has about ten green, tired leaves. Then I look toward my house, where the tree grows full and the flowers are beautiful and my mother comes to meet me.

This reminds me of times when I was very small in First School and my mother's work hours ended before I got home. She and Bram sometimes walked up the street to meet my train. They never made it far because Bram stopped to look at everything along the way. "That kind of attention to detail might be a sign that he's meant to be a sorter," my father used to say, until Bram got older and it became apparent that he lost his ability to pay attention to detail along with his baby teeth.

When I reach my mother she hugs me right there on the sidewalk. "Oh, Cassia," she says. Her face looks pale and tired. "I'm so sorry. I missed your first official outing with Xander."

"You missed something else last night, too," I say, my face against her shoulder. She is taller than I am and I don't think I will ever catch up. I'm slight and short, like my father's family. Like Grandfather. I smell my mother's familiar smell of flowers and clean fabric, and I breathe in deeply. I'm so glad she's back.

"I know." My mother never speaks against the government. The most defiant she's ever been was when the Officials searched my father. I don't expect her to rant and rave about the unfairness of the Officials taking the artifacts, and she doesn't. It occurs to me that if she did, she'd be ranting and raving against her own husband. He is, after all, an Official, too.

Though he isn't the one who held out his hand and asked us to drop our prized possessions into it, he did that to other people.

When my father came home last night, he gave Bram and me each a long hug and then went straight to his room without saying anything. Maybe because he couldn't stand to see the pain in our faces and remember that he had caused that same pain in others.

"I'm sorry, Cassia," my mother says now as we walk home. "I know how much that compact meant to you."

"I feel sorry for Bram."

"I know. I do, too."

When we enter the front door I hear the chime that means our food has arrived. But when I go into the kitchen only two portions sit in the delivery area. "What about Papa and Bram?"

"Papa requested dinner early so he and Bram could go for a walk before Bram's free-rec hours."

"Really?" I ask. We don't often make such requests.

"Yes. Your father thought that Bram could use something special after everything that's happened lately."

I'm happy, especially for Bram's sake, that the nutrition Officials granted Papa's request. "Why didn't you go too?"

"I wanted to see you." She smiles at me and then looks around the kitchen. "We haven't eaten together in a long time. And of course, I want to hear about your outing with Xander."

We sit across from each other at the table, and I notice again how tired she looks. "Tell me about your trip," I say, before she can ask about last night. "What did you see?"

"I'm still not sure," she says softly, almost to herself. Then she straightens up. "We went to another Arboretum to look at some crops. After that, we had to go to some Farmlands. It all took some time."

"But now everything's back to normal, right?"

"For the most part. I have to write a formal report and submit it to the Officials in charge of the other Arboretum."

"What's the report about?"

"I'm afraid that's confidential information," my mother says regretfully.

We both fall silent, but it is a good silence, a mother-daughter one. Her thoughts are far away somewhere, perhaps back at the Arboretum. Maybe she's writing the report in her mind. That's all right with me, though. I relax and let my own thoughts go where they want, which is to Ky.

"Thinking about Xander?" my mother says, giving me a knowing smile. "I always daydreamed about your father, too."

I smile back. There's no point telling her that I'm thinking about the wrong boy. No, not the *wrong* boy. Ky may be an Aberration but there's nothing about *him* that is defective. It's our Government and their classification system and all their systems that are wrong. Including the Matching System.

But if the system is wrong and false and unreal, then what about the love between my parents? If their love was born because of the Society, can it still be real and good and *right*? This is the question that I can't get out of my mind. I want the answer to be *yes*. That their love is true. I want it to have beauty and reality independent of anything else.

"I should get ready to go to the game center," I tell her, and she yawns. "*You* should go to sleep. We can talk more tomorrow."

"Well, maybe I'll rest for a little while," she says. We both stand up: I take her foilware container to the recycling bin for her and she carries my water bottle to the sterilizer for me. "Come say good-bye before you leave, though, won't you?"

"Of course."

My mother goes into her room and I slip into mine. I have a few minutes before I'm due to meet everyone. Do I have time to read a little more of Ky's story? I decide that I do. I pull the crumpled napkin from my pocket.

I want to know more about Ky before I see him tonight. I feel as if the two of us are our true selves when we hike in the trees on the hills. When we're with everyone else on Saturday nights, though, it becomes difficult. We go through a forest that is complicated and full of tangles and there are no stone cairns to guide us except the ones we build ourselves.

Sitting on my bed to read, I glance again at the spot in my closet where I kept the compact. I feel a sharp pain of loss and turn back to Ky's story. But as I read and the tears slip down my cheeks, I realize that I do not know anything about loss.

In the middle of the crease Ky drew a village, little houses, little people. But all the people lie supine, on their backs. No one stands straight, except the two Kys. The young one's hands are no longer empty; they carry something. One hand holds the word *Mother*, slumping over the edge of his hand, shaped a little like a body. The top of the *t* tips up, like an arm flung askew.

The other hand holds the word *Father*, and that word lies still too. And the young Ky's shoulders are bent with the weight of these two little words, and his face is still tipped to the sky, where I see now the rain has turned into something dark, something deadly and solid. Ammunition, I think. I've seen it in the showing.

The older Ky has turned his face away from the village in the middle, from the other boy. His hands are no longer open. They are clenched. Behind him, people in Official uniforms watch him. His lips curve in a smile that never touches his eyes; he wears plainclothes, a line indicating the crisp crease where he's ironed them neat.

> *at first when the rain fell*
> *from the sky so wide and deep*
> *it smelled like sage, my favorite smell*
> *I went up on the plateau to watch it come*
> *to see the gifts it always brought*
> *but this rain changed from blue to black*
> *and left*
> *nothing.*

＊

There's a drought of Officials at the game center, even though the center itself brims with people playing, winning, losing. I see three Officials, watching the largest of the game tables. They look earnest and on edge in their white uniforms, their faces showing more stress than usual. This is strange. Usually, we have twelve or more lower-level Officials in the center, keeping the peace, keeping score. Where are the rest of them tonight?

Somewhere, things aren't going quite right.

But here, as far as I'm concerned, at least one thing has. Ky's with us. I look at him once as we weave our way through the masses of people, following Xander, hoping that Ky understands from that look that I have read his story, that I care. He walks right behind me and I want to reach back and take his hand but there are too many people. The one thing I can do for Ky is to help keep him safe, to hold onto what I want to say until there is a good place to say it. And to remember the words he wrote, the pictures he made, even though I wish that part of the story had never happened to him.

His parents died. He saw it happen. Death came from the sky, and that's what he remembers. Every time it rains.

Xander stops and so we all do, too. To my surprise, he gestures to a game table where the games played are one-on-one. Games Xander doesn't usually play. He likes to take on a group, to win when the stakes are higher and more players are involved. It's a better test of his abilities—more challenging, more variables. Less personal. "You want to play?" Xander asks.

I turn to see who he means.

Ky.

"All right," Ky says without hesitation, nothing revealed in his voice. He keeps his eyes on Xander, waiting for the next move.

"What kind of game do you want to play? Skill or chance?" Is there a trace of challenge in Xander's voice? His face remains perfectly even, as does Ky's.

"I don't care," Ky answers.

"How about a game of chance, then," Xander says, which surprises me again. Xander hates games of chance. He much prefers ones that involve actual skill.

Em and Piper and I stay, watching, as Xander and Ky sit down and scan their cards into the datapod at the table. Xander sets out the playing cards, red with black markings in the center, first stacking the edges even with two sharp hits of the deck against the metal. "Want to go first?" Xander asks Ky, and Ky nods and reaches to draw.

"What game are they playing?" someone asks next to me. Livy. She's here for Ky, I'm sure of it, her eyes possessive as she watches his hands over the cards.

His hands are not yours to watch, I think to her, and I remember again that they aren't mine, either. I should be watching Xander. I should be hoping for Xander to win.

"Prisoner's dilemma," Em says next to me. "They're playing prisoner's dilemma."

"What's that?" Livy asks.

She doesn't know the game? I turn to her in surprise. It's one of the simplest, most common games. Em tries to explain it to Livy in a low voice so she doesn't disturb the players. "They each put down a card at the same time. If they both have an even card, they each get two points. If they're both odd, then they each get one point."

Livy interrupts Em. "What if one has even and one has odd?"

"If one is even and one is odd, the person who puts down the odd card gets three points. The person who puts down the even one gets zero."

Livy's eyes fix on Ky's face. Jealously, I think that even if she sees him in the same amount of detail that I do—which I doubt—she doesn't know anything about him. Would she still be so interested in Ky if she knew about his status as an Aberration?

I have a thought that strikes me cold: Would *I* be so interested if I *didn't* know that he's an Aberration? I never paid Ky particular attention before I knew about his classification.

And before you saw his face on the microcard, I remind myself. *Naturally, that piqued your interest. Besides. You weren't supposed to be interested in* anyone *until you were Matched.*

I feel a little sick thinking that Livy might see Ky's true worth in a way that is somehow more pure; she's simply interested in *him*. No hidden reasons. No tangles. No extra layers beneath her basic attraction to him.

But then again, I realize, I never know. She could be hiding something, as I am. We could all be hiding something.

I turn my attention back to the game and I watch Ky's and Xander's faces closely. Neither one of them blinks an eye, pauses before a move, shows their hand.

In the end, it doesn't matter. Ky and Xander end the rounds with an even number of points. They've each won, and lost, an equal amount of hands.

"Let's go walk around for a minute," Xander says, reaching for me. I want to look at Ky before I twine my fingers with Xander's, but I don't. I have to play the game, too. Surely Ky will understand.

But would Xander? If he knew about Ky and me, and the words we share on the Hill?

I push the thought away as I walk from the table with Xander. Livy immediately slides into his place and starts up a conversation with Ky.

Xander and I go out in the hallway alone. I wonder if he's about to kiss me and I wonder what I'm going to do if he does, but then he whispers to me instead, his words soft and close. "Ky throws the games."

"What?"

"He loses the games on purpose."

"You tied. He didn't lose." I don't know what Xander's getting at.

"Not tonight. Because it wasn't a game of skill. Those are the ones he usually throws. I've been watching him for a while. He's careful about how he does it, but I'm sure that's what he's doing."

I stare back at Xander, not sure how to respond.

"It's easy to throw a game of skill, especially when it's a big group. Or a game like Check, when you can put your pieces in harm's way and make it look natural. But today, in a game of chance, one-on-one, he didn't lose. He's no fool. He knew that I was watching." Xander grins. Then his face gets puzzled. "What I don't understand is *why*?"

"Why what?"

"Why would he throw so many games? He knows the Officials watch us. He knows they're looking for people who can play well. He knows our play probably influences what vocations they assign us. It doesn't make sense. Why wouldn't he want them to know how smart he is? Because he *is* smart."

"You're not going to tell anyone about this, are you?" Suddenly I am very worried for Ky.

"Of course not," Xander says, thoughtfully. "He must have his reasons. I can respect that."

Xander's right. Ky does have his reasons, and they *are* good ones. I read them on the last napkin, the one with the stains that I know must be tomato sauce but that look like blood. Old blood.

"Let's play one more time," Ky says when we get back, his eyes on Xander. They flicker once, and I think he's looked down at my hand in Xander's, but I can't be sure. His face shows nothing.

"All right," Xander says. "Chance or skill?"

"Skill," Ky suggests. And something in his expression suggests that he might not throw the game this time. He might be in it to win.

Em rolls her eyes at me and gestures at the boys as if to say, "Can you believe how primitive this is?" But we both follow them to another table. Livy comes, too.

I sit between Ky and Xander, equidistant from both of them. It's as if I'm a piece of metal and they are two magnets and there's a pull from either side. They've both taken risks for me—Xander with the artifact, Ky with the poem and the writing.

Xander is my Match and my oldest friend and one of the best people I know. When I kissed him, it was sweet. I'm drawn to him and tied to him with the cords of a thousand different memories.

Ky is not my Match, but he might have been. He's the one who taught me how to write my name, how to keep the poems, how to build a tower of rocks that looks like it should fall but doesn't. I have never kissed him and I don't know if I ever will, but I think it might be more than sweet.

It is almost uncomfortable, this awareness of him. Each pause, each movement when he places a piece on the black-and-gray board. I want to reach out and grab his hand and hold it to me, right over my heart, right where it aches the most. I don't know if doing that would heal me or make my heart break entirely, but either way this constant hungry waiting would be over.

Xander plays with daring and intelligence, Ky with a kind of deep and calculated intuition; both are strong. They are so evenly matched.

It's Ky's move. In the quiet before Ky takes his turn, Xander watches him carefully. Ky's hand hovers over the board. For a moment, as he holds the piece in the air, I see where he could put it to win and I know he sees it, too, that he planned the whole game for that last move. He looks at Xander and Xander looks back, both of them locked in some kind of challenge that seems to run deeper and older than what's happening here on this board.

Then Ky moves his hand and puts his piece down in a spot where Xander can eventually overtake him for the win. Ky doesn't hesitate once he places the piece; he sets it down with a solid sound and leans back in his chair, looking up at the ceiling. I think I see the slightest hint of a smile on his lips but I can't be sure; it's gone faster than a snowflake on an air-train track.

Ky's move may not be the brilliant one I know he could have made, but it's not stupid, either. He made the move of an average player. When he looks back down from the ceiling, he meets my gaze and holds it, as he held the game piece earlier before putting it down. He tells me something in that silent pause that he cannot say out loud.

Ky can play this game. He can play all of their games, including the one in front of him that he just lost. He knows exactly how to play, and that's why he loses every time.

CHAPTER 21

I have a hard time concentrating at sorting the next day. Sundays are for work; there are no leisure activities, so I won't likely see Ky until Monday. I can't talk to him about his story until then; I can't say, "I'm sorry about your parents." I said those words before, when he first came to live with the Markhams and we all welcomed him and expressed our condolences.

But it's different now that I really know what happened. Before, I knew they died, but I didn't know how. I didn't know that he saw it rain down from the sky while he watched, helpless. Burning the napkin with that part of his story on it is one of the hardest things I've ever done. Like the books out at the Restoration site, like Grandfather's poem, Ky's story, bit by bit, is turning into ash and nothing.

Except. He remembers it, and now I do, too.

A message from Norah appears on my screen, interrupting my sort. *Please report to the supervisor's station*. I lift my head to look across the sorting slots toward Norah, and then I stand straight up in surprise.

The Officials are back for me.

They watch me as I walk along the aisles of other workers and I think I see approval in their eyes. I feel relieved.

"Congratulations," the gray-haired Official tells me when I reach them. "You scored very well on your test."

"Thank you," I say, as I always do to the Officials. But this time I mean it.

"The next step is a real-life sort," the Official tells me. "At some point in the near future, we will come and escort you to the site of the test."

I nod. I've heard about this, too. They'll take you to sort something real—actual data, like news, or actual people, or a small subset of a school class—to see if you can apply things in the real world. If you can, you move on to the next step, which is likely your final work position.

This is happening quickly. In fact, everything seems hurried lately: the hasty removal of the artifacts from personal residences, my mother's sudden trip, and now this, more and more of us leaving school early in the year.

The Officials wait for me to respond.

"Thank you," I say.

In the afternoon my mother receives a message at work: Go home and pack. She is needed for another trip; it may be even longer than the last one. I can tell my father doesn't like this; and neither does Bram. Neither do I, as a matter of fact.

I sit on the bed and watch her as she packs. She folds her two extra sets of plainclothes. She folds her pajamas, underclothes, socks. She opens her tablet container and checks the tablets.

She's missing one, the green tablet. She glances up at me and I look away.

It makes me think that perhaps these trips are harder than they seem and I realize that in seeing the missing tablet, I haven't seen an example of her weakness but an example of her strength. What she's dealing with is difficult enough to make her take the green tablet, so it must also be difficult to keep inside, to not share with us. But she is strong and she keeps the secrets because it protects us.

"Cassia? Molly?" My father walks into the room and I stand up to leave. I move quickly over to my mother to embrace her. When I step back, our eyes meet and I smile at her. I want her to know that I know that I shouldn't have looked away earlier. I'm not ashamed of her. I know how hard it is to keep a secret. I may be a sorter like my father and my grandfather before me, but I am also my mother's daughter.

On Monday morning, Ky and I walk into the trees and find the spot where we stopped the time before. We start marking again with red flags. I wish it were so easy to begin where we left off in other ways. At first I hesitate, not wanting to disturb the peace of these woods with the horror of the Outer Provinces, but he has suffered so long alone that I can't bear to make him wait one more minute.

"Ky. I'm so sorry. I'm so sorry they are gone."

He doesn't say anything but bends to tie a red cloth around a particularly thorny shrub. His hands shake a bit. I know what that brief moment of losing control means for someone like Ky and I want to comfort him. I place my hand on his back, gently, softly, just enough so that he knows I am there. As my hand meets the cloth of his shirt he spins around and I pull back when I see the pain in his eyes. His look begs me not to say any more; it is enough that I know. It may be too much.

"Who's Sisyphus?" I ask, trying to think of something to distract him. "You mentioned his name once. When the Officer told us that we were going to start coming to the Hill."

"Someone whose story has been told for a long time." Ky stands up and starts walking again. I can tell that he needs to keep moving today. "It was one of my father's favorite stories to tell. I think he wanted to be like Sisyphus, because Sisyphus was crafty and sneaky and always causing trouble for the Society and the Officials."

Ky's never talked about his father before. Ky's voice sounds flat; I can't tell from his tone how he feels about the man who died years ago, the man whose name Ky held in his hand in the picture.

"There's a story about how Sisyphus once asked an Official to show him how a weapon worked and then he turned it on the Official."

I must look shocked, but Ky seems to have anticipated my surprise. His eyes are kind as he explains. "It's an old story, from back when the Officials carried weapons. They don't use them anymore."

What he doesn't say, but what we both know, is *They don't have to*. The threat of Reclassification is enough to keep almost everyone in line.

Ky turns back, pushes his way ahead. I watch him move, the muscles in his back inches away from me; I follow close so that I can slip through the branches he holds back for me. The smell of the forest seems, for a moment, to be simply the smell of him. I wonder what sage smells like, the smell he said was his favorite in his old life. I hope that the smell of this forest is his favorite now. I know it is mine.

"The Society decided that they needed to give Sisyphus a punishment, a special one, because he dared to think he could be as clever as one of them, when he wasn't an Official, or even a citizen. He was nothing. An Aberration from the Outer Provinces."

"What did they do to him?"

"They gave him a job. He had to roll a rock, a huge one, to the top of a mountain."

"That doesn't sound so terrible." There's relief in my voice. If the story ends well for Sisyphus, maybe it can end well for Ky.

"It wasn't as easy as it sounds. As he was about to reach the top, the rock rolled back to the bottom and he had to start again. That happened every time. He never got the rock to the top. He went on pushing forever."

"I see," I say, realizing why our hikes on the little hill reminded Ky of Sisyphus. Day after day we did the same thing: climbed back up and came back down. "But we did make it to the top of the little hill."

"We were never allowed to stay there for long," Ky points out.

"Was he from *your* Province?" I stop for a moment, thinking I've heard the Officer's whistle, but it's merely a shrill birdcall from the canopy of leaves above us.

"I don't know. I don't know if he's real," Ky says. "If he ever existed."

"Then why tell his story?" I don't understand, and for a second I feel betrayed. Why did Ky tell me about this person and make me feel empathy for him when there's no proof that he ever lived at all?

Ky pauses for a moment before he answers, his eyes wide and deep like the oceans in other tales or like the sky in his own. "Even if *he* didn't live his story, enough of us have lived lives just like it. So it's true anyway."

I think about what Ky said while we move again, quickly, tying off areas and helping each other around and through the tangled parts of the forest. There's a smell here that I have smelled before: a smell of decay, but it doesn't seem rotten. It smells almost rich, the scent of the plants returning to the earth, of wood giving way to dust.

But the Hill could be hiding something. I remember Ky's

words and pictures and I realize that no place is completely good. No place is completely bad. I've been thinking in terms of absolutes; first, I believed our Society was perfect. The night they came for our artifacts, I believed it was evil. Now I simply don't know.

Ky blurs the lines for me. He helps me see clearly, too. And I hope I do the same for him.

"Why do you throw the games?" I ask him as we pause in a small clearing.

His face tightens. "I have to."

"Every time? Don't you even let yourself think about winning?"

"I *always* think about winning," Ky tells me. There's fire in his eyes again, and he snaps a branch off a tree to make room for us to go through. He tosses the first branch to the side and holds another one back, waiting for me to pass, but I stay right there next to him. He looks down at me, shadows from the leaves crossing his face, and also sun. He's looking at my lips, which makes it hard to speak, even though I know what I want to say.

"Xander knows you lose on purpose."

"I know he does," Ky says. A smile tugs at the corners of his mouth, like the one I thought I saw last night. "Any other questions?"

"Just one," I say. "What color *are* your eyes?" I want to know what he thinks, how he sees himself—*the real Ky*—when he dares to look.

"Blue," he says, sounding surprised. "They've always been blue."

"Not to me."

"What do they look like to you?" he says, puzzled, amused. Not looking at my mouth anymore, looking into *my* eyes.

"Lots of colors," I say. "At first, I thought they were brown. Once I thought they were green, and another time gray. They *are* most often blue, though."

"What are they now?" he asks. He widens his eyes a little, leans closer, lets me look as long and as deep as I want.

And there's so much to see. They are blue, and black, and other colors, too, and I know some of what they've seen and what I hope they see now. Me. Cassia. What I feel, who I am.

"Well?" Ky asks.

"Everything," I tell him. "They're everything."

Neither of us moves for a moment, locked instead in each other's eyes and in the branches of this Hill we might never finish climbing. I'm the one who moves first. I step past him and push my way through some more tangled leaves, climb over a small fallen tree.

Behind me I hear Ky doing the same.

I'm falling in love. I am in love. And it's not with Xander, although I do love him. I'm sure of that, as sure as I am of the fact that what I feel for Ky is something different.

As I tie another red flag on the trees and wish for the fall of our Society and its systems, including the Matching

System, so that I can be with Ky, I realize that it is a selfish wish. Even if the fall of our Society would make life better for some, it would make it worse for others. *Who am I to try to change things, to get greedy and want more? If our Society changes and things are different, who am I to tell the girl who would have enjoyed the safe protected life that now she has to have choice and danger because of me?*

The answer is: I'm not anyone. I'm just one of the people who happened to fall in the majority. All my life, the odds have been on my side.

"Cassia," Ky says. He snaps another branch off and bends down in a swift movement to write in the thick dirt on the forest floor. He has to push away a layer of leaves and a spider hurries away. "Look," he says, showing me another letter. *K.*

Thankful for the distraction, I crouch down beside him. This letter is more difficult and it takes me several tries to even come close. In spite of my practice with the other letters my hands are still not used to this; to writing in any way but tapping. When I finally get it right and look up, I see that Ky is grinning at me.

"So, I've learned *K*," I say, grinning back. "That's strange. I thought we were going alphabetically."

"We were," Ky tells me. "But I think *K* is a good letter to know."

"What's my next letter, then?" I ask with mock innocence. "Could it be *Y*?"

"It could," Ky agrees. He's no longer smiling but his eyes are mischievous.

The whistle sounds behind and below us. Hearing it, I wonder how I could have ever thought that the birdcall I heard earlier sounded anything like the Officer's whistle. One sounds metallic and man-made and the other is high and clear and lovely.

I sigh and brush my hand across the dirt, returning the letters to the earth. Then I reach for a rock to make a cairn. Ky does the same. Together we build the tower piece by piece.

When I put the last rock on top of the pile, Ky puts his hand over mine. I do not pull it away. I do not want anything to fall and I like the feeling of his rough warm hand on top of mine with the cool smooth surface of the rocks underneath. Then I turn my hand slowly so that my palm is up and our fingers intertwine.

"I can never be Matched," he says, looking first at our hands and then into my eyes. "I'm an Aberration." He waits for my reaction.

"But you're not an Anomaly," I say, trying to make light of things, knowing immediately that it's a mistake; there's nothing light about this.

"Not yet, anyway," he says, but the humor in his voice sounds forced.

It is one thing to make a choice and it is another thing to never have the chance. I feel a sharp cold loneliness deep within me. What would it be like to be alone? To know that you could never choose anything else?

That's when I realize that the statistics the Officials give us do not matter to me. I know there are many people who are happy and I am glad for them. But this is Ky. If he is the one person who falls by the wayside while the other ninety-nine are happy and fulfilled, that is not right with me anymore. I realize that I don't care about the Officer pacing below or the other hikers among the trees or really anything else at all, and that is when I realize how dangerous this truly is.

"But if you *were* Matched," I say softly, "what do you think she'd be like?"

"You," he says, almost before I've finished. *"You."*

We do not kiss. We do nothing but hold on and breathe, but still I know. I cannot go gently now. Not even for the sake of my parents, my family.

Not even for Xander.

CHAPTER 22

A few days later, I sit in Language and Literacy, staring at the instructor as she talks about the importance of composing succinct messages when communicating via port. Then, as if to illustrate her point, one such message comes through the main port in the classroom.

"Cassia Reyes. Procedural. *Infraction*. An Official will arrive to escort you shortly."

Everyone turns to look at me. The room goes silent: students stop tapping on their scribes; their fingers stilled. Even the instructor allows an expression of pure surprise to cross her face; she doesn't try to keep teaching. It's been a long time since someone here committed an Infraction. Especially one announced publicly.

I stand up.

In some ways, I am ready for this. I expect it. No one can break as many rules as I have and not get caught somehow, sometime.

I gather my reader and scribe, dropping them into my bag with my tablet container. It seems very important, suddenly, to be ready for the Official. For I have no doubt which Official will come this time. The first one, the one from the greenspace near the game center, the one who told me everything would be all right and nothing would change with my Match.

Did she lie to me? Or did she tell the truth, and my choices made a lie of her words?

The teacher nods to me as I leave the room, and I appreciate this simple courtesy.

The hall is empty, long, the floor slick-surfaced from a recent cleaning. Yet another place where I cannot run.

I don't wait for them to come for me. I walk down the hall, setting my feet precisely on the tile, careful, careful, not to slip, not to fall, not to run while they are watching.

She is there in the greenspace next to the school. I have to walk across the paths to sit on another bench under her eye. She waits. I walk.

She does not stand to greet me. When I come close to her, I do not sit down. It's bright out here, and I squint my eyes against the white of her uniform and the metal of the bench, both dazzling, sharp, crisp in the sunlight. I wonder if she and I see things differently now that we don't just see what we hope to see.

"Hello, Cassia," she says.

"Hello."

"Your name has come up lately in several Society departments." She gestures for me to sit. "Why do you think that is?"

There could be any number of reasons, I think to myself. *Where do I begin? I've hidden artifacts, read stolen poems, learned how to write. I've fallen in love with someone who's not my Match and I'm keeping that fact from my Match.*

"I'm not sure," I say.

She laughs. "Oh, Cassia. You were so honest with me the last time we talked. I should have known it might not last." She points at the spot on the bench next to her. "Sit down."

I obey. The sun shines almost directly overhead, the light unflattering. Her skin looks papery and misted with sweat. Her edges seem blurred, her uniform and its insignia small, less powerful than the last time we talked. I tell myself this so that I won't panic, so that I won't give anything away, especially Ky.

"There's no need to be modest," she says. "Surely you have some idea of how well you performed on your sorting test."

Thank goodness. Is that why she's here? But what about the Infraction?

"You have the highest score of the year. Of course, everyone is fighting to get you assigned to their department for your vocation. We in the Match Department are always looking for a good sorter." She smiles at me. Like last time, she offers relief and comfort, reassurance about my place in the Society. I wonder why I hate her so much.

In a moment I know.

"Of course," she says, her tone now touched with what sounds like regret, "I had to tell the testing Officials that, unless we see a change in some of your personal relationships, we would be averse to hiring you. And I had to mention to them that you might also be unfit for other sorting-related work if these things keep up."

She doesn't look at me as she says all of this; she watches the fountain in the center of this greenspace, which I suddenly notice has run dry. Then she turns her gaze on me and I feel my heart racing, my pulse pounding clear to my fingertips.

She knows. Something, at least, if not everything.

"Cassia," she says kindly. "Teenagers are hot-blooded. Rebellious. It's part of growing up. In fact, when I checked your data, you were predicted to have some of these feelings."

"I don't know what you're talking about."

"Of course you do, Cassia. But it's nothing to worry about. You might have certain feelings for Ky Markham now, but by the time you are twenty-one, there is a ninety-five percent chance that it will all be over."

"Ky and I are friends. We're hiking partners."

"Don't you think this happens quite often?" the Official says, sounding amused. "Almost seventy-eight percent of teenagers who are Matched have some kind of youthful fling. And most of those occur within the year or so after the Matching. This is not unexpected."

I hate the Officials the most when they do this: when they act as if they have seen it all before, as if they have seen *me* before. When really they have never seen *me* at all. Just my data on a screen.

"Usually, all we do in these situations is smile and let things work themselves out. But the stakes are higher for you because of Ky's Aberration status. Having a fling with a member of Society in good standing is one thing. For the two of you, it's different. If things continue, you could be declared an Aberration yourself. Ky Markham, of course, could be sent back to the Outer Provinces." My blood runs cold, but she isn't finished with me yet. She moistens her lips, which are as dry as the fountain behind her. "Do you understand?"

"I can't quit speaking to him. He's my hiking partner. We live in the same neighborhood—"

She interrupts me. "Of course you may talk with him. There are other lines you should not cross. Kissing, for example." She smiles at me. "You wouldn't want Xander to know about this, would you? You don't want to lose him, do you?"

I am angry, and my face must show it. And what she says is true. I don't want to lose Xander.

"Cassia. Do you regret your decision to be Matched? Do you wish that you had chosen to be a Single?"

"That's not it."

"Then what is it?"

"I think people should be able to choose *who* they Match with," I say lamely.

"Where would it end, Cassia?" she says, her voice patient. "Would you say next that people should be able to choose how many children they have, and where they want to live? Or when they want to die?"

I am silent, but not because I agree. I am thinking of Grandfather. *Do not go gentle.*

"What Infraction have I committed?" I ask.

"Excuse me?"

"When they called me out of school over the port, the message said I'd committed an Infraction."

The Official laughs. Her laugh sounds easy and warm, which makes a shiver of cold prickle my scalp. "Ah, that was a mistake. Another one, it seems. They seem to keep happening where you are concerned." She leans a little closer. "You haven't committed an Infraction, Cassia. Yet."

She stands up. I keep my eyes on the dry fountain, willing the water back to it. "This is your warning, Cassia. Do you understand?"

"I understand," I say to the Official. The words are not entirely a lie. I *do* understand her, on some level. I know why she has to keep things safe and stable and some part of me respects that. I hate that most of all.

When I finally meet her gaze, her expression is satisfied. She knows she's won. She sees in my eyes that I won't risk making things worse for Ky.

"There's a delivery for you," Bram tells me when I arrive home, his face eager. "Someone brought it by. It must be something good. I had to have my fingerprint entered in their datapod when I accepted it."

He follows me into the kitchen where a small package

sits on the table. Looking at the pulpy brown paper wrapped around it, I think how much of Ky's story he could put on those pages. But he can't do that anymore. It's too dangerous.

Still, I can't help but open the paper carefully. I smooth it out neatly, taking my time. This almost drives Bram crazy. "Come on! Hurry up!" Deliveries don't happen every day.

When Bram and I finally see what's in the package we both sigh. Bram's is a sigh of disappointment and mine is a sigh of something else I can't quite define. Longing? Nostalgia?

It's the scrap of my dress from the Match Banquet. In keeping with tradition they have placed the silk between two pieces of clear glass with a small silver frame around the edge. The glass and the material both reflect the light, blinding me for a moment and reminding me of the glass mirror in my lost compact. I stare at the fabric, trying to remember the night at the Match Banquet when we were all pink and red and gold and green and violet and blue.

Bram groans. "That's all it is? A piece of your dress?"

"What did you think, Bram?" I say, and the acid in my tone surprises me. "Did you think they were going to send our artifacts back? Did you think this was going to be your watch? Because it's not. We're not getting any of it back. Not the compact. Not the watch. Not Grandfather."

Shock and hurt register on my brother's face, and before I can say anything he leaves the room. "Bram!" I call after him. "Bram—"

I hear the sound of his door closing.

I pick up the box that the framed sample came in. As I do, I realize that it *is* the perfect size to hold a watch. My brother dared to hope, and I mocked him for it.

I want to take this frame and walk to the middle of the greenspace. I'll stand next to that dry fountain and wait until the Official finds me. And when she does and asks me what I'm doing, I'll tell her and everyone else that I know: they are giving us pieces of a real life instead of the whole thing. And I'll tell her that I don't want my life to be samples and scraps. A taste of everything but a meal of nothing.

They have perfected the art of giving us just enough freedom; just enough that when we are ready to snap, a little bone is offered and we roll over, belly up, comfortable and placated like a dog I saw once when we visited my grandparents in the Farmlands. They've had decades to perfect this; why am I surprised when it works on me again and again and again?

Even though I am ashamed of myself, I take the bone. I worry it between my teeth. Ky has to be safe. That's what matters.

I don't take the green tablet; I'm still stronger than they are. But not strong enough to burn the last bit of Ky's story before reading it, the piece he pressed into my hand earlier on our way back down through the forest. *No more after this*, I tell myself. *Only this, no more.*

This picture is the first one with color. A red sun, low in the sky, right on the napkin crease again so that it is part of both boys, both lives. The younger Ky has dropped the words of *father* and *mother*; they have vanished from the picture. Forgotten, or left behind, or so much a part of him that they don't have to be written anymore. He looks over at the older Ky, reaches for him.

> *they were too much to carry*
> *so I left them behind*
> *for a new life, in a new place*
> *but no one forgot who I was*
> *I didn't*
> *and neither did the people who watch*
> *they watched for years*
> *they watch now*

The older, current Ky's hands are in handlocks in front of him, an Official on each side. He's colored his hands red, too—I don't know if he means to represent the way they look after he's been working, or if he means something else. His parents' blood still on his hands from all those years ago, even though he did not kill them.

The hands of the Officials are red, too. And I recognize one of them; he's caught her face in a few lines, a few sharp strokes.

My Official. She came for him, too.

CHAPTER 23

The next morning I wake to a shrieking so high and keening that I bolt straight out of bed, tearing the sleep tags from my skin.

"Bram!" I scream.

He is not in his room.

I run down the hall to my parents' room. My mother came home from her trip last night; they should both be there. But their room is empty, too, and I can tell they left in a hurry: I see twisted sheets and a blanket on the floor. I draw back. It's been a long time since I've seen their bed unmade and, even in the fear of the moment, the intimacy of that tangled bedding catches my eye.

"Cassia?" My mother's voice.

"Where are you?" I call in a panic, turning around.

She hurries down the hall toward me, still wearing her sleepclothes. Her long, blond hair streams behind her, and she looks almost unearthly until she pulls me into arms that feel real and strong. "What happened?" she asks me. "Are you all right?"

"The screaming—" I say, looking around her for the source. Just then I hear another sound added to the screaming: the sound of metal on wood.

"It's not screaming," my mother says, her voice sad. "You're hearing the saws. They're cutting down the maple trees."

I hurry out onto the front steps where Bram and my father also stand. Other families wait outside, too, many of them still wearing their sleepclothes like us. This is another intimacy so shocking and unusual that I am taken aback. I can't think of another time when I've seen any of my neighbors dressed like this.

Or maybe I can. The time when Patrick Markham went out and walked up and down the street in his sleepclothes after his son died, and Xander's father found him and brought him home.

The saw bites into the trunk of our maple tree, slices through so fast and clean that at first I think nothing happened except the scream. The tree seems fine for a brief moment, but it is dead as it stands. Then it falls.

"Why?" I ask my mother.

When she doesn't answer right away, my father puts his arm around her and tells me. "The maple trees have become too much of a problem. The leaves get too messy in the fall. They're not growing uniformly. For example, ours grew too big. Em's is too small. And some of them have diseases, so they all need to be chopped down."

I look at our tree, at its leaves still reaching for the sun, still working to turn light into food. They don't know they are dead yet. Our yard looks like a different place without the tree standing tall in front of our house. Things seem smaller.

I look over at Em's house. Her yard, on the other hand, doesn't look much different now that their sad little tree is gone, the one that never quite grew. It was never much more than a stick-stalk of a tree with a little burst of leaves on the top. "It's not as bad for Em," I say. "Her tree isn't as much of a loss."

"It's sad for all of us," my mother says fiercely.

Last night when I couldn't sleep, I crouched down near the wall to listen to her talk with my father. They spoke so softly that I couldn't make out any of the words, but she sounded tired and sad. Eventually I gave up and climbed back into bed. Now she looks angry, standing in front of the house with her arms folded across her chest.

The workers with the saws have already moved on to another house now that our tree is down. That part was easy. Tearing up the roots will be the hard part.

My father holds my mother close. He doesn't love the trees the way she does; but he loves other things that were destroyed and he understands. My mother loves the plants; my father loves the history of things. They love each other.

And I love them both.

It isn't only myself and Ky and Xander I'll hurt if I commit an Infraction. It's all these other people I love.

"It's a warning," my mother says, almost to herself.

"I didn't do anything!" Bram exclaims. "I haven't even been late to school in weeks!"

"The warning isn't for you," my mother says. "It's for someone else."

My father puts his hands on my mother's shoulders and it is as though they are alone, the way he looks at her. "Molly, I promise. I didn't . . ."

And at the same time, I open my mouth to say something—I don't know what—something about what I have done and how this is all my fault. But before my father can finish and I can begin, my mother speaks.

"It's a warning for *me*."

She turns and goes back into the house, brushing a hand across her eyes. As I watch her go, the guilt slices quick through me like the cuts in the tree.

I don't think the warning is for my mother.

If the Officials truly can see my dreams, they should be happy with what I dreamed last night. I burned the last of Ky's story in the incinerator, but afterward I kept thinking of what it showed, what it told me: The sun was red and low in the sky when the Officials came to get him.

So then, when I dreamed, I saw scene after scene of Ky surrounded by Officials in their white uniforms with a red sky behind him, a glimpse of sun waiting on the horizon. Whether it was rising or setting, I could not tell; I had no sense of direction in the dream. In each dream he did not show any fear. His hands did not shake; his expression remained calm. But I knew he was afraid, and when the red light of the sun hit his face it looked like blood.

I do not want to see this scene played out in real life. But I have to know more. How did he escape last time? What happened?

The two desires struggle within me: the desire to be safe, and the desire to know. I cannot tell which one will win.

My mother hardly speaks as we ride the train to the Arboretum together. She looks over at me and smiles now and then, but I can tell she's deep in thought. When I ask her questions about her trip, she answers carefully, and finally I stop.

Ky rides the same air train we do, and he and I walk together toward the Hill. I try to act friendly but reserved— the way we once were around each other—even though I want to touch his hand again, to look in his eyes and ask him about the story. About what happened next.

It only takes a few seconds in the forest before I lose control and I have to ask him. I put my hand on his arm as we follow our path to the spot where we last marked. When I touch him he smiles at me, and it warms my heart and makes it hard to take my hand away, to let go. I don't know if I can do this, despite wanting him to be safe even more than I want *him*.

"Ky. An Official contacted me yesterday. She knows about us. They know about us."

Ky nods. "Of course they do."

"Did they talk to you, too?"

"They did."

For someone who has spent his entire life avoiding attention from the Officials, he seems remarkably composed about this. His eyes are deep as ever but there is a calm there that I haven't seen before.

"Aren't you worried?"

Ky doesn't answer. Instead, he reaches into the pocket of his shirt and pulls out a paper. He hands it to me. It's different from the brown paper of napkins and wrappings that he's been using—whiter, smoother. The writing on it is not his own. It's from some kind of port or scribe, but something about it seems foreign.

"What is this?" I ask.

"A late birthday present for you. A poem."

My jaw drops—a poem? *How?*—and Ky hurries to reassure me. "Don't worry. We'll destroy the paper soon so we don't get in trouble. It won't take long to memorize." His face is alight with happiness and I suddenly realize that Ky looks the slightest bit like Xander, with his face open and joyful like this. I am reminded of the shifting faces on the portscreen the day after I got my Match, when I saw Xander, then Ky. But now, I see only Ky. Only Ky and no one else.

A poem. "Did you write it?"

"No," he says, "but it's by the same man who wrote the other poem. *Do not go gentle.*"

"How?" I ask him. There were no other poems by Dylan Thomas in the port at school.

Ky shakes his head, evading my question. "It's not the whole thing. I could only afford part of a stanza." Before I can ask what he gave in exchange for the poem, he clears his throat a little nervously and looks down at his hands. "I liked it because it mentions a birthday and because it reminds me of you. How I felt when I saw you that first day, in the water at the pool." He looks confused and I see a trace of sadness on his face. "Don't you like it?"

I hold the white paper, but my eyes are so blurred with tears that I can't read it. "Here," I say, thrusting the poem back at him. "Will you read it to me?" I turn away and start walking through the trees, staggering almost, so blinded am I by the beauty of his surprise and so overwhelmed by possibility and impossibility.

Behind me, I hear Ky's voice. I stop and listen.

My birthday began with the water—
Birds and the birds of the winged trees flying my name
Above the farms and the white horses
And I rose
In rainy autumn
And walked abroad in a shower of all my days.

I begin walking again, not bothering with cairns or cloths or anything that might slow me down. I'm careless and I disturb a group of birds, which flutters up and away from us into the sky. White on blue, like the colors of City Hall. Like the colors of angels.

"They're flying your name," Ky says from behind me.

I turn around and I see him standing in the forest, the white poem in his hand.

The birds' cries fly away on the air with them. In the quiet that follows I don't know who moves first, Ky or me, but soon there we are, standing close but not touching, breathing in but not kissing.

Ky leans toward me, his eyes holding mine, near enough that I can hear the slight crackle of the poem as he moves.

I close my eyes as his lips touch warm on my cheek. I think of the cottonwood seeds brushing against me that day on the air train. Soft, light, full of promise.

CHAPTER 24

Ky gives me three gifts for my birthday. A poem, a kiss, and the hopeless, beautiful belief that things might work. When I open my eyes, as I put my hand up to the place on my cheek where his lips touched, I say, "I didn't give you anything on your birthday, I don't even know when it is." And he says, "Don't worry about that," and I say, "What can I do?" and he answers, "Let me believe in this, all of this, and you believe it, too."

And I do.

For one entire day I let his kiss burn on my cheek and into my blood, and I don't push the memory away. I have kissed and been kissed before. This is different. This, more than my real birthday the day of the Match Banquet, feels like a day to mark time by. This kiss, these words, they feel like beginning.

I let myself imagine futures that can never be, the two of us together. Even when I sort later that day, I keep my mind on the task at hand by pretending each number sorted is a code, a message to Ky that I will keep our secret. I will keep us safe; I won't reveal a thing. Each sort I perform correctly keeps attention away from us.

Since it is not my turn for the sleep tags that night, I let my dreams take me where they will. To my surprise, I don't dream of Ky on the Hill. I dream of him sitting on the steps in front of my house, watching the wind shuffle the leaves of the maple tree. I dream of him taking me to the private dining hall and pulling my chair out, bending so close to me that even the pretend candles flutter at his presence. I dream of the two of us digging up the newroses in his yard and of Ky teaching me how to use the artifact. Everything I dream is something simple and plain and everyday.

That's how I know they are dreams. Because the simple and plain and everyday things are the ones that we can never have.

"How?" I ask him the next day on the Hill, once we are deep enough into the forest that no one can hear us. "How can we believe this might work? The Official threatened to send you back to the Outer Provinces, Ky!"

Ky doesn't answer for a moment, and I feel as though I've yelled when really I kept my voice as low as possible. Then we walk past the cairn from our last hike and he looks straight at me and I swear I feel that kiss again. But this time, I feel it on my lips instead.

"Have you ever heard of the prisoner's dilemma?" Ky asks me.

"Of course." Is he teasing me? "It's the game you played against Xander. We've all played it before."

"No, not the game. The Society changed the game. I mean the theory *behind* the game."

I don't know what he's talking about. "I guess not."

"If two people commit a crime together, are caught, and then separated and interrogated, what happens?"

I am still lost. "I don't know. What?"

"That's their dilemma. Do they tell on each other in hopes that the Officials will go easy on them—a plea bargain? Do they refuse to say anything that would betray their partner? The best scenario is for both to say nothing. Then they can both be safe."

We've stopped near a group of fallen trees. "Safe," I say.

Ky nods. "But that never happens."

"Why not?"

"Because one prisoner will almost always betray the other. They'll tell what they know to get a break."

I think I know what he's asking me. I'm getting better at reading his eyes, at knowing his thoughts. Perhaps it comes from knowing his story, from finally knowing more of him. I hand him a red cloth; neither of us try anymore not to let our fingers touch, come together, cling before letting go.

Ky continues. "But in the perfect scenario, neither would say anything."

"And you think we can do that?"

"We'll never be safe," Ky says, brushing my face with his hand. "I finally understand that. But I trust you. We'll keep each other as safe as we can for as long as we can."

Which means that our kisses have to stay promises, promises left like his first kiss, soft on my cheek. Our lips do not meet. Not yet. For once we do that, the Infraction will have been committed. The Society will be betrayed. And so will Xander. We both know this. How much time can we steal from them? From ourselves? Because I can see in his eyes that he wants that kiss as much as I do.

There are other parts to our lives: many hours of work for Ky; sorting and Second School for me. But when I look back, I know those moments won't be remembered the way I remember each detail of those days with Ky, hiking on the Hill.

Except one memory, of a strained Saturday night at the showing theater where Xander holds my hand and Ky acts as though nothing is different. There is a terrible moment at the end when the lights go up and I see the Official from the greenspace looking around. When she meets my eyes and sees my hand in Xander's she looks at me and gives me a tiny smile and disappears. I glance over at Xander after she's gone and an ache of longing goes through me, an ache so deep and real that I can still feel it later, when I think of that night. The longing isn't for Xander, it's for the way things used to be between us. No secrets, no complications.

But still. Though I feel guilty about Xander, though I worry for him, these days belong to Ky, to me. To learning more stories and writing more letters.

Sometimes Ky asks me if I remember things. "Remember Bram's first day of school?" he asks me one day as we move fast through the forest to make up for all the time we spent writing earlier on the hike.

"Of course," I say, breathless from hurrying and from thinking about his hands on mine. "Bram wanted to stay home. He caused a scene at the air-train stop. Everyone remembers that." Children start First School the autumn after they turn six. It's supposed to be an important rite of passage, a prequel to the Banquets to come. At the end of the first successful day, the children bring a small cake home to eat after dinner, along with a tangle of brightly colored balloons. I don't know which Bram was more excited about—the cake, which we have so rarely, or the balloons, which are unique to the occasion of the First Day. That was also the day he would receive his reader and scribe, but Bram didn't care one bit about that part of it.

When the time came to board the train to First School, Bram wouldn't get on. "I don't want to go," he said. "I'll stay here instead."

It was morning and the station brimmed with people leaving for work and school. Heads turned to look at us as Bram refused to board the air train with my parents. My father looked worried but my mother took it in stride. "Don't worry," she whispered to me. "The Officials in charge of his pre-School care center warned me this might happen. They predicted he'd have a little trouble with this milestone." Then she knelt down next to him and told him, "Let's get on the train, Bram. Remember the balloons. Remember the cake."

"I don't want them." And then, to everyone's surprise, he began to cry. Bram never cried, not even back when he was very small. All the confidence left my mother's face, and she put her arms around him and held him tight. Bram is the second child she thought she might never have. After having me quickly and easily, it took her years to become pregnant with him, and he was born weeks before her thirty-first birthday, the cutoff age for having children. We all feel lucky to have Bram, but my mother especially.

I knew if the crying kept up much longer we'd be in trouble. Back then, an Official assigned to watch out for problems lived on each street.

So I said loudly to Bram, "Too bad for you. No reader, no scribe. You'll never know how to write. You'll never know how to read."

"That's not true!" Bram yelled. "I can learn."

"How?" I asked him.

He narrowed his eyes, but at least he stopped crying. "I don't care if I can't read or write."

"That's fine," I said, and out of the corner of my eye I saw someone knocking on the Official's door at the house right next to the air-train stop. *No. Bram already has too many citations from the care center.*

The train swooshed to a stop and in that moment I knew what I had to do. I picked up his schoolbag and held it out to him. "It's up to you," I said, looking right into his eyes and holding his gaze. "You can grow up or you can be a baby."

Bram looked hurt. I shoved the bag into his arms and whispered into his ear, "I know a way to play games on the scribe."

"Really?"

I nodded.

Bram's face lit up. He took the bag and went through the air-train doors without a backward glance. My parents and I climbed on after him, and my mother hugged me tight once we were inside. "Thank you," she said.

There weren't any games on the scribe, of course. I had to invent some, but I'm not a natural sorter for nothing. It took Bram months to figure out that none of the other kids had older siblings who hid patterns and pictures in screens full of letters and then timed them to see how fast they could find them all.

That was why I knew before anyone else that Bram would never be a sorter. But I still invented levels and records of achievement and spent almost all my free time during those months coming up with games I thought he would like. And even when he figured it out, he wasn't mad. We'd had too much fun, and after all, I hadn't lied. I *had* known a way to play games on the scribe.

"That was the day," Ky says now, and stops.

"What?"

"The day I knew about you."

"Why?" I say, feeling hurt somehow. "Because you could see I followed the rules? That I made my brother follow them, too?"

"No," he says, as if it should be obvious. "Because I saw the way you cared about your brother and because I saw that you were smart enough to help him." Then he smiles at me. "I already knew what you looked like, but that day was when I first knew about *you*."

"Oh," I say.

"What about me?" he asks.

"What do you mean?"

"When did *you* first see *me*?"

For some reason I can't tell him. I can't tell him that it was his face on the screen the morning after my Match Banquet—the mistake—that made me first begin to think of him this way. I can't tell him that I didn't see him until they told me to look.

"On the top of the first hill," I say instead. And I wish that I did not have to tell him this lie, when he knows more of my truth than anyone else in the world.

Later that night I realize that Ky did not give me any more of his story and I did not ask. Perhaps it is because now I live in his story. Now I am a part of his, and he of mine, and the part we write together sometimes feels like the only part that matters.

But still, the question haunts me: *What happened when the Officials took him away and the sun was red and low in the sky?*

CHAPTER 25

Our time together feels like a storm, like wild wind and rain, like something too big to handle but too powerful to escape. It blows around me and tangles my hair, leaves water on my face, makes me know that I am alive, alive, alive. There are moments of calm and pause as there are in every storm, and moments when our words fork lightning, at least for each other.

We hurry up the Hill together, touching hands, touching trees. Talking. Ky has things to tell me and I have things to tell him and there is not enough time, not enough time, never enough time.

"There are people who call themselves Archivists," Ky says. "Back when the Hundred Committee made their selections, the Archivists knew the works that didn't get selected would become a commodity. So they saved some of them. The Archivists have illegal ports, ones they've built themselves, for storing things. They saved the Thomas poem I brought you."

"I had no idea," I say, touched. I never thought that someone might think far enough ahead to save some of the poems. Did Grandfather know this? It doesn't seem like he did. He never gave them *his* poems to save.

Ky puts his hand on my arm. "Cassia. The Archivists aren't altruistic. They saw a commodity and they did what they could to preserve it. Anyone can have it who's willing to pay, but their prices are high." He stops as though he's revealed too much—that this poem cost him something.

"What did you trade with them?" I ask, suddenly afraid. As far as I know, Ky has two things of value: his artifact and the words of the *Do not go gentle* poem. I don't want him to give up the artifact, his last tie to his family. And for some reason, the thought of our poem being traded repulses me. Selfishly, I don't want just anyone to have it. I realize that I'm not much better than the Officials in this regard.

"Something," he says, and his eyes are amused. "Don't worry about the price."

"Your artifact—"

"Don't worry. I didn't trade that. I didn't trade our poem, either. But Cassia, if *you* ever need to, they don't know about the poem. I asked how many Dylan Thomas writings they had and they didn't have much. The birthday poem, and a story. That was all."

"If I ever need to what?"

"Trade," he says carefully. "Trade for something else. The Archivists have information, connections. You could tell them one of the poems your grandfather gave you." He frowns. "Although proving authenticity might be a problem, since you don't have the original paper . . . still, I'm sure they would be worth something."

"I'd be too afraid to trade with people like that," I say, and then I wish I hadn't. I don't want Ky to think I get scared easily.

"They're not completely evil," he says. "I'm trying to get you to see that they're no better or worse than anyone else. No better or worse than the Officials. You have to be careful with the Archivists the same way you have to be careful with everyone else."

"Where would I find them?" I ask him, frightened by his need to let me know this. What does he think is going to happen? Why does he think I might need to know how to sell our poem?

"The Museum," he tells me. "Go to the basement and stand in front of the exhibit about the Glorious History of Oria Province. No one ever goes there. If you stay long enough, someone will ask you if you want them to tell you more about the history. You say yes. They'll know you want contact with an Archivist."

"How do you know this?" I ask him, surprised again at all the ways he knows how to survive.

He shakes his head. "It's better if I don't tell you."

"What if someone goes there who really *does* want to know more about the history?"

Ky laughs. "No one ever does, Cassia. No one here wants to know anything about the past."

We hurry on, hands still touching through the branches. I hear Ky humming a piece of one of the Hundred Songs, the

269

one we heard together. "I love that one," I say, and he nods. "The woman who sings it has such a beautiful voice."

"If only it were real," he says.

"What do you mean?" I ask him.

He looks at me, surprised. "Her voice. She's not real. It's generated. The perfect voice. Like all of the singers, in all of the songs. Didn't you know that?"

I shake my head, disbelieving. "That can't be right. When she's singing, I can hear her breathe."

"That's part of it," Ky says, his eyes distant, remembering something. "They know that we like to feel that things are authentic. We like to hear them breathe."

"How do you know?"

"I've heard real people singing," he says.

"So have I, at school. And my father sang to me."

"No," he says. "I mean, singing out, as loud as you can. Whenever you felt like it. I've heard people sing like that, but not here. And even the most beautiful voice in the world didn't sound anywhere near as perfect as that voice in the music hall."

For a split second, I imagine him at home in that landscape he has drawn for me, listening to others sing. Ky glances up at the sun blinking through the trees above us. He's gauging the time. He trusts the sun more than his watch. I've noticed this. As he stands there, shielding his eyes with one hand, another line from the Thomas poem comes to mind

Wild men who caught and sang the sun in flight

I would like to hear Ky sing.

Ky reaches into his pocket, pulls out my birthday poem. "Do you know it well enough yet?"

I know what he's saying. It's time to destroy the poem. It's dangerous to keep it for too long.

"Yes," I say. "But let me look at it one more time." I read it over and look back up at Ky. "It's not as sad to destroy this one," I say, telling him and reminding myself. "Other people know it. It still exists somewhere else."

He nods at me.

"Do you want me to take it home and incinerate it?" I ask.

"I thought we could leave it here," he says. "Bury it, in the ground."

I'm reminded of planting with Xander. But this poem has nothing tied to it; it's severed, neat and clean, from where it came. We know the name of the author. We don't know anything about him, don't know what he wanted the poem to mean, what he thought when he formed the words, how he wrote it. That long ago, were there scribes? I can't remember from the Hundred History Lessons. Or did he write it as Ky writes, with his hands? Did the poet know how *lucky* he was, to have such beautiful words and a place to put them and keep them?

Ky reaches for the poem.

"Wait," I say. "Let's not bury all of it." I hold out my hand for the paper and he gives it to me, smoothing it flat over my palm. There's not much to the poem; it's small, one verse. It will be easily buried. I tear carefully along the line that talks about the birds:

Birds and the birds of the winged trees flying my name

I tear it smaller, smaller, until the pieces are tiny and light. Then I toss them into the breeze, to let them fly for a moment. They are so small that I don't see where most of them settle, but one lands soft on a branch near me. Perhaps a real bird will use it for a nest, will tuck it away from everyone else, as I have the other Thomas poem.

We *do* know about the author, I realize as Ky and I bury the rest of the paper. We know him through his words.

And someday I will have to share the poems. I know it. And someday I will have to tell Xander what is happening here on the Hill.

But not yet. I burned poetry before to be safe. I can't do it now. I hold tight to the poetry of our moments together, protecting them, protecting us. All of us.

"Tell me about your Match Banquet," Ky says another time.

He wants me to tell him about Xander?

"Not about Xander," he says, reading my mind and smiling that smile I love. Even now, when he smiles more often, I am still greedy for it. Sometimes, I reach out and touch his lips with my hand when he does it. I do that now, feel them move as he says, "About you."

"I was nervous, excited . . ." I stop.

"What did you think about?"

I wish I could tell him that I thought about him, but I lied to him once and I won't do it again. And besides, I wasn't thinking about Xander either.

"I thought about angels," I say.

"Angels?"

"You know. The ones in the old stories. How they can fly to heaven."

"Do you think anyone believes in them anymore?" he asks.

"I don't know. No. Do you?"

"I believe in you," he says, his voice hushed and almost reverent. "That's more faith than I ever thought I'd have."

We move quickly through the trees. I feel more than see that we must be nearing the top of the Hill. Eventually, our work here will be done and this time will be over. It doesn't take long anymore to traverse the first part of the Hill; everything is tamped down and well marked and we know where we are going, at least initially. But there is still unexplored territory left. There are still things to discover. For that I am grateful. I'm so grateful that I wish I did believe in angels so that I could express my gratitude to someone or something.

"Tell me more," Ky says.

"I wore a green dress."

"Green," he says, glancing back at me. "I've never seen you in green."

"You've never seen me in anything but brown or black," I tell him. "Brown plainclothes. Black swimwear." I flush.

"I take back what I said," he says later, as the whistle blows. "I *have* seen you in green. I see you in green everyday, here in the trees."

The next day, I ask him, "Can you tell me why you cried in the showing that day?"

"You saw me?"

I nod.

"I couldn't help it." His gaze is distant, hard now. "I didn't know they had footage like that. It could have been my village. It was definitely one of the Outer Provinces."

"Wait." I think of the people, dark shadows running. "You're saying this was—"

"Real," he finished. "Yes. Those aren't actors. It's not a stage. It happens in all the Outer Provinces, Cassia. When I left, it was happening more and more."

Oh no.

The whistle will blow soon, I can tell. He knows, too. But I reach for him and hold on here in the forest where the trees screen us and the birdcalls cover our voices. The entire Hill is complicit in our embrace.

I pull away first because I have something to write before our time ends. I've been practicing in air, but I want to carve in earth.

"Close your eyes," I say to Ky, and I bend down, his

breathing above me while he waits. "There," I say, and he looks at what I've written.

I love you.

I feel embarrassed, as though I am a child who has tapped out these words on her scribe and held them out for a boy in her First School class to read. My writing is awkward and straggly and not smooth like Ky's.

Why are some things easier to write than say?

Still, I feel undeniably brave and vulnerable as I stand there in the forest with words that I cannot take back. My first written words, other than our names. It's not much of a poem, but I think Grandfather would understand.

Ky looks at me. For the first time since the showing, I see tears in his eyes.

"You don't have to write it back," I say, feeling self-conscious. "I just wanted you to know."

"I don't want to write it back," he tells me. And then he says it, right out there on the Hill, and of all the words I have hidden and saved and treasured, these are the ones I will never forget, the most important ones of all.

"I love you."

Lightning. Once it has forked, hot-white, from sky to earth, there is no going back.

It's time. I feel it, I know it. My eyes on him, his on me, and both of us breathing, watching, tired of waiting. Ky closes his eyes, but mine are still open. What will it feel like, his lips on mine? Like a secret told, a promise kept? Like that line in the poem—*a shower of all my days*—silvery rain falling all around me, where the lightning meets the earth?

The whistle blows below us and the moment breaks. We are safe.

For now.

CHAPTER 26

We hurry back down from the Hill. I see glimpses of white through the trees, and I know they are not the birds we saw earlier. These white figures aren't made for flight. "Officials," I say to Ky, and he nods.

We report to the Officer, who looks a bit preoccupied with the visitors waiting for us. I wonder again how he ended up with this assignment. Even supervising the marking of the big Hill seems like a waste of time for someone of his rank. As I turn away, I see all the lines that discipline has etched in his face and I realize again that he is not very young.

The Officials, I discover when I get closer, are ones I've seen before. The ones who tested my sorting abilities. The blond female Official takes charge this time; apparently this is her portion of the test to administer. "Hello, Cassia," she says. "We're here to take you to your on-site portion of the sorting test. Can you come with us now?" She glances over at the Officer with a touch of deference in her look.

"Go on," the Officer says, glancing at the others who have returned from the Hill. "You can all go. We'll meet here again tomorrow."

A few of the other hikers look at me with interest but

not concern; many of us await our final work positions and Officials always seem to be a part of that process. "We'll take the air train," the blond Official says to me. "The test will only last a few hours. You should be home in time for your evening meal."

We walk toward the air-train stop, two Officials on my right and one on my left. There's no escaping them; I don't dare look back at Ky. Not even when we climb onto the train he takes into the City. When he walks past me, his "hello" sounds perfect: friendly, unconcerned. He continues on down the length of the car and sits next to a window. Anyone watching would be convinced that he doesn't feel anything at all for me. He's almost convinced *me*.

We don't get off the air train at the City Hall stop, or at any of the other stops in the City proper. We keep going. More and more blue-clothed workers climb on, laughing and talking. One of them cuffs Ky on the shoulder and Ky laughs. I don't see any other Officials or anyone else wearing student plainclothes like me. The four of us sit together in the sea of blue, the train twisting and turning like a river running, and I know it's hard to fight against a current as strong as the Society.

I look out the window and hope with all my heart that this isn't what I think it is. That we aren't going to the same place. That I won't be sorting Ky.

Is this a trick? Are they watching us? *That's a stupid question,* I think to myself. *Of course they're watching us.*

Hulking gray buildings crowd around in this part of town; I see signs, but the air train moves too fast for me to read them. But it's clear where we are: the Industrial District.

Up ahead, I see Ky shift, stand. He doesn't have to reach up for the grips hanging from the ceiling; he keeps himself level and balanced as the train slides to a stop. For a moment, I think everything will be fine. The Officials and I will keep going, past these gray buildings, beyond the airport with its landing strips and bright red traffic flags whipping in the wind like kites, like markers on the Hill. We'll go on out to the Farmlands, where they'll have me sort nothing more important than a crop or some sheep.

Then the Officials next to me stand up and I have no choice but to follow them. *Don't panic*, I tell myself. *Look at all these buildings. Look at all these workers. You could be sorting anything or anyone. Don't jump to conclusions.*

Ky doesn't look to see if I've gotten off, too. I study his back and his hands to see if I can find any of the tension running through him that runs through me. But his muscles are relaxed and his stride even as he walks around to the side of the building where the employees enter. Many of the other workers wearing blue plainclothes go through the same door. Ky's hands are loose at his sides, open. Empty.

As Ky disappears into the building, the blond Official leads me around to the front, to a kind of antechamber. The other Officials hand her datatags and she places them behind my ear, at my pulse points on my wrists, under the neck of my shirt. She's quick and efficient about it; now that I'm being monitored, I try even harder to relax. I don't want to seem unusually nervous. I breathe deep and I change the words of the poem. I tell myself to go gentle, just for now.

"This is the food distribution block of the City," the Official informs me. "As we mentioned before, the goal of the real-life sort is to see if you can sort real people and situations within certain parameters. We want to see if you can help the Government improve function and efficiency."

"I understand," I say, although I'm not sure I do.

"Then let's get started." She pushes open the doors and another Official comes to greet us. He's apparently the Official in charge of this building, and the orange and yellow bars on his shirt mean he's involved in one of the most important Departments of all, the Nutrition Department. "How many do you have today?" he asks, and I realize that I'm not the only one taking the test and completing real-life sorts here. The thought makes me relax a little.

"One," she says, "but this is our high scorer."

"Excellent," he says. "Let me know when you finish." He strides away and I stand still, overwhelmed by the sights and smells around me. And by the heat.

We stand in a gaping space, a chamber larger than the gymnasium at Second School. This room looks like a steel box: metal floors dotted with drains, gray-painted concrete walls, and stainless-steel appliances lining the sides and bisecting the middle of the room in rows. Steam mists and writhes around the room. Vents at the top and sides of the building open to the outside, but there are no windows. The appliances, the foilware trays, the steaming hot water coming out of the faucets: Everything is gray.

Except for the dark-blue workers and their burned-red hands.

A whistle blows and a new stream of workers comes in from the left while the other workers exit on the right. Their bodies sag, tired, weighted. They all wipe their brows and leave their work without a backward glance.

"The new workers have been in a sterilization chamber to remove all outside contaminants," the Official tells me conversationally. "That's where they pick up their numbers and adhere them to their uniforms. This new shift is the one you'll be concerned with."

She gestures up and I notice several outlook points throughout the room: small metal towers with Officials standing at the top. There are three towers; the one in the middle of the floor is empty. "We'll be up there."

I follow her up the metal stairs, the kind that we have at air-train stops. But these stairs end on a small platform with barely enough space for the four of us to stand. Already the gray-haired Official perspires heavily and his face is red. My hair sticks to the back of my neck. And all we have to do is stand and watch. We don't even have to work.

I knew Ky's job was hard but I had no idea.

Tubs and tubs of dirty containers stand next to small

stations with sinks and recycling tubes. Through a large opening at the end of the building, the soiled foilware arrives in a never-ending stream, flowing from the recycling bins in our residences and meal halls. The workers wear clear protective gloves, but I don't see how the plastic or latex doesn't melt into their skin as they spray off the foilware containers with hot water. Then they put the clean foilware down into the recycling tubes.

It goes on and on and on, a steady flow of steam and scalding water and foilware. My mind threatens to glaze over and shut down as it does when I'm confronted with a particularly difficult sort on the screen and I feel overwhelmed. But these aren't numbers on the screen. These are people.

This is Ky.

So I force myself to stay clear and focused. I force myself to watch those bent backs and those burning hands and the vastness of all the refuse sliding silver along the tracks.

One of the workers raises his hand, and an Official comes down from his perch to confer with the worker. He gives a foilware container to the Official, who scans the bar code on the side of the container with his datapod. After a moment, he takes the foilware container with him and disappears into an office at the edge of the large open room. The worker is already back at work.

The Official looks at me as if she's waiting for something. "What do you think?" she asks.

I'm not sure what she wants, so I hedge. "Of course, the most efficient thing to do would be to get machines."

"That is not an option," the Official says pleasantly. "Food preparation and distribution needs to be handled by personnel. Live personnel. It's a rule. But we would like to free up more of the workers for other projects and vocations."

"I don't see how to make it any more efficient," I say. "There's the other obvious answer . . . to make them work more hours . . . but they look exhausted as it is . . ." My voice trails off, a wisp of steam too small to matter.

"We're not asking you to come up with a solution." The Official sounds amused. "Those who are higher up than you have already done that. Hours will be extended. Leisure hours will cease. Then some of the personnel from this area can be spared for another vocation."

I'm beginning to understand and I wish I weren't. "So if you don't want me to sort the other variables in the work situation, you want me to—"

"Sort the people," she says.

I feel sick.

She holds out a datapod. "You have three hours to watch. Enter the numbers of the workers you think are the most efficient, those who should be sent to work on an alternative project."

I look at the numbers on the back of the workers' shirts. This *is* like a sort on the screen; I'm supposed to watch for the faster patterns among the workers. They want to see if my mind will automatically register the workers who move the most quickly. Computers could do this job and probably have. But now they want to see if I can do it, too.

"And Cassia," the Official says from the metal stairs. I look down at her. "Your sort will hold. That's part of the test. We want to see if you can make decisions well when you know they have actual results."

She sees the shock on my face and continues. I can tell she's trying to be kind. "It's one shift of one group of menial laborers, Cassia. Don't worry. Just do your best."

"But what's the other project? Will they have to leave the City?"

The Official looks shocked. "We can't answer that. It's not relevant to the sort."

The gray-haired Official, still breathing heavily, turns back to see what's happening. She nods to him that she's on her way down, and then tells me gently, "Better workers get the better work positions, Cassia. That's all you need to know."

I don't want to do this. For a moment, I contemplate throwing the datapod into one of the sinks, letting it drown.

What would Ky do if he were the one standing up here?

I don't throw the datapod. I take deep breaths. Sweat runs down my back and a piece of my hair falls into my eyes. I push the hair back with one hand and then I straighten my shoulders and look out at the workers. My eyes dart from place to place. I try not to see faces, only numbers. I look for fast patterns and slow ones. I start to sort.

The most disturbing part of the whole experience is that I am very, very good at it. Once I tell myself to do what Ky would do, I don't look back. Over the course of the sort, I watch for pacing and patterns and I watch for stamina. I see the slower, more steady ones who get more done than you might think. I see the quick, deft ones who are the very best. I see the ones who can't quite keep up. I see their red hands move amid the steam, and I see the pile of foilware moving along in its silver stream as it turns from dirty to clean.

But I don't see people. I don't see faces.

When the three hours are almost over my sort is complete and I know it's a good one. I know I've classified the best workers in the group by their numbers.

But I can't resist. I look at the number of the very middle worker, the one who is right in between the best and the worst of the group.

I look up. It's the number on Ky's back.

I want to laugh and cry. It's as though he's sending me a message. No one fits in the way he does; no one else has mastered the art of being exactly average so well. For a few seconds I let myself watch the boy in blue plainclothes with the dark hair. My instincts tell me to put him with the more efficient group; I know that's where he belongs. That's the group that gets the new vocation. They might have to leave the City, but at least he wouldn't be trapped here forever. Still, I don't think I could do it. What would my life be like if he left?

I let myself imagine climbing down from that ladder and pulling Ky close in the middle of all this heat and sound. And then I imagine something even better. I imagine walking over and taking his hand and leading him out of this place into light and air. I could do this. If I sort him into the higher group, he won't have to work here anymore. His life will be better. I could be the one to change that for him. And suddenly that desire, the desire to help him, is even stronger than my selfish desire to keep him close.

But I think of the boy in the story he's given me. The boy who has done everything he can to survive. What would that boy's instincts say?

He would want me to put him in the lower group.

"Almost finished?" the Official asks me. She waits on the metal steps a few feet below. I nod. She climbs toward me, and I pull up another number of someone who is near the middle so that she doesn't know I've been looking at Ky.

She stands next to me, looking at the number and then out at the person on the floor. "The middle workers are always the most difficult to sort," she says with sympathy in her voice. "It's hard to know what to do."

I nod, but she's not finished.

"Menial laborers like these don't usually live to eighty," she says. Her voice hushes. "Many of them are Aberration status, you know. The Society doesn't worry as much about them reaching optimal age. Many die early. Not horribly early, of course. Not pre-Society early, or Outer Province early. But sixty, seventy. Lower-level vocations in nutrition disposal are particularly dangerous, even with all the precautions we take."

"But . . ." The shock on my face doesn't surprise her, and I realize that this must be part of the test, too. Coming across an unknown factor in the middle of an otherwise straightforward sort just when you thought you were done. And I wonder: *What's going on here? Why are the stakes so high for a test sort?*

There's something happening that is something bigger than me, bigger than Ky.

"This is all confidential information, of course," the Official says. Then she glances down at her datapod. "You have two minutes."

I need to concentrate but my mind is off on another sort of its own, asking questions and lining them up to make an answer:

Why do the laborers die early?

Why couldn't Grandfather share the food from his plate at the Final Banquet?

Why do so many Aberrations work in food cleanup?

They poison the food for the elderly.

It's all clear now. Our Society prides itself on never killing anyone, having done away with the death penalty, but what I see here and what I've heard about the Outer Provinces tells me that they have found another way to take care of things. The strong survive. Natural selection. With help from our Gods, of course—the Officials.

If I get to play God, or angel, then I have to do the best I can for Ky. I can't let him die early and I can't let him spend his life in this room. There has to be something better out there for him. I have enough faith left in my Society to think that; I have seen many people living good lives, and I want one of those lives to be Ky's. Whether or not I can be a part of it.

I sort Ky into the higher group and close the datapod as if the decision has cost me nothing at all.

Inside, I scream.

I hope I made the right choice.

"Tell me more about where you're from," I say to Ky on the Hill the next day, hoping he doesn't hear the desperation in my voice, hoping he doesn't ask about the sort. I have to know more about his story. I have to know if I did the right thing. The sort has changed things between us; we feel watched, even here in the trees. We speak softly; we don't look at each other too long.

"It's red and orange there. Colors you don't see here very often."

"That's true," I say, and I try to think of things that are

red. Some of the dresses at the Match Banquet. The fires in the incinerators. Blood.

"Why is there so much green and brown and blue here?" he asks me.

"Maybe because they are growing colors and so much of our Province is agricultural," I say. "You know. How blue is the color of water, and brown the color of fall and harvest. And green is the color of spring."

"People always say that," Ky says. "But red is the first color of spring. It's the real color of rebirth. Of beginning."

He's right, I realize. I think of the ruddy color of the tight new buds on the trees. Of the red of his hands the day before in the nutrition disposal center and the new beginning I hope I have given him.

CHAPTER 27

*W*arning. *Warning.* The light on the tracker flashes and words scroll across the screen. *You have reached maximum speed earlier than recommended for this exercise session.*

I punch the numbers so that I go even faster.

Warning. Warning. You have exceeded your optimal heart rate.

Usually, when I push too hard on the tracker I stop in time. I take things to the edge but I never jump. But if I go to the edge enough times, I'm going to get pushed over or fall right in.

Maybe it's time to jump. But I can't do it without dragging all the people I love with me.

Warning. Warning.

I'm going too fast. I'm too tired. I know it. But my fall still surprises me.

My foot slips and before I know it I'm down, down on the tracker with the belt still going and burning, burning, burning my skin. I lie there for a moment, in shock and on fire, and then I roll off as fast as I can. The tracker keeps going, but it will notice my absence in a moment. It will stop and then they will know I couldn't keep up. But if I get back on fast enough, no one has to know what happened.

I glance at my skin, rubbed raw and red from the moving belt. *Red*.

I jump up. I tense my muscles and spring at just the right time and I hit the tracker running. Pound. Pound. Pound pound pound.

My knees and elbows stream blood and I have tears in my eyes, but I am still going. The plainclothes will hide my wounds tomorrow and no one will ever know that I fell. No one will ever know what happened until it is too late.

When I come back upstairs after running on the tracker, my father gestures me toward the port. "Just in time," he says. "There's a communication for you."

The sorting Officials wait on the screen. "Your sort looks excellent," the blond Official tells me. "Congratulations on passing the test. I'm sure you'll hear news regarding your work position soon."

I nod my head, sweat dripping off me and blood from my cuts running down my knees and my arms. She can only see the sweat, I think to myself. I tug my sleeves down a little to make sure they cover everything, so that no one will know that I am injured and bloody.

"Thank you. I look forward to it." I step back, sure that the portscreen communication is finished, but the Official has one last question for me.

"Are you sure that there aren't any changes you want to make before the sort is implemented?"

My last chance to take back what I've done. I almost say it. I have his number memorized; it would be so easy. Then I remember what she told me about life expectancy, and the words turn to rocks in my mouth and I can't speak around them.

"Cassia?"

"I'm sure."

I turn away from the port and almost run into my father. "Congratulations," he says. "Sorry. I hope you don't mind that I•listened. They didn't say it was a private communication."

"It's fine," I say. Then I ask, "Did you ever wonder . . ." I pause, unsure of how to phrase this. How to ask him if he ever doubted his Match with my mother. If he ever wanted someone else.

"Did I ever wonder what?" he asks me.

"Never mind," I say, because I think I already know the answer. Of course he didn't. They fell in love immediately and never looked back.

I go into my room and open my closet. Once it held the compact and the poem. Now it is empty except for clothes and shoes and the small, framed piece of my dress. I don't know where my silver box is and I panic. Did they accidentally take it when they took the artifacts? No, of course not. They know what the silver boxes are. They'd never mistake them for something from the past. The Match Banquet boxes are clearly for the future.

I'm hunting around through my meager belongings

when my mother comes into the room. She returned late last night from her third trip out of Oria. "Are you looking for something?" she asks.

I straighten up. "I found it," I say, holding up the fragment of green under glass. I don't want to tell her that I can't find the Match Banquet box.

She takes the square from me and holds it up, the green fabric from the dress catching the light. "Did you know that there used to be windows with colored glass?" she asks. "People put them in places where they worshipped. Or in their own homes."

"Stained glass," I say. "Papa's told me about it." It does sound beautiful: light shining through color, windows as art or tribute.

"Of course he has," she says, laughing at herself. "I finally submitted that report today, and now I'm so tired I can't think well."

"Is everything all right?" I ask. I want to ask her what she meant about the trees that day, why she thought their loss was a warning to her, but I don't think I want to know. After the real-life sort I feel like I can't take any more pressure; I feel as though I already know too much. Besides, my mother seems happier now than she's seemed in weeks, and I don't want to change that.

"I think it will be," she says.

"Oh, good," I say. We're both silent for a moment, looking at my dress under glass.

"Are you going to have to travel again?"

"No, I don't think so," she says. "I think that's finished. I hope." She still looks exhausted, but I can see that submitting the report has lifted a burden.

I take the memento back from her, and as I do, I have an idea. "Can I see the piece of *your* dress?" The last time I looked at it was the night before my Match Banquet. I was a little nervous, and she brought me the dress fragment and told me again the story of their Match with its happy ending. But so much has changed since then.

"Of course," she says, and I follow her into her bedroom. The framed bit of fabric sits on a little shelf inside the closet she shares with my father, along with two silver boxes—hers and Papa's—that held their microcards and, later, the rings for their Contract. The rings are purely ceremonial, of course—they don't get to keep them—and they give the microcards back to the Officials at the Contract celebration. So my parents' silver boxes are empty.

I pick up her dress fragment and hold it up. My mother's gown was blue and thanks to preservation techniques, the satin is still bright and lovely in its frame.

I put it next to mine along the windowsill. Together, side by side, I imagine that they look a little like a stained-glass window. The light behind them brightens them, and I can almost imagine that I could look through the colors and see a world made beautiful and different.

My mother understands. "Yes," she says. "I imagine the windows looked something like that."

I want to tell her everything but I can't. Not now. I am too fragile. I am trapped in glass and I want to break out and breathe deep but I'm too afraid that it will hurt.

My mother puts her arm around me. "Can you tell me what's wrong?" she asks gently. "Is it something to do with your Match?"

I reach for my dress fragment and take it down from the window so my mother's sits up there alone. I don't trust myself to speak, so I shake my head. How can I explain to my perfectly Matched mother everything that has happened? Everything I've risked? How can I explain to her that I'd do it again? How can I tell her that I hate the system that created her life, her love, her family? That created *me*?

Instead, I ask, "How did you know?"

She reaches for her frame and takes it down, too. "At first, I could see that you were falling deeper and deeper in love, but I didn't worry about it because I thought your Match was perfect for you. Xander is wonderful. And you might be able to stay in Oria, nearby, since both of your families live here. As a mother, I couldn't imagine a better scenario."

She pauses, looking at me. "And then I was so busy with work. It took until today for me to realize that I was wrong. You weren't thinking of Xander."

Don't say it, I beg her with my eyes. *Don't say that you know I'm in love with someone else. Please.*

"Cassia," she tells me, and the love in her eyes for me is pure and true and that's what makes her next words cut deep, because I know she has my best interests at heart. "I'm married to someone wonderful. I have two beautiful children and a job I love. It's a good life." She holds out the piece of blue satin. "Do you know what would happen if I broke this glass?"

I nod. "The cloth would disintegrate. It would be ruined."

"Yes," she says, and then it's almost as if she's speaking to herself. "It would be ruined. Everything would be ruined."

Then she puts her hand on my arm. "Do you remember what I said the day they cut the trees down?"

Of course I do. "About how it was a warning for you?"

"Yes." She flushes. "That wasn't true. I was so worried that I wasn't acting rationally. Of course it wasn't a warning for me. It wasn't a warning for anyone. The trees simply needed to come down."

I hear in her voice how badly she wants to believe that what she says is true, how she almost *does* believe it. Wanting to hear more, but not wanting to push too hard, I ask, "What was so important about the report? What makes it different from other reports you've done?"

My mother sighs. She doesn't answer me directly; instead, she says, "I don't know how the workers at the medical center stand it when they're working on people or delivering babies. It's too hard to have other lives in your hands."

My unspoken question hovers in the air: *What do you mean*? She pauses. She seems to be deciding whether or not to answer me, and I hold perfectly still until she speaks again. Absentmindedly she picks up her dress fragment and begins polishing the glass.

"Someone out in Grandia, and then in another Province, reported that there were strange crops popping up. The one in Grandia was in the Arboretum, in an experimental field that had been fallow for a long time. The other field was in the Farmlands of the second Province. The Government asked me and two others to travel to the fields and submit reports about the crops. They wanted to know two things: Were the crops viable as foodstuffs? And were the growers planning a rebellion?"

I draw in my breath. It's forbidden to grow food unless the Government has specifically requested it. They control the food; they control us. Some people know how to grow food, some know how to harvest it, some know how to process it; others know how to cook it. But none of us know how to do all of it. We could never survive on our own.

"The three of us agreed that the crops were definitely usable as foodstuffs. The grower at the Arboretum had an entire field of Queen Anne's lace." My mother's face changes suddenly, lights up. "Oh, Cassia, it was so beautiful. I've only seen a sprig here and there. This was a whole field, waving in the wind."

"Wild carrot," I say, remembering.

"Wild carrot," she agrees, her voice sad. "The second grower had a crop I'd never seen before, of white flowers even more beautiful than the first. Sego lilies, they called them. One of the others with me knew what they were. You can eat the bulb. Both growers denied knowing you could use the plants for food; they both asserted that their interest was in the flower. They insisted the plants were new to them and that they cultivated them as research, for the blossoms."

Her voice, which has been soft and sad since she mentioned the field of Queen Anne's lace, grows stronger. "The three of us argued the whole way back after the second trip. One expert was convinced the growers were telling the truth. The other thought they were lying. They submitted conflicting reports. Everyone waited for mine. I asked for one last trip to be sure. After all, these growers will be Relocated or Reclassified based on our reports. Mine would tip the balance one way or the other."

She stops polishing the glass and looks down at the piece of blue cloth as though there is something written there for her to see. And I realize that for her, there is. That blue cloth represents the night she was Matched to my father. She reads her life, the life she loves, in that square of blue satin.

"I knew all along," she whispers. "I knew when I saw the fear in their eyes when we first arrived. They knew what they were doing. And something the Queen Anne's lace grower said on my second visit convinced me even more of the truth.

He acted as though he'd never seen the plant outside of a portscreen before until he raised the crop, but he grew up in a town near mine, and I knew I'd seen the flower there growing wild.

"But I still hesitated. And then when I came home again and saw all of you, I realized I had to report the truth. I had to fulfill my duty to the Society and guarantee our happiness. And keep us all safe."

That last word, *safe*, is as soft and hushed as the swish of silk.

"I understand," I tell her, and I do. And the hold she has over me is much greater than the Officials, because I love her and admire her.

Back in my room I find the silver box where it fell inside one of my winter boots. I open it up and take out the microcard with all of Xander's information and the courtship guidelines. If there hadn't been a mistake, if I'd just seen his face and everything had been normal, none of this would have happened. I wouldn't have fallen in love with Ky and the choice wouldn't have been so hard to make in the sort. Everything would have been fine.

Everything can still be fine. If the sort is what I suspect, if Ky leaves for a better life, will I pick up the pieces of my life here? The biggest piece, my Match with Xander, would not be hard to shape a life around. I could love him. I *do* love him. And because I do, I have to tell him about Ky. I do not mind stealing from the Society. But I will not steal from Xander any longer. Even if it hurts, I have to tell him. Because either way, whichever life I build, has to be built on truth.

Thinking of telling Xander hurts almost as much as thinking of losing Ky. I roll over and hold the tablet container tight in my palm. *Think of something else.*

I remember the first time I saw Ky on top of that little hill, leaning back, sun on his face, and I realize that *is* when I fell in love with him. I didn't lie to him after all. I didn't see him differently because I saw his face on the portscreen the morning after my Match; I saw him differently because I saw him outside, unguarded for a moment, with eyes the color of the sky in the evening before it goes down into dark. I saw him seeing me.

Lying in bed, my body and soul bruised and tired, I realize that the Officials are right. Once you want something, everything changes. Now I want everything. More and more and more. I want to pick my work position. Marry who I choose. Eat pie for breakfast and run down a real street instead of on a tracker. Go fast when I want and slow when I want. Decide which poems I want to read and what words I want to write. There is so much that I want. I feel it so much that I am water, a river of want, pooled in the shape of a girl named Cassia.

Most of all I want Ky.

"We're running out of time," Ky says.

"I know." I've been counting the days, too. Even if Ky's

new work position is still here in the City, the summer leisure activities are almost over. I won't see Ky nearly as much. I allow myself to daydream for a few seconds—what if his new position is one that allows him more time? He could come to all of the Saturday night activities. "Only a couple of weeks of hiking left."

"That's not what I mean," he says, moving closer. "Don't you feel it? Something's changing. Something's happening."

Of course I feel it. For me, everything is changing.

His eyes are wary, as though he still feels watched. "Something big, Cassia," he says, and then he whispers softly, "I think the Society is having trouble with their war on the borders."

"What makes you say that?"

"I have a feeling," he says. "From what you told me about your mother. From the shortage of Officials during free-rec hours. And there are changes coming at work. I can tell." He glances at me and I duck my head.

"Do you want to tell me why you were there?" he asks gently.

I swallow. I've been wondering when he would want to know. "It was a real-life sort. I had to sort the workers into two groups."

"I see," he says, and he waits to see if I will say more.

And I wish I could. But I can't get the words out. Instead, I say, "You haven't given me any more of the story. What happened after the Officials came to get you? When did that happen? I know it wasn't long ago, because . . ." My voice trails off.

Ky ties a red cloth on the tree slowly, methodically, and then he looks up. After years of seeing only surface emotions from him, the new and deeper ones startle me sometimes. The expression on his face now is not one I have seen before.

"What's wrong?" I ask.

"I'm afraid," he says simply. "Of what you're going to think."

"About what? What happened?" After everything he's been through, Ky's afraid of what I might think?

"It was in the spring. They came to talk with me at work, pulled me aside into a room there. They asked if I ever wondered what my life would be like if I weren't an Aberration." Ky's jaw tightens at this and I feel sorry for him. He glances up and sees it on my face and his jaw becomes even more set. He does not want my pity, so I turn my face away to listen.

"I said I never thought about that much. I said I didn't worry about things I couldn't change. Then they told me there had been a mistake. My data had been entered into the Matching pool."

"Your data?" I ask, surprised. *But the Official told me it was a mistake on the microcard, Ky's picture where it shouldn't be. She told me that he* hadn't *been entered into the pool.*

She lied. The error was much bigger than she said it was.

Ky keeps talking. "I'm not even a full citizen. They said the whole incident was completely irregular." He smiles, a bitter twist to his mouth that it hurts me to see. "Then they showed me a picture. The girl who would have been my Match if I weren't what I am." Ky swallows.

"Who was she?" I ask. My voice sounds harsh, grating. *Don't say that it was me. Don't say that it was me, because then I will know that you saw me because they told you to look.*

"You," he says.

And now I see. Ky's love for me, which I thought was pure and unblemished by any Officials or data or Matching pools, is not. They have touched even this.

I feel like something is dying, ruined beyond repair. *If the Officials orchestrated our whole love affair, the one thing in my life I thought happened in* spite *of them*—I can't finish the thought.

The forest around me blurs into green and without the red flags marking the way, I would not know my way down. As it is, I tear at them wildly, pulling them off the branches.

"Cassia," he says behind me. "Cassia. Why does it matter?"

I shake my head.

"Cassia," he calls after me. "You're keeping something from me, too."

A whistle sounds sharp and clear below us. We have come so far but never made it to the top.

"I thought you were eating lunch at the Arboretum," Xander says. The two of us sit together in the meal hall at Second School.

"I changed my mind," I tell him. "I wanted to eat here today." The nutrition personnel frowned at me when I asked for one of the extra meals they keep on hand, but after checking my data, they handed over the meal without further comment. They must have seen that I hardly ever do this. Or maybe there's some other flag on my data that I can't think about right now. Not after the revelation from Ky.

I realize how much food my container holds this time, now that it's a general portion and not labeled specifically for me. My portions *have* been getting smaller. *What purpose does that serve? Am I too fat?* I look down at my arms and legs, strong from all the hiking. I don't think so. And I realize again how distracted my parents must be; under normal circumstances, they would have noticed my smaller portions and had plenty to say to the nutrition personnel about them.

Things are wrong everywhere.

I push back my chair. "Will you come with me?"

Xander glances at his watch. "Where? Class starts soon."

"I know," I say. "We're not going far. Please."

"All right," Xander says, looking at me with a puzzled expression on his face.

I lead him down the hall to the classroom area and push open the door at the end. There, in a small area like a courtyard, is the Applicable Sciences botany pond. Xander and I are alone.

I have to tell him. This is Xander. He deserves to know

about Ky, and he deserves to hear it from me. Not from an Official in a greenspace, today or some other day.

Drawing a deep breath, I look down at the pond. It isn't blue like the pool where we swim. This water is brownish-green under its silvery surface, messy with life.

"Xander," I say, my voice as quiet as if we were hidden in trees on the Hill. "I have something to tell you."

"I'm listening," he says, waiting, looking at me. Always steady. Always Xander.

It's better to say this quickly, before I find myself unable to say it at all. "I think I'm falling in love with someone else." I speak so softly, I almost can't hear my own voice. But Xander understands.

Almost before I've finished, he's shaking his head and saying, "*No*," putting up his hand to stop me before I say more. But it isn't either of those gestures or that word that makes me fall silent. It's the hurt in his eyes. And what they are saying isn't *No*. It's: *Why?*

"No," Xander says again, turning away from me.

I can't bear that, so I move in front of him, try to see him, too. He won't look at me for a long moment. I don't know what to say. I don't dare to touch him. All I can do is stand there, hoping he will look back.

When he does, the pain is still there.

And something else too. Something that doesn't look like surprise. It looks like recognition. Did some part of him know this was happening? Is that why he challenged Ky to the games?

"I'm sorry," I say, rushing. "You're my friend. I love you too." It is the first time I've said those words to him, and it comes out all wrong. The sound of it, hurried and strained, makes the words seem like less than they are.

"You love me *too*?" Xander says, his voice cold. "What game are you playing?"

"I'm not playing a game," I whisper. "I do love you. But it's different."

Xander says nothing. An hysterical giggle rises up in me; it's exactly like the last time we had an argument and he refused to speak to me. Years ago, when I decided that I didn't like playing the games as much as I once had. Xander was mad. "But no one else plays like you," he said. And then, when I wouldn't give in, he wouldn't talk to me. I still wouldn't play.

It took two weeks before our peace was brokered, that day he saw me jump into the pool from the diving board after Grandfather jumped first. I surfaced, frightened and exhilarated, and Xander swam over to congratulate me. In the rush of the moment all was forgotten.

What would Grandfather think of this jump I'm taking? Would this be one time he would tell me to hang on to the edge with all my might? Would he say to cling to the side of the board until my fingers became bloody and scraped? Or would he say that it was all right to let go?

"Xander. The Officials played a game with *me*. The morning

after the Match Banquet, I put the microcard in the port. Your face came up on the screen and it disappeared." I swallow. "And then someone else's face appeared instead. It was Ky's."

"Ky Markham?" Xander asks, disbelieving.

"Yes."

"But Ky's not your Match," Xander says. "He can't be, because—"

"Because why?" I ask. Does Xander know about Ky's status after all? How?

"Because *I* am," Xander says.

For a long moment, neither of us speak. Xander doesn't look away and I don't think that I can stand this. If I had a green tablet in my mouth now, I'd bite, taste the bitterness before the calm. I think back to that day in the meal hall when he told me Ky could be trusted. Xander believed that. And he believed he could trust *me*.

What does he think of us both now?

Xander leans closer. Blue eyes holding mine, hand hovering next to mine. I close my eyes, both to shut out the pain in his gaze and to stop myself from turning my hand up, weaving my fingers through his, leaning forward, meeting his lips. I open my eyes and look at Xander again.

"I came up on the screen, too, Cassia," he says quietly. "But he was the one you chose to see." And then, quick as a player making his last move, he turns away and pushes through the doors. He leaves me behind.

Not at first! I want to tell him. *And I still see you!*

One by one, the people I can talk to have gone. Grandfather. My mother. And now, Xander.

You are strong enough to go without it, Grandfather told me about the green tablet.

But, Grandfather. Am I strong enough to go without you? Without Xander?

The sun shines down on me where I have chosen to stand. No trees, no shade, no height from which I can look down on what I've done. And even if there were, I cannot see for the tears.

CHAPTER 28

At home that night, I take out the green tablet again. I know what it can do for me; I saw what it did for Em. *It will make me calm.* That word, *calm*, sounds impossibly beautiful, gloriously uncomplicated. A water-smooth word, a word that can take the edge away from fear, gloss it over, make it shiny. *Calm. Gentle.*

I put the tablet back in the container and snap it shut, turning to another kind of green next to me. My framed piece of dress in its bit of glass. I wrap my hand in one of my socks and then press down, hard. A faint snap. I lift my hand.

It's harder to break something than you would think. I wonder if the Society is finding this to be true of me as well. I put my hand down again, push harder.

It would be easy if no one watched, if no one could hear me. If these walls weren't so thin and my life weren't so transparent, I could throw the glass against the wall, smash it with a rock, destroy with abandon and noise. I think the glass would make a glittery sound when it broke; I would like to see it burst into a million pieces and shine all the way down. But instead, I have to be careful.

Another long silvery crack runs across the surface of the

glass. Underneath, the smooth ice-green cloth is undisturbed. Carefully I pull the pieces of glass apart, lift the largest one up, and pull out the fabric.

I take off the sock and hold up my hand. I'm not even cut, not even bleeding.

After the scratchy wool of my sock, the silk feels cool in my hand, luxurious, like water. *My birthday began with the water*, I think as I fold the material, and I smile.

After I've tucked both the fabric and the tablet container into the pocket of tomorrow's plainclothes, I climb into bed with that image in my mind. Water. I will drift away tonight on my dreams. That way the datatags won't pick up a thing in my mind except me, Cassia, floating on the waves, letting them carry my weight for a little while.

The Officer is not at hiking today.

Instead, we have a junior Official who bites his words out quick and fast, as though he thinks this is how the Officers speak. His eyes sweep over us, happy with the power to oversee, to direct. "The decision has been made to shorten leisure activities this summer. Today's your last day of hiking. Take down as many of the red flags as you can and knock over the cairns."

I glance over at Ky, who does not seem surprised. I try not to let my gaze linger on his face, try not to look for answers in his eyes. We were both polite and normal on the air-train ride to the Arboretum this morning; we both know how to perform when we're being watched. All the time I wondered what he thought of me running away from him on the Hill yesterday. What he will think of me once he finds out about the sort, and if he will accept the gift I want to give him today.

Or if he will do to me what I did to Xander and turn me away.

"Why?" Lon asks in a whine. "We spent half the summer marking these paths!"

I think I see a faint smile on Ky's face and I realize that he likes Lon. Who asks the questions no one else will ask even though he never gets an answer. It strikes me that this is a kind of bravery. A wearing-down kind of bravery, but bravery nonetheless.

"Don't ask questions," the Official snaps at Lon. "Get started."

And so, for the last time, Ky and I begin to climb the Hill.

When we are far enough onto our own path that no one else can see us, Ky grabs my hand as I reach to untie a red cloth from one of the shrubs. "Forget it all," he says. "We're going to the top."

Our eyes meet. I've never seen him look so reckless. I open my mouth to say something but he interrupts me. "Unless you don't want to try?"

There's a challenge in his voice I haven't heard before. His voice isn't cruel, but he's not just curious. He *needs* to know the answer; what I do now tells him something about me. He doesn't say anything about yesterday. His face is open, his eyes alight, his body tense, every muscle saying *It's time. Now.*

"I want to try," I tell him. To prove it, I lead the way along the path we've marked together. It isn't long before I feel his hand brush mine and when our fingers intertwine I feel the same urgency he does. *We have to make it to the top.*

I don't turn around but I hold on tight.

As we break into the last part of the forest, the part we haven't charted, I stop. "Wait," I say. If we're really going to clear this Hill, I want to pull out the last tangles and twists so we can stand on the top free and open.

Behind the patience on Ky's face I see worry, worry that we aren't going to make it in time. Even now, the whistle could be shrilling below us and I wouldn't hear it over the beating of our hearts and the sound of our breathing in and out, in and out, the same air. "I was scared yesterday."

"Of what?"

"That we fell in love because of the Officials," I say. "They told you about me. They told *me* about *you*, the morning after my Match, when your face came up on my microcard by mistake. You and I knew each other all along, but we never did anything about it until . . ." I can't finish my sentence, but Ky knows what I mean.

"You don't throw something away just because they predicted it," he protests.

"But I don't want to be defined by their choices," I say.

"You're not," he says. "You never have to be."

"Sisyphus and the rock," I say, remembering. Grandfather would have understood that story. He rolled the rock, he lived the life the Society planned for him, but his thoughts were always his own.

Ky smiles. "Exactly. But *we*," he tugs at my hand, gently, "are going to make it to the top. And maybe even stand there for a minute. Come on."

"I have to tell you something else," I say.

"Is it about the sort?" he asks.

"Yes—"

Ky interrupts me. "They told us. I'm part of the group that's going to get a new work position. I already know."

Does he know? Does he know his life will be shorter if he keeps working at the disposal center? Does he know he was right on the line between those who stayed and those who moved on? Does he know what I did?

He sees the questions in my eyes. "I know you had to sort us into two groups. I know I was probably right in the middle."

"Do you want to know what I did?"

"I can guess," he says. "They told you about the life expectancy and the poisons, didn't they? That's why you put me where you did."

"Yes," I say. "You know about the poisons, too?"

"Of course. Most of us figure it out. But none of us are

in a position to complain. Our lives are still much longer here than they'd be in the Outer Provinces."

"Ky." It's hard to ask, but I have to know. "Are you leaving?"

He looks up. Above us, fierce and golden, the sun climbs the sky. "I'm not sure. They haven't told us yet. But I know we don't have much time."

When we reach the top of the Hill it feels completely different in some ways and not in others. He is still Ky. I am still Cassia. But we stand together in a place where neither of us has been before.

It's the same world, gray and blue and green and gold, that I've seen all my life. The same world I saw from Grandfather's window and from the top of the little hill. But I am higher now. If I had wings, I could spread them. I could soar.

"I want you to have this," Ky says, handing me the artifact.

"I don't know how to use it," I say, not wanting to reveal how much I want to accept his gift. How deeply I ache to hold and have something that is part of his story and part of him.

"I think Xander can teach you," he says gently, and I draw in my breath. Is he telling me good-bye? Is he telling me to trust in Xander? To be with Xander?

Before I can ask, Ky pulls me close and his words are in

my ear, warm and whispered. "It will help you find me," he says. "If I ever do go anywhere."

My face fits perfectly into the spot against his shoulder, near his neck, where I can both hear his heart and smell his skin. I'm safe here, too. Some essential part of me is safer with Ky than anywhere else.

Ky presses another piece of paper into my hand. "The last part of my story," he says. "Will you save it? Don't look at it yet."

"Why?"

"Just wait," he says, voice quiet, strong. "Wait a little while."

"I have something for you, too," I say, pulling away just a little, reaching into my pocket. I give him the scrap of fabric, the green silk from my dress.

He holds it up to my face to see how I looked that night at the Match Banquet. "Beautiful," he says, gently.

He puts his arms around me on the top of the Hill. From where we stand I see clouds and trees and the dome of City Hall and the tiny houses of the Boroughs in the distance. For one brief moment, I see it all, this world of mine, and then I look back at Ky.

Ky says, "Cassia," and closes his eyes, and I close mine too so that I can meet him in the dark. I feel his arms around me and the smoothness of the green silk as he presses his hand against the small of my back and pulls me closer, closer.

"Cassia," he says once more, softly, so close his lips meet mine, at last. At last.

I think he might have meant to say something more, but when our lips touch, there is no need, for once, for any words at all.

CHAPTER 29

There is screaming in the Borough again and this time it is human.

I open my eyes. It is so early in the morning that the sky is more black than blue, the slice of dawn at the edge of the horizon more promise than reality.

My door slams open and in the rectangle of light I see my mother. "Cassia," she says in relief, and she turns back to call to my father, "She's fine!"

"Bram, too," he calls back, and then we are all in the hall, going toward the front door, because someone on our street is screaming and the sound of it is so uncommon it cuts deep. We may not hear the sound of pain often in Mapletree Borough, but the instinct to try to help has not yet been Matched out of us.

My father throws open the door and we all look out.

The streetlights seem dimmer; the Officials' coats dull and gray. They walk fast, a figure between them. Behind them, a few more people. Officers.

And someone else, screaming. Even in the muted glow of the streetlights, I recognize her. Aida Markham. Someone who has borne pain before and who bears it again now as she chases the figure surrounded by Officials and Officers.

Ky.

"Ky!"

For the first time in my life, I run as fast as I can in public. No tracker to slow me, no branches to stop me. My feet fly over grass, over cement. I cut across the lawns of my neighbors and through their flowers, trying to catch up to the lead group moving toward the air-train stop. An Officer detaches from them and hurries toward Aida. She's drawing too much attention; other houses have open doors and people standing on the steps watching.

I run faster; my feet hit the sharp, cool grass of Em's lawn. *A few houses more.*

"Cassia?" Em calls from her doorway. "Where are you going?"

Ky hasn't heard me over Aida's screams. They're almost to the steps that go up to the air-train platform. When they walk under the light at the bottom, I see they've locked Ky's hands together.

Just like they did in the picture.

"Ky!" I scream again, and his head snaps up. He turns his face toward me, but I am not close enough to see his eyes. I have to see his eyes.

Another Officer breaks away from the group and heads in my direction. I should have waited until I was closer before I called out, but I am still fast. I'm almost there.

Part of my mind tries to process what is happening. *Are they taking him away for his new work position? If so, why so early in the morning? Why is Aida so upset? Wouldn't she be happy to know he has a new chance, something better than washing foilware? Why is he wearing handlocks? Did he try to fight them?*

Did they see the kiss? Is that why this is happening?

I see the air train sliding along the tracks toward the station, but it's not the air train we usually ride, the silvery-white one. It's the charcoal-gray long-distance train, the kind that only departs from the City Center. I can hear it coming, too; it's heavier, louder, than the white one.

Something isn't right.

And if I didn't know that already, the word Ky calls to me as they push him up the steps confirms everything. Because there in front of everyone, all his survival instincts leave him and a different instinct takes over.

He calls my name. *"Cassia!"*

In that one word, I hear it all: That he loves me. That he's afraid. And I hear the good-bye he was trying to tell me yesterday on the Hill. He knew. He's not just leaving for a new work position; he's going somewhere and he doesn't think he'll come back.

I hear footsteps behind me, soft on the grass and footsteps in front of me, hard on the metal. I glance back and see an Officer hurrying toward me; forward, and an Official rushes down the metal stairs. Aida's no longer screaming; they want to stop me the way they stopped her.

I can't get to him. Not this way. Not now. I can't push past the Officer on the stairs. I'm not strong enough to fight them or fast enough to outrun them—

Do not go gentle.

I don't know if Ky speaks the words to my mind somehow or if I think them to myself or if Grandfather might be out there somewhere in this almost-night, calling words on the wind, words with wings like angels.

I veer to the side of the platform, feet fast on the cement. Ky sees what I'm doing and he twists away, a sharp movement that earns him a second of freedom before their hands clamp down on him again.

It is enough.

For a moment, he leans over the edge of the lighted platform and I see what I need to see. I see his eyes, bright with life and fire, and I know he won't stop fighting. Even if it's the kind of quiet fight on the inside that you can't always see. And I won't stop fighting either.

The calls of the Officials and the sound of the air train sliding to a stop will cover my words. Ky won't be able to hear anything I say.

So in the middle of all the noise, I point to the sky. I hope he understands what I mean, because I mean so many things: My heart will always fly his name. I won't go gentle. I'll find a way to soar like the angels in the stories and I will find him.

And I know he understands as he looks straight at me,

deep into my eyes. His lips move silently, and I know what he says: the words of a poem that only two people in the world know.

Tears well up but I blink them away. Because if there is one moment in my life that I want to see clearly, this is it.

The Officer reaches me first, grabbing my arm and pulling me back.

"Leave her alone," my father says. I had no idea he could run so fast. "She's done nothing." My mother and Bram hurry across the grass toward us. Xander and his family follow behind.

"She's causing a disturbance," the Officer says grimly.

"Of course she is," my father retorts. "They've taken her childhood friend away in the early hours of the morning while his mother screams. What's going on?"

I hear how loud my father's voice is as he dares to ask this question, and I dart a glance over at my mother to see how she feels about this. Her face shows nothing but pride as she looks at him.

To my surprise, Xander's father speaks up. "Where are they taking the boy?"

A white-coated Official takes charge, his voice loud so that everyone gathering can hear. His words are clipped and formal. "I'm sorry your morning has been disrupted. This young man received a new work position and we were merely picking him up to transport him. Since the position is outside of Oria Province, his mother became overwrought and upset."

But why all the Officers? Why all the Officials? Why the

handlocks? The Official's explanation makes no sense, but after a short pause, everyone nods, accepting it. Except Xander. He opens his mouth as if to speak but then he glances over at me and closes it.

All the adrenaline from trying to catch up to Ky leaves me and a horrible realization begins to sink in. *Wherever Ky went, it's because of me. Because of my sort, or because of my kiss. Either way, this is my fault.*

"Lies," Patrick Markham says. Everyone turns to look at him. Even standing there in his sleepclothes, his face drawn and thin from all he has suffered, he still has a quiet dignity—a quality no one can touch. It is something I have only seen in one other person. Though Patrick and Ky are not related by blood, they both possess the same kind of strength.

"The Officials told Ky and other workers," he says, looking at me, "that they'd been given a new work position. A better one. But in reality, they're sending them to the Outer Provinces to fight."

I reel backward as if I've been struck, and my mother reaches out her hand to steady me.

Patrick is still talking. "The war with the Enemy isn't going well. They need more people to fight. All the original villagers are dead. *All* of them." He pauses, speaks as if to himself. "I should have known they'd take Aberrations first. I should have known Ky would be on the list . . . I thought, since we'd been through so much . . ." His voice shakes.

Aida turns on him, furious, forgiving. "We forgot, sometimes. But he never did. He knew it was coming. Did you see him fight? Did you see his eyes when they took him away?" She throws her arms around Patrick's neck and he holds her close, her sobs ringing out in the cool morning. "He's going to die. It's a death sentence back there." Then she pulls away, screams at the Officials, "He's going to *die!*"

Two of the Officials move quickly, pinning Patrick's and Aida's hands behind their backs and pulling the Markhams away. Patrick's head snaps back as one of them gags him to keep him from talking, and they do the same to Aida to stifle her screams. I've never seen or heard of Officials using such force. Don't they realize that doing so gives truth to Patrick's and Aida's words?

An air car descends near us and disgorges more Officials. The Officers push the Markhams toward it and Aida reaches for her husband's hand. Their fingers miss by centimeters and she is denied that touch, the one thing in the world that could comfort her now.

I close my eyes. I wish I couldn't hear her screams echoing in my ears and the words I know I will never forget. *He's going to die.* I wish my mother could take me back inside my house, tuck me back in bed like she did when I was a child. When I watched night fall outside my window without a worry, when I did not know what it was like to want to break free.

"Excuse me."

I know that voice. It's my Official, the one from the greenspace. Next to her stands an Official with the insignia of the highest level of government: three golden stars, shining visibly under the streetlight. A hush falls over us.

"Everyone, please take out your tablet containers," he says pleasantly. "Remove the red tablet."

We all obey. My hand closes on the small container with its three tablets secured inside my pocket. Blue and red and green. Life and death and oblivion always at my fingertips.

"Now, keep the red tablets and hand Official Standler"— he gestures to my Official, who holds a square plastic receptacle—"your containers. Shortly after we've finished here you'll receive new containers and a new set of tablets."

Once again, we obey. I drop the little metal cylinder in with the others, but I do not meet my Official's eyes.

"We'll need you to take your red tablets. Official Standler and I will make sure you do. There's nothing to worry about."

Officers seem to multiply. They walk down the street, keeping everyone who stayed in their houses where they are and isolating the dozen or so of us who stand near the airtrain stop—the handful of us who know what happened today in Mapletree Borough and across the country. I imagine other scenes went more smoothly than this; likely none of the other Aberrations had parents or family high up enough to know what was really happening. And even Patrick Markham could do nothing to save his son.

And it's all my fault. I didn't play God or angel; I played Official. I let myself think that I knew what was best and changed someone's life accordingly. It doesn't matter whether or not the data backed me up; in the end, I made the decision myself. And the kiss—

I can't let myself think about the kiss.

I look down at the red tablet, so small in my hand. Even if it means death, I think I would welcome that now.

But wait. I promised Ky. I pointed to the sky and promised him. And now, moments later, I'm going to give up?

I drop the tablet on the ground, trying to be discreet. For a second I see it small and red in the grass, and I remember what Ky said about red being the color of birth and renewal. *"To a new beginning,"* I say to myself, and I shift my feet the tiniest bit so that I crush the tablet; it bleeds beneath my feet. It reminds me of the time I saw Ky's face across the crowded room at the game center just as my feet crushed the lost tablets beneath me.

Except now, when I look up, he is nowhere to be found.

No one has followed the orders yet. Even though the Official is the highest-ranking one we've ever seen and he's ordered us to do it, we've heard years of rumors about the red tablet.

"Would anyone like to go first?"

"I will," my mother says, stepping forward.

"No," I say, but a look from my father stops me. I know what he's trying to tell me, *She's doing this for us. For you.* And somehow, he knows it's going to be all right.

"I will, too," he says, moving to stand next to her. Together, as we all watch, they both swallow their tablets down. The Official checks my parents' mouths and nods briefly. "They dissolve within seconds," he tells us. "Too quickly for you to try and throw it back up, but it's unnecessary anyway. It won't hurt you. All it does is clear your mind."

All it does is clear your mind. Of course. I know now why we're going to take them. So we forget what happened to Ky, so we forget that the Enemy is winning the war in the Outer Provinces, that the villagers there are all dead. And I realize why they didn't have us take the tablets when something happened to the first Markham boy: because we needed to remember how dangerous Anomalies can be. How vulnerable we would be without the Society to keep them all away.

Did they let that Anomaly out on purpose? To remind us?

What will they tell us happened to Ky, later? What story will we all believe instead of his true one? Will we take the green tablet next, a calm after the forgetting?

I don't want to be calm anymore. I don't want to forget.

As much as it hurts, I have to hold onto the whole story of him, the painful parts, too.

My mother turns to look at me and I worry I'll see blank eyes or a vacant, slack expression. But she looks fine. So does my father.

Soon, everyone lines up, red tablets in their palms, ready to get this over with and go back to their lives. What will I do when they find out I got rid of mine? I glance down at the grass beneath my feet, almost expecting to see a tiny patch of it seared and obliterated, wiped clean. Instead it looks exactly as it did before. I can't even see the red fragments in the grass. I must have crushed them completely.

Bram looks terrified but excited. He's still not old enough to carry his own red tablet, so my father gives him the extra one he carries.

My Official starts checking people, too. She moves closer and closer to me, but I can't take my eyes from Bram and then from Em as she takes the tablet. For a moment, I remember my dream and I feel horror as I watch her. But nothing happens. Nothing that I can see, anyway.

And then it is Xander's turn. He glances over and sees me watching him, and an expression crosses his face that is nothing but pain. I want to look away, but I don't. I watch as Xander nods to me and lifts the red tablet toward me, almost in a toast.

Before I see him take it, someone blocks my view of everyone and theirs of me. It's my Official.

"Let me see your tablet, please," she says.

"I have it." I hold out my hand but I don't open my palm.

I think I almost see her smile. Even though I know she carries extra tablets—I've seen them—she doesn't offer me one yet.

Her glance flickers down to the grass at my feet and

then back up to my face. I lift my arm and pretend to put something in my mouth and then I swallow, hard. And she moves on to the next person.

Even though this is what I want, I hate her. She *wants* me to remember what happened here. What I've done.

CHAPTER 30

When the darkness finally lifts, it is a flat, hot, steel-colored morning, a morning without dimension or depth. The houses around me could be the set for a showing; they could be pictures on a bigscreen. I feel that if I walk too far I'll walk right into canvas or through a paper wall and then out into black-nothing and the end of everything.

Somehow I've run out of fear; I feel lethargic instead, which is almost worse. Why care about a flat planet populated by flat people? Who cares about a place where there is no Ky?

This is one of the reasons I need Ky, I realize. Because when I am with him, I *feel*.

But he is gone. I saw it happen.

I made it happen.

Did Sisyphus have to do this, too? I wonder. *Stop for a minute and concentrate on holding firm, on pushing the rock just enough to keep it from rolling down and crushing him, before he could even think about trying to climb again?*

The red tablet took effect almost immediately after the Officers and Officials shepherded us home. The events of the past twelve hours have been wiped from my family's minds.

Within the hour, a delivery of new containers and tablets arrived with a letter of explanation that ours were found to be defective and removed earlier this morning. Everyone else in my family accepts the explanation without question. They have other things to worry about.

My mother is confused—where did she put her datapod for work when she finished with it last night? Bram can't remember whether he finished writing his assignment on his scribe.

"Well, turn it on and check, honey," my mother says, flustered. My father looks a little blank, too, but not as confused. I think he's experienced this before, possibly many times in his line of work. While the tablet still works, he seems less bewildered by the feeling of disorientation.

Which is good, because the Officials haven't finished with our family yet.

"Private message for Molly Reyes," the generic voice from the port calls out.

My mother looks up, surprised. "I'll be late for work," she protests softly, although whoever sent this message can't hear her. They also can't see her straighten her shoulders before she walks over to the port and puts on the earpiece. The screen darkens, the picture on it only visible from the exact spot in which she stands.

"What now?" says Bram. "Should I wait?"

"No, go on to school," my father tells him. "We don't want you to be late."

On his way out the door, Bram complains, "I always miss

everything." I wish I could tell him that wasn't true; but then again, would I really want him to keep the memory of what happened this morning?

Something happens to me when I look at Bram leaving our house, and things become real again. Bram is real. I am real. Ky is real, and I need to get started on finding him. *Now.*

"I'm going into the City for the morning," I tell my father.

"Don't you have hiking?" he asks, and then he shakes his head as if to clear it. "Sorry. I remember. Summer leisure activities ended early this year, right? That's why Bram's already on his way to school instead of swimming. My mind's foggy this morning." He doesn't seem surprised by that fact, and I think again that this is something that's happened to him before. And I remember how he let my mother take the red tablet first; somehow he knew it wouldn't hurt her.

"They didn't assign us anything else to do yet to take the place of hiking," I tell my father. "So I have time to go into the City before Second School." This in itself is an oversight, another little hitch in the well-oiled machine of our Society that proves something is wrong somewhere.

My father doesn't answer. He stares at my mother, whose face is ashen and pale as she stares at the portscreen. "*Molly?*" he says. You're not supposed to interrupt a private message, but he takes a few steps closer. And then closer again.

Finally, when he puts his hand on her shoulder, she

turns away from the screen. "This is my fault," my mother says, and for the first time in my life, I see her look through my father, not at him, her gaze fixed on some distant point beyond. "We've been Relocated to the Farmlands, effective immediately."

"What?" my father asks. He shakes his head, glances back behind her at the port. "That's impossible. You submitted the report. You told the truth."

"I suppose they don't want those of us who saw the rogue crops to continue working in positions of authority," my mother says. "We know too much. We might be tempted to do the same. They'll put us out in the Farmlands where we won't be in charge. Where they can watch us and wear us out planting what they tell us to plant."

"But at least," I say, trying to comfort her, "we'll be closer to Grandmother and Grandfather."

"Not the Farmlands in Oria," my mother says. "The Farmlands in a different province. We leave tomorrow." Then that blank, stunned gaze of hers shifts to my father and I see her begin to feel again. I watch realization and emotion come back into her face. As I see it happen to her, I feel a sense of urgency so strong I don't know if I can bear it. *I have to find out where they sent Ky. Before we leave.*

"I've always wanted to live in the Farmlands," my father says, and my mother leans her head on his shoulder, too tired to cry and too overcome to pretend that everything is all right.

"But I did what I was supposed to do," she whispers. "I did exactly what they asked."

"It will be all right," he whispers to my mother and to me. Maybe if I had taken the red tablet I could believe him.

Down the street, there's an Official air car in front of the Markhams' house. Our Borough has had entirely too much attention from the Officials in the past few weeks.

Em bounces out the door of her treeless house. "Did you hear?" she asks, excited. "The Officials are gathering the Markhams' things. Patrick has been transferred to work in the Central Government! It's such an honor. And he's from *our* Borough!" She frowns. "It's too bad we didn't get to say good-bye to Ky. I'll miss him."

"I know," I say, and my heart aches, and I stop again under my stone, pushing back against the weight of being the only one who knows what really happened this morning.

Except for a few select Officials. And even they don't know that I know. Only two people truly know what took place, that I didn't take the red tablet. Me. And my Official.

"I have to go," I tell Em, and I start moving again, toward the air-train stop. I don't look back at the Markhams' house. Patrick and Aida, gone for good, too. Have they been assigned Aberration status or a quiet Retirement somewhere far from here? Have they taken the red tablet, too? Do they look around their new place with surprise, wondering what happened to their second son? I'll have to try to find them, too, for Ky, but right now I have to find Ky. There's only one place I can think of to look for information about where they might have sent him.

On the ride to City Hall, I keep my head down. There are too many places I can't look: at the seats where Ky used to sit; at the floor of the air-train car where he set his feet and kept his balance, always making it seem easy, natural. I can't bring myself to look out the windows at all, knowing that I might catch a glimpse of the Hill where Ky and I stood yesterday. Together. When the train stops to let more people on and a breeze wafts in, I wonder if the strips of red cloth that Ky and I left there flutter in the wind. Signal flags of a new beginning, though not the kind we wanted.

Finally, I hear the announcer's voice, calling my destination.

City Hall.

My idea won't work. I know it the minute I stand on the steps of the Hall for only the second time in my life. This is not the place of open doors and twinkling lights that welcomed me, invited me to catch a glimpse of my future. In the daylight, this is a place with armed guards, a place of business, a place where past and present are locked safe inside. They won't let me in, and even if they did, they wouldn't tell me anything.

They might not know there was anything to tell. Even Officials carry red tablets.

I turn back and there across the street I see possibility and my heart flutters. *Of course. Why didn't I think of this first? The Museum.*

The Museum is long, low, white, blind. Even its windows are made of frosted white opaque glass to keep the artifacts inside safe from the light. City Hall, across the street, has tall, clear windows. City Hall sees everything. Still, the Museum might have something for me behind its tightly closed eyes. Hope quickens my step as I cross the street, gives me strength as I push open the enormous white doors.

"Welcome," says a curator, sitting at a round white desk. "Can I help you find anything?"

"I'm wandering," I say, trying to look relaxed. "I have some extra time today."

"And you came here," the curator says, pleased, puzzled. "Wonderful. You might want to try the second level. Some of our most popular displays are up there."

I don't want to draw too much attention to myself, so I nod and climb the steps, their metal echo reminding me painfully of Ky's feet on the stairs at the station. *Don't think about that now. Stay calm. Remember coming here that time in First School, before Ky came to the Borough? Back when we had time to consider the past, before we went to Second School where all that matters is the future? Remember walking into the dining hall in the basement of the Museum with the other schoolchildren, all of us so excited to be eating somewhere new and different? Remember Xander's bright blond head among the rest, the way he pretended to listen to the curator's speech but kept making jokes to the side that no one else could hear?*

Xander. If I leave him here, will another piece of my heart be torn away, too?

Of course it will.

A sign points to the Hall of Artifacts and I veer right, suddenly, wanting to see the display. Wanting to see where they put all those things they took. Perhaps I'll see my compact, Xander's cuff links, Bram's watch. I could bring him here one more time before we leave for the Farmlands.

I stop in the middle of the hall, realizing that none of those things are here.

The other cases are still crammed with artifacts, but the new display is nothing but a long glass case, huge and empty. A sign in the middle of it, printed in lettered words that look so different from Ky's cursive, reads: ADDITIONAL ARTIFACTS COMING SOON. A light from above illuminates the sign in its empty, cavernous case. That sign could last forever in this sealed and pristine environment. Like the scrap of my dress from the Match Banquet.

But I've already broken the glass; I've given the green away; I've made my choice. I'm already dying without Ky here and now I have to make sure I live to find him.

I realize that our artifacts will likely never make it into the case. The sign is the only display there may ever be. I don't know what they've done with them.

Now I know for myself that there is nothing left.

I walk down the stairs into the basement. Where they keep the Glorious History of Oria Province, where I meant to go all along before the chance to glimpse what was lost distracted me from what must be found.

I stand close to the glass and look at the map of our Province with its city, farmlands, and rivers, listening to the footsteps on the marble floor behind me. A small, uniformed man comes to stand next to me. "Would you like me to tell you more about the history of Oria?" he asks.

Our eyes meet: mine searching, his sharp and bright.

I look at him and realize: I will not sell our poem. I am selfish. Besides the scrap of fabric, it is all I had to give Ky, and we are the last two people in the world who know the whole thing. Even this is a dead end, even this last idea of mine won't work. I could trade the poem but it would gain me nothing. This isn't something I can barter; it's something I have to do.

"No, thank you," I tell the man, even though I *would* like to know the true history of this place where I live. But I don't think anyone knows it anymore.

Before I leave, I look once more at the geographic map of our Society. There, in the middle of the map, fat and happy, sit the large plump shapes of the Provinces. And around their edges are all the Outer Provinces, the lines dividing them into sections, but none of them named.

"Wait," I call out to the man.

He turns and looks back at me expectantly. "Yes?"

"Does anyone know the names of the Outer Provinces?"

He waves his hand, uninterested now that he knows he isn't going to get something worth trading from me. "That *is* their name," he calls back. "The Outer Provinces."

Those blank, divided Outer Provinces on the map hold my gaze. The map is thick with letters and information, and it's hard to make out all the names. I scan them over, not really reading them, not sure what I'm looking for.

Then. Something stands out to me, one piece of information lodges in my sorting brain: Sisyphus River. It threads through some of the Western Provinces and then through two of the Outer Provinces and off into the void of the Other Countries.

Ky must be from one of those two Outer Provinces. And since that's where the attack came when he was young, that could be where the trouble is now. I lean closer to the map to memorize the location of the two places that might be his.

I hear footsteps coming closer, again, and I turn. "Are you *sure* I can't help you with anything?" the small man asks.

I don't want to trade anything! I almost exclaim to him, and then I realize that he seems to be sincere.

I point to the Sisyphus River on the map, one tiny black thread of hope running along the paper. "Do you know anything about this river?"

His voice hushes. "I heard a story about it once when I was younger. A long time ago the river turned toxic partway down and no one could live near its banks. But that's all I've heard."

"Thank you," I tell him, because now I have an idea, thanks to what I've learned about the way our elderly die. Could our Society have poisoned the waters on their way down to the enemy country? But Ky and his family weren't poisoned. Perhaps they lived farther up, in the higher of the two Provinces along that river.

"It's only a story," the man warns me. He must have seen the hope flash across my face.

"Isn't everything?" I say.

I walk out of the Museum and I do not look back.

My Official waits for me in the greenspace outside the Museum. Wearing white, sitting on a white bench, backed by a white-yellow sun. It's too much; I blink.

If I close my eyes a little I can pretend that this is the greenspace next to the game center, where I will meet my Official for the first time. I can pretend that she's going to tell me that there's a mistake with my Match. But this time things will take a different turn, go down a different path, one where Ky and I can be together and happy.

But there is no such path, not here in Oria.

She gestures for me to come and sit by her on her bench. It strikes me that she's chosen a strange place to meet, right here next to the Museum doors. Then I remember that it's a perfect place, still and empty. Ky was right. No one here is interested in the past.

The bench is carved of stone and feels solid and cool from the hours it spends in the shade of the Museum. I put my hand against the rock after I sit down, wondering where they quarried the stone. Wondering who had to move the rocks.

This time I speak first. "I made a mistake. You have to bring him back."

"Ky Markham has already had one exception made for him. Most Aberrations don't even have that," she says. "You're the one who sent him away. You've proven our point. People who let the data slide, who let emotions get involved, create a mess for themselves."

"*You* did this," I say. "You set up that sort."

"But you performed it," she says. "Perfectly, I might add. You might be upset; his family might be devastated, but it was the right decision, as far as his ability was concerned. You knew he was more than he pretended to be."

"He should be the one who decides whether to go or stay. Not me. Not you. Let him choose."

"If we did, everything would fall apart," she says, patiently. "Why do you think we can guarantee such long life spans? How do you think we eradicated cancer? We Match for *everything*. Genes included."

"You guarantee these long life spans but then you kill us at the end. I know about the poison in the food for people like Grandfather."

"We can also guarantee a high quality of life up until the very last breath. Do you know how many miserable people in how many miserable societies across the years would have given almost anything for that? And the method of administering the—"

"Poison."

"Poison," she says, unflinching, "is unbelievably humane. Small doses, in the patient's favorite foods."

"So we eat to die."

She dismisses my concern. "Everyone eats to die, regardless of what we do. Your problem is that you don't respect the system and what it offers you, even now."

This almost makes me want to laugh. The Official sees the twist of my lips and launches into a list of examples, of ways I've broken with the Society's rules in the past two months—and she doesn't even know the worst of them—but she doesn't cite a single example from all the years before. If she had a way to track all my memories, she would see they are pure. That I truly wanted to fit in and be Matched and do everything the right way. That I truly believed.

That part of me still believes.

"It was time for this little experiment to end anyway," the Official says, sounding regretful. "We don't have the manpower to focus on it anymore. And, of course, situations being what they are—"

"What experiment?"

"The one with you and Ky."

"I already know," I say. "I know that you told him. And I know it was a bigger mistake than you led me to believe that first time we spoke. Ky was actually *in* the Matching pool."

"It was no mistake," she says.

And I am falling again, just when I thought I had hit the bottom.

"*We* decided to put Ky into the Matching pool," she says. "Now and then we do that with an Aberration, simply to gather additional data and watch for variation. The general public doesn't know about it; there's no reason they should. What's important for you to know was that *we* were in control of the experiment all along."

"But the odds of him Matching with me—"

"Are virtually impossible," the Official agrees. "So you can see why we were intrigued. Why we let you see Ky's picture so that *you* would be curious. Why we made sure you were assigned to the same hiking group, and then to the same pairs. Why we had to follow it through, at least for a time."

She smiles. "It was so intriguing; we could control so many variables. We even reduced your meal portions to see if that would make you more stressed, more likely to give up. But you didn't. Of course, we were never cruel. You always had sufficient calories. And you're strong. You never did take the green tablet."

"Why does that matter?"

"It makes you more interesting," she says. "A very intriguing subject, in fact. Ultimately predictable, but still unusual enough to want to watch. It would have been interesting to see your situation play out to the final predicted outcome." She sighs, a sigh of genuine sadness. "I planned to write an article about it, available only to select Officials, of course. It would have been an unparalleled proof of the validity of Matching. That's why I didn't want you to lose your memory of what happened this morning at the air-train station. All my work would have been for nothing. Now, at least I can see you make your final choice while you still know what happened."

The anger fills me so full that there is no room for thought or speech. *It would have been interesting to see it play out to the final predicted outcome.*

It was all planned from the start. *Everything.*

"Unfortunately, my skills are needed elsewhere now." She runs her hand along the datapod in front of her. "We simply don't have the time to monitor the situation anymore, so we can't extend it any longer."

"Why tell me all of this?" I ask. "Why do you want me to know every last detail?"

She looks surprised. "Because we care about you, Cassia. No more or less than we care about all our citizens. As the subject of an experiment, you have the right to know what happened. The right to make the choice we know you'll make now instead of waiting any longer."

It's so funny, her use of the word *choice*, so unintentionally hysterical that I would laugh if I didn't think it would come out sounding like a cry. "Did you tell Xander?"

She looks offended. "Of course not. He's still your Match. In order for the experiment to be controlled, he had to remain in the dark. He knows nothing about any of this."

Except what I told him, I think, and I realize that she doesn't know.

There are things she doesn't know. With this realization, it is as though something has been given back to me. The knowledge drops into my anger and distills it into something pure and clear. *And one of the things she knows nothing about is love.*

"Ky, however, was different," she says. "We told him. We pretended we were warning him, but of course we were hoping to give him impetus to try to be with you. And that worked as well." She smiles, smug, because she also thinks that I don't know this part of the story. But, of course, I do.

"So you watched us all the time," I say.

"Not all the time," she answers. "We watched you enough to get an effective sample of what your interactions were like. We couldn't watch all of your interactions on the Hill, for example, or even on the smaller hill. Officer Carter still had jurisdiction over that area and did not look kindly on our being there."

I wait for her to ask; somehow I know she will. Even though she thinks she has an accurate sample, there is a part of her that has to know more.

"So what *did* happen between you and Ky?" she asks.

She doesn't know about the kiss. That was not what sent him away. That moment on the Hill is still ours, mine and Ky's. *Ours*. No one has touched it but the two of us.

This will be what I have to hold onto as I go forward. The kiss, and the poem, and the I love you's we wrote and said.

"If you tell me, I can help you. I can recommend you for a work position in the City. You could stay here; you wouldn't have to leave for the Farmlands with your family." She leans closer. "Tell me what happened."

I look away. In spite of everything, the offer *is* tempting. I'm a little afraid of leaving Oria; I don't want to leave Xander and Em. I don't want to leave the places that hold so many memories of Grandfather. And most of all I don't want to leave this City and my Borough because they are where I found and loved Ky.

But he's not here anymore. I have to find him somewhere else.

The prisoner's dilemma. Somewhere Ky keeps faith with me and I can do the same for him. I won't give up.

"No," I say clearly.

"I thought you'd say that," she tells me, but I hear the disappointment in her tone and I suddenly want to laugh. I want to ask her if it ever gets tedious being right all the time. But I think I know what her answer would be.

"So what *is* the final predicted outcome?" I ask.

"Does it matter?" she smiles. "It's what will happen. It's what you'll do. But I'll tell you if you'd like."

I realize that I don't need to hear it; I don't need to hear anything she has to say or any predictions she thinks she can make. They do not know that Xander hid the artifact, that Ky can write, that Grandfather gave me poetry.

What else doesn't she know?

"You say you planned this all along," I say suddenly, on instinct, acting as though I want to be certain. "You're telling me you put Ky into the Matching pool *yourselves*."

"Yes," she answers. "We did."

This time, I look right at her when she speaks and that's when I see it. The faintest twitch of muscle in her jaw, a slight shift of her eyes, the smallest ring of performance in the tone of her voice. She doesn't often have to lie; she's never been an Aberration, so this doesn't come easily to her, she hasn't had as much practice. She can't keep her face perfectly still the way Ky does when he's playing a game and he knows what he has to do, whether it's better to win or lose.

And although she's been told how to play, she doesn't know exactly which cards she's holding.

She doesn't know who put Ky into the Matching pool.

If the Officials didn't, who did?

I look at her again. She doesn't know, and she isn't listening to her own words. If the almost-impossible happened before—my being Matched to two boys I already knew—then it can happen again.

I can find him.

I stand up to leave. I think I smell rain in the air, even though there isn't a cloud in the sky, and I remember. I still have a piece of Ky's story left.

CHAPTER 31

Xander sits on the steps of my house.

It's a familiar place for him to be in the summer, and his position looks familiar, too. Legs outstretched, elbows resting on the step behind him. The shadow he casts in the summer sun is smaller than he is, a darker, compacted version of Xander next to the real one.

He watches me as I walk up the path, and when I get close, I see the pain still there in his eyes, a shadow behind the blue.

I almost wish the red tablet had wiped away more than the past twelve hours for Xander. That he didn't remember what I told him, how much it ached. Almost. But not quite. Even though telling the truth has caused us both hurt, I don't see how I could have given Xander anything different. It was all I had to give and he deserved to have it.

"I've been waiting for you," Xander says. "I heard about your family."

"I was in the City," I tell him.

"Come sit by me," Xander says. I hesitate—does he mean this? Does he want me to sit by him, or is he helping me

348

put on a show for whoever might be watching? Xander keeps looking up at me, waiting. "Please."

"Are you sure?" I ask.

"Yes," he says, and then I know that he is. He's in pain. I am, too. It strikes me that perhaps this is part of what we are fighting to choose. Which pain we feel.

Not much time has passed since the Match Banquet, but we are different now, stripped of our fancy clothes, our artifacts, our belief in the Match System. I stand there, thinking about this. How much has changed. How little we knew.

"You always have to make me speak first, don't you?" Xander asks, a hint of a smile on his face. "You always win our arguments in the end."

"Xander," I say, and I sit down and slide right next to him. His arm goes around me, and I put my head on his shoulder and he bends his head to rest on mine. I sigh, so deep it is almost a shudder, at the relief I feel. At how good this is, to be held like this. None of it is for the Society, watching, always. It is all real, for me. I will miss him so much.

Neither of us says anything for a moment, as we look out at our street together one last time. I might come back, but I won't live here again. Once you've been Relocated, you don't return except to visit. Clean breaks are best. And I will make the cleanest break of all, when I go to find Ky. That is the kind of Infraction that no one can overlook.

"I heard you leave tomorrow," Xander says, and I nod, my head moving against his cheek. "I have to tell you something."

"What is it?" I ask. I look ahead, feeling his shoulder move under the shirt of his plainclothes as he shifts position slightly, but I don't move away. What will he tell me? That he can't believe I betrayed him? That he wishes he'd been Matched with anyone but me? Those are the things I deserve to hear, but I don't think he will say them. Not Xander.

"I remember what happened this morning," Xander whispers to me. "I know what really happened to Ky."

"How?" I sit upright, look at him.

"The red tablets don't work on me," he whispers, soft into my ear, so no one else can hear. He looks down the street, back toward the Markhams' house. "They didn't work on Ky, either."

"*What?*" How is it that these two boys who are so different are connected in such unexpected, deep ways? Maybe we all are, I think, and we don't know how to see it anymore. "Tell me."

Xander still gazes at the little house with the yellow shutters where Ky lived hours ago. Where Ky watched and learned how to survive. Xander taught him some of that, without knowing it. And perhaps Xander has been learning from Ky, too.

"I dared him to take it once, a long time ago," Xander says quietly. "It was when he first got here. I acted friendly to him, but inside I was jealous. I saw how you looked at him."

"Really?" I don't remember this at all, but suddenly I hope Xander's right. I hope part of me fell in love with Ky before anyone else told me to.

"It's not a memory I'm proud of," Xander tells me. "I asked him to come swimming with me one day and then on the way I told him I knew about his artifact. I knew about it because once, one Borough over, I was coming back from taking something to a friend and I caught Ky using it, trying to find his way home. He was so careful. I think it was the one time he got it out, ever, but he had bad timing. I saw him."

This image almost breaks my heart; it's another side of Ky I haven't seen before—lost. Taking risks. As well as I know him, as much as I love him, there are still parts of him I don't know. It's that way with everyone, even Xander, who I never could have pictured being so cruel.

"I dared him to find and steal two red tablets. I thought it would be impossible. I said that if he didn't bring them to swimming the next day to prove he could, I'd tell everyone about the compass—the artifact—and get Patrick in trouble."

"What did he do?"

"You know Ky. He wouldn't risk his uncle." Then Xander starts to laugh. Shocked, I ball my fists up in anger. Does he think this is *funny*? What, in this story, could there possibly be to laugh at?

"So Ky got the tablets. And guess who he stole them from?" Xander says, still laughing. "Just guess."

"I don't know. Tell me."

"My parents." Xander stops laughing. "Of course, it wasn't funny at the time. That night my parents were upset because their red tablets were missing. I knew right away what had happened, but of course I couldn't say anything. I couldn't tell them about the dare." Xander looks down and I notice that he has a large brown paper envelope in his hand. It makes me think of Ky's story. I'm hearing another part of it now. "It was a big mess. Officials came and everything. I don't know if you remember that."

I shake my head. I don't.

"They checked to make sure we hadn't taken the tablets, and they could tell somehow that we hadn't, and my parents were pretty convincing, saying they didn't know what happened. They were completely panicked. Finally, the Officials decided that my parents must have lost the tablets when *they* were swimming earlier in the week and that they'd been negligent not to notice it sooner. They'd never caused any trouble before, so they got off without an Infraction. Just a citation."

"Ky did *that*? Took the tablets from your *parents*?"

"He did." Xander takes a deep breath. "I went to his house the next day ready to tear him apart. He stood on the front steps waiting for me. When I got there he held out the two red tablets, right for everyone to see.

"Of course, I was so scared I grabbed them out of his hand and asked him what he was trying to do. That's when he told me that you don't play with other people's lives." Xander seems ashamed, remembering. "And then he told me that we could start over if I wanted. All we had to do was take the red tablets, one for each of us. He promised me we wouldn't get hurt."

"That's cruel of him, too," I say in shock, but to my surprise Xander disagrees with me.

"He knew the tablets didn't work on him; I don't know how, but he did. He thought they *would* work on me. He thought I wouldn't remember how horrible I'd been and that I'd be able to start clean."

"How many other people do you think are walking around out there, pretending that their tablets worked when they didn't?" I ask, wondering.

"As many as want to stay out of trouble," Xander says. He glances at me. "Apparently they don't work on you, either."

"It's not exactly like that," I say, but I don't want to tell him the whole story. He already carries enough of my secrets.

Xander studies me for a moment, but then when I don't say more, he speaks again. "While we're talking about tablets," he says, "I have a gift for you. A farewell gift." He hands me the envelope and whispers, "Don't open it now. I put some things in there to remind you of the Borough, but the real gift is a bunch of blue tablets. In case you have to go on another long journey or something."

He knows I'm going to try to find Ky. And he's helping me. In spite of everything, Xander hasn't betrayed me. And I realize, too, that I never wondered, as I ran down the street after Ky, if it was Xander who had set those events in motion. I knew he hadn't. He kept faith with me. It's the prisoner's dilemma. This dangerous game that I must play with Ky, and again with Xander. But what I know, and the Official doesn't, is that all of us will do our best to keep each other safe. "Oh, Xander. How did you get these?"

"They keep extra supplies in the pharmacy at the medical center," Xander says. "These were slated for disposal. They're about to expire, but I think they'll still work for a few months past expiration."

"The Officials will still miss them."

He shrugs. "They will. I'll be careful, and you should be, too. I'm sorry I couldn't bring you real food."

"I can't believe you're doing all of this for me," I say to Xander.

He swallows hard. "Not just for you. For all of us."

It all makes sense now. If we could change things, in time, maybe . . . maybe we could *all* choose.

"Thank you, Xander," I say. I think about how I might have a chance to find Ky, thanks to Ky's compass and Xander's tablets, and I realize that, in so many ways, Xander is the one who made it possible for me to love Ky.

"Ky thought you might be able to help me learn how to use the artifact," I tell him. "Now I know why. Did you recognize it that day, when I gave it to you?"

"I thought I did. But it had been a long time and I kept my promise. I didn't open it."

"But you know how to use it."

"I figured out the basic principles of what it was after I'd seen it. I used to ask him questions about it once in a while."

"It might help me find him."

"Even if I could show you, why would I?" And Xander can't cover it anymore; bitterness and anger mingle with the pain. "So you can go off and be happy with him? Where does that leave me? *What* does that leave me?"

"Don't say that," I tell him. "You gave me the blue tablets so I could find him, right? If I'm gone, and we can change things, maybe you can choose someone, too."

"I did," he says, looking at me.

I don't know what to say.

"So I have to wish for the end of the world as I know it?" Xander asks, another hint of his old laugh in his voice.

"Not the end of the world. For the beginning of a better one," I say, and I am frightened, too. Is this what we really want to wish for? "One where we can get Ky back."

"Ky," Xander says, and there's sadness in his voice. "Sometimes it seems like everything I've done has been to help you be ready for someone else."

I don't know what to say, how to tell him that he is wrong, how *I* was wrong moments ago when I thought the same thing. Because yes, Xander has helped Ky and me time and time again. But how can I explain to Xander that *he* is a reason for wanting a new world, too? That he is important? That I love him?

"I can teach you," Xander says, finally. "I'll send you some instructions in a message over the port."

"But anyone can read those."

"I'll make it so it looks like a love letter. We *are* still Matched, after all. And we're good at pretending." Then he whispers, "Cassia . . . If we *could* choose, would you ever have chosen me?"

I'm surprised he has to ask. And then I realize that he doesn't know that at one point I *did* choose him. When I first saw his face on the screen and then Ky's over it, I wanted safe and known and expected. I wanted good and kind and handsome. I wanted Xander.

"Of course," I say.

We both look at each other and start to laugh. Then we can't stop. We're laughing so hard that tears roll down our faces and Xander pulls away from me, leaning over and gasping for air. "We could still end up together," he says. "After all this."

"We could," I agree.

"Then why do any of it?"

I'm serious now. All this time it's taken me to understand what Grandfather meant. Why he didn't want to have the sample stored; why he didn't want a chance to live forever on someone else's terms. "Because it's about making our own choices," I tell him. "That's the point. Isn't it? This is bigger than us now."

He looks up. "I know." Maybe for Xander it has always been bigger than us; since he's seen more, known more, for years. As Ky has.

"How many times?" I whisper to Xander.

He shakes his head, confused.

"How many times have the rest of us taken the tablet, and we can't remember?" I ask.

"Once, that I know of," Xander says. "They don't use it much on citizens. I was sure they'd make us take it after the Markhams' son died, but they didn't. But, one day, I'm pretty sure everyone in the Borough took it."

"Did I?"

"I'm not positive," he says. "I didn't actually see you do it. I don't know."

"What happened?" I ask.

Xander shakes his head. *"I'm not going to say,"* he whispers.

I don't press him further. I haven't told him everything—about the kiss on the Hill, the poem—and I cannot ask him to do what I have not. This is a difficult balance, telling the truth: how much to share, how much to keep, which truths will wound but not ruin, which will cut too deep to heal.

So I gesture to the envelope instead. "What did you put in here? Besides the tablets?"

He shrugs. "Not much. I was mostly trying to hide the tablets. A couple of newrose blooms, like the ones we planted. They won't last long. I printed a copy of one of the Hundred Paintings from the port, that picture you did a report on a long time ago. That won't last long either." He's right; the paper from the ports always deteriorates quickly. Xander looks at me, sad. "You'll have to use all of it in the next couple of months."

"Thank you," I tell him. "I didn't get anything for you—everything happened so fast this morning—" I fall silent again. Because I used what time I did have for Ky. I chose him, again, over Xander.

"It's all right," he says. "But maybe—you could—"

He looks into my eyes, deep, and I know what he wants. A kiss. Even though he knows about Ky. Xander and I are still connected; this is still good-bye. I know already that that kiss would be sweet. It would be what he would hold on to, as I hold on to Ky's.

But that's something I don't think I can give. "Xander—"

"It's all right," he says, and then he stands up. I do, too, and he reaches for me, pulls me close. Xander's arms are as warm and safe and good around me as they have always been.

We both hold on, tight.

Then he lets go and walks down the path, without another word. He doesn't look back. But I watch him go. I watch him all the way home.

The journey to our new home is fairly straightforward: ride the air train to the City Center, change to a long-distance air train for the Farmlands of Keya Province. Most of our belongings fit into one small case each; the few things that don't will be sent later.

As the four of us walk to the air-train stop, neighbors and friends come out to say good-bye and wish us well. They know we're being Relocated but they don't know why; it isn't considered polite to ask. As we come to the end of the street we see that a new sign has been hammered into place: Garden Borough. Without the trees and without the name, Mapletree Borough is gone. It's as though it never existed. The Markhams are gone. We are gone. Everyone else will live on here in Garden Borough. They've already added extra newroses to all the flower beds.

The quickness with which Ky disappeared, with which the Markhams disappeared, with which we will disappear, makes me cold. It is as if we never happened. And I suddenly remember a time back when I was small, when I used to look for the air train home to Stony Borough and we had paths made of low flat stones that led to our doors.

This happened before. This Borough keeps changing names. What other bad things lie beneath the surface of our Borough? What have we buried underneath our rocks and trees and flowers and houses? That time Xander won't talk about, when we all took the red tablet—what happened? When other people left, where did they really go?

They could not write their names, but I can write mine, and I will again, somewhere where it will last for a long, long time. I will find Ky, and then I will find that place.

Once we are on the long-distance air train, my mother and Bram both fall asleep, exhausted from the emotion and exertion of the journey.

I find it strange, with everything else that happened, that it was my mother's obedience which spelled the need for our Relocation. She knew too much and she admitted it in that report. She couldn't do otherwise.

The ride is long and there are other travelers. No soldiers like Ky. They keep them on their own trains. But there are tired families who look much like ours, a group of Singles who laugh and talk excitedly about their jobs, and, in the last car, a few rows of young women about my age going on a work detail for a few months. I watch these girls with interest; they are girls who did not get work positions and therefore will float around wherever they are needed for a time. Some of them seem sad and faded, disappointed. Others have faces turned to the windows with interest in their eyes. I catch myself glancing over at them more than I should. We're supposed to keep to ourselves. And I need to concentrate on finding Ky. I have equipment now: blue tablets, the artifact called a compass, knowledge of the Sisyphus River, memories of a grandfather who did not go gentle.

My father notices me watching the girls. While my mother and Bram sleep he says softly, "I don't remember what happened yesterday. But I know the Markhams left the Borough and I think that has hurt you."

I try to change the subject. I glance over at my sleeping mother. "Why didn't they use a red tablet on her? Then we wouldn't have had to leave."

"A red tablet?" my father asks, surprised. "Those are only for extreme circumstances. This isn't one of them." Then, to my surprise, he says more. He speaks to me like an adult; more than that, like an equal. "I'm a sorter by nature, Cassia," he says. "All the information adds up to something being wrong. The way they took the artifacts. Your mother's trips to the other Arboretums. The gap in my memory from yesterday. Something is wrong. They are losing a war and I can't tell who it's against—people on the inside or people on the outside. But there are signs of cracking."

I nod. Ky told me almost the same thing.

But my father goes on. "And I've noticed other things, too. I think you're in love with Ky Markham. I think you want to find him, wherever he's gone." He swallows.

I glance over at my mother. Her eyes are open now. She looks at me with love and understanding, and I realize: She knows what my father did. She knows what I want. She knows and even though she would not destroy a tissue sample or love someone who was not her Match, she still loves *us*, even though we have done those things.

My father has always broken the rules for those he loves, just as my mother has always kept them for the same reason. Perhaps that is yet another reason why they make a perfect

Match. I can trust in my parents' love. And it strikes me that that is a big thing to trust, a big thing to have had, no matter what else happens.

"We can't give you the life you want," my father says, his eyes wet. He looks at my mother and she nods at him to continue. "We wish we could. But we can help you have a chance to decide which life you want."

I close my eyes and ask the angels and Ky and Grandfather for strength. Then I open them and look straight at my father. "How?"

CHAPTER 32

My hands are in the soil; my body is tired, but I will not let this work take away my thoughts. Because that is what the Officials here want: workers who work but do not think.

Do not go gentle.

So I fight. I fight the only way I know how, with thinking of Ky, even though the pain of missing him is so strong I can hardly stand it. I put the seeds into the ground and cover them with soil. Will they grow toward the sun? Will something go wrong so that they never push, never turn into anything, just stay here rotting in the ground? I think of him, I think of him, I think of him.

I think of my family. Of Bram. Of my parents. I have learned something about love through all of this—about the love I have for Ky and the love I have for Xander and the love my parents and Bram and I have for one another. When we reached our new home, my parents requested that I be sent on a three months' work detail because I showed signs of rebellion. The Officials in our new village checked my data; it correlated with my parents' statement. My father mentioned a particular work detail he had in mind: hard farming, planting an experimental winter crop in a Western Province through which the river of Sisyphus runs. He and Xander and my mother keep me updated on anything they learn about where Ky might be. I am closer to him here; I feel it.

I think of Xander. We could have been happy, I know that, and it is perhaps the hardest thing to know. I could have held his hand, warm and strong, and we could have had what my parents have, and it would have been beautiful. It would have been beautiful.

We wear no chains. We have nowhere to go. They wear us down with work; they don't beat us or hurt us. They simply want to make us tired.

And I am tired.

When I think I might give up after all, I remember the last part of the story that Ky gave me, the part I finally read before we left our home for the last time:

Cassia, he wrote at the top of the page, in letters that were tall and clear and unafraid, that curled and moved and turned my name into something beautiful, something more than a word. A declaration, a piece of a song, a bit of art, framed by his hands.

There was only one Ky drawn on the napkin. Smiling. A smile in which I could see both who he had been and who he became. His hands were empty again, and open, and reaching a little. Toward me.

Cassia.

I know which life is my real one now, no matter what happens. It's the one with you.

For some reason, knowing that even one person knows my story makes things different. Maybe it's like the poem says. Maybe this is my way of not going gentle.

I love you.

I had to burn that part of his story, too, but I held the heat of that *I love you* close, like red, like a new beginning.

Without knowing the pieces of Ky's story and the words of my poems I might give up. But I think of my words and of the cache of tablets and compass hidden away and my family and Xander who send me messages on the work camp portscreen that tell me they are still looking; they are still helping me.

Sometimes, when I look down at the pale seeds I scatter in the black dirt, it reminds me of the night of my Banquet when I imagined that I could fly. The darkness behind doesn't worry me; neither do the stars ahead. I think of how perhaps the best way to fly would be with hands full of earth so you always remember where you came from, how hard walking could sometimes be.

And I look at my hands, too, which move in the shape of my own inventions, my own words. It is hard to do, and I am not good at it yet. I write them in the soil where I plant and then step on them, dig holes in them, drop seeds in them to see if they will grow. I steal a piece of black burned wood from one of the cropfires and write on a napkin. Later, at another cropfire; my hand brushes over the flames with the napkin, and the words die. Ash and nothing.

My words never last long. I have to destroy them before anyone sees them.

But. I remember them all. For some reason, the act of writing them down makes me remember. Each word I write brings me closer to finding the right ones. And when I see Ky again, which I know will happen, I will whisper the words I have written in his ear, against his lips. And they will change from ash and nothing into flesh and blood.

Q WHERE DID THE BRILLIANT IDEA FOR *MATCHED* COME FROM?

A *Matched* was inspired by several events – specific ones, like a conversation with my husband and chaperoning a high-school prom – and general ones, like falling in love and becoming a parent.

Q HOW LONG DID IT TAKE YOU TO WRITE IT?

A It took me about nine months to write *Matched* – I worked on it from Fall 2008 to Summer 2009.

Q WHAT IS YOUR WRITING PROCESS?

A I write every day except Sunday. I can't write when my kids are awake – I'm the worst multitasker in the world! – so I usually put in the time during their naps or after they have gone to bed. I write fairly slowly – about 1,000 words a day – when I'm drafting, and I write terrible first drafts. Once I've finished a first full draft, I'll go over it literally dozens of times to finesse it and smooth out the plot.

Q WHO IS YOUR FAVORITE CHARACTER IN *MATCHED* AND WHY?

A My favorite character in *Matched* is Cassia, because she experiences the most growth. I always think that is the most interesting part of the novel to write – the character's evolution.

Q HOW DID YOU COME UP WITH THE NAMES CASSIA, XANDER AND KY?

A I went through several names to get the right name for Cassia. I had some rather specific criteria for the name: I wanted something classical, unusual, and botanical. I also love names that start with 'C'. My sister was the one who drew my attention to the name Cassia, which fits all of these criteria and also just seemed to fit the girl on the page. Xander and Ky were easier. Their names came to mind almost immediately – I wanted names that sounded familiar but also looked a little different and unusual.

Q WHY DID YOU CHOOSE TO WRITE FOR A TEENAGE AUDIENCE?

A I used to teach high school, and so when I started writing, I automatically began writing for young adults. I think teenagers are interesting, honest, passionate – I loved working with them and I love writing for them.

Q WHICH BOOKS DID YOU LOVE TO READ WHEN YOU WERE A TEENAGER?

A I read a lot of Agatha Christie, Anne Tyler, and Wallace Stegner. I must have read Tyler's *Saint Maybe* fifteen times in high school. Really, I loved to read anything I could get my hands on!

Q WHEN YOU TAKE A
BREAK FROM WRITING
NOW, WHAT DO YOU LIKE
TO READ?
A The same – I revisit Stegner
and Christie every year, and I'm
always looking forward to what
ever Anne Tyler is working on next.
In recent years, I've fallen in love with the writing of Marilynne
Robinson and M. T. Anderson, among others, and Alan Bradley's
mystery series is excellent. My son and I just read Grace Lin's
fantastic *Where the Mountain Meets the Moon*, one of the most
beautiful books I've read in a very long time.

Q SPEAKING OF WRITING, WHEN CAN WE LOOK FORWARD TO
MEETING CASSIA AGAIN?
A We're hoping to have the second book out about one year after
the release of the first. So, if all goes well, it won't be too long!

Q LASTLY – HOW DID YOU FEEL WHEN YOU HEARD *MATCHED* WAS
GOING TO BE PUBLISHED, AND HOW DID YOU CELEBRATE?
A To be honest, I cried. Just sat there and cried, and then I called
my husband, who has been incredibly supportive and lovely, and
then we both cried. Later that night, after we got our three little boys
to sleep, we got takeout for dinner from our favorite restaurant.
That's when the hysterical laughter began – the 'Can you believe this
might really be happening?!?' laughter. It was a very fun, very
emotional day.

IN THE *SOCIETY*,
OFFICIALS DECIDE

WHO I LOVE.

WHERE I WORK.

WHEN I DIE.

WHO WILL BE YOUR

MATCH?